So I clarified myself. "The stress of maintaining control of the internal operations of the station was overwhelming enough. Fighting off an interloper was too much to handle."

"Yes. That is exactly right." Rold stopped to stare at the metallic banding across his knuckles. "I wonder one thing about her death."

"And that would be?"

"We were all shipped off the Baderes before Duriken pulled the switch. There may have been a stowaway, but I really doubt it. The last time I checked, all personnel had been evacuated from the station. There was only a single life sign as we jettisoned off. At least, that is what the scanners indicated."

I finished for him, seeing where he was going with his determination. "In other words, you think the person or entity that killed Sunteel was from another dimension."

He nodded, but his only audible response was a beeping sigh.

Don't miss the first book in the series . . .

THE ASTROLOGER: Heart of Stone

Ace Books by Denny DeMartino

THE ASTROLOGER SERIES

HEART OF STONE
WAYWARD MOON

✦ THE ASTROLOGER ✦

WAYWARD
------ MOON

DENNY DeMARTINO

ACE BOOKS, NEW YORK

If you purchased this book without a cover, you should be aware that this book is stolen property. It was reported as "unsold and destroyed" to the publisher, and neither the author nor the publisher has received any payment for this "stripped book."

This is a work of fiction. Names, characters, places, and incidents either are the product of the author's imagination or are used fictitiously, and any resemblance to actual persons, living or dead, business establishments, events, or locales is entirely coincidental.

THE ASTROLOGER: WAYWARD MOON

An Ace Book / published by arrangement with the author

PRINTING HISTORY
Ace mass-market edition / July 2001

All rights reserved.
Copyright © 2001 by Denise Vitola
Cover art by Fred Gambino

This book, or parts thereof, may not be reproduced in any form without permission.
For information address: The Berkley Publishing Group, a division of Penguin Putnam Inc., 375 Hudson Street, New York, New York 10014.

The Penguin Putnam Inc. World Wide Web site address is www.penguinputnam.com

Check out the ACE Science Fiction & Fantasy newsletter and much more on the Internet at Club PPI!

ISBN: 0-441-00830-5

ACE®
Ace Books are published by The Berkley Publishing Group, a division of Penguin Putnam Inc., 375 Hudson Street, New York, New York 10014.
ACE and the "A" design are trademarks belonging to Penguin Putnam Inc.

PRINTED IN THE UNITED STATES OF AMERICA

10 9 8 7 6 5 4 3 2 1

To Nancy and Michael Davis

1

The fire of zero-point gravity purified her. She liked playing in this heat. It made her sweat in every crack and crevice of her body, and for Duriken Sunteel, there were quite a few places for the moisture to collect.

"Testing range complete, Progenitor. Shutting down external scanning devices. Warning buoys are now deployed. There should be no interference from passing space traffic."

Sunteel did not turn from the space station's main viewing porthole to address her assistant. Instead, she stared through the pitted window toward the world below. It would be the last time she would ever watch the icy pink colors swirling in the atmosphere and marvel at the sparkle of the wide ring system surrounding the planet. Such a view was enough to bring a glycerine tear to the eye. She wasn't an emotional being—at least, that's what she claimed to anyone who would listen.

"You may disengage, Immaculate. I will complete the final maneuvers alone."

Her assistant, Rold, faltered in complying with her orders. Sunteel felt his hesitation to terminate the link he held through the synaptic cloth of the station's cyber bonnet without turning around. With all this direct contact, she was still uncertain what his pause meant. It niggled at her awareness, but seconds later, he confirmed the reason he had delayed.

"Are you certain, Progenitor?" he asked quietly. "I

will gladly continue with the gravitic measurements until it is time for me to leave."

"No. I will do it all. Please retreat to the run-pod and return to Istos to make your report of the activities here."

Sunteel sensed Rold's compliance, but suddenly she scraped in some of his anger. He did not conceal his emotions well. There was something greatly out of balance in his physical construction. It would be good to have him away from the station.

When she was sure Rold had left the cyber bonnet, she spoke again, though she didn't look at him. "I thank you for your help and your loyalty. This would not have been possible without you."

He did not respond, or if he did, she could not hear him, because the celestial wind had started to blow through Sunteel, opening the coded chambers of her DNA. After he was gone, she slid into the slick metal chair before the activation console, pausing to wriggle her blunt fingers like a harpist readying herself to play.

Sunteel was an Idealian, a proud member of a species of organic-mechanoids who had quietly inhabited the galaxy's eastern and northern arms. Her species was comprised of hulking but peaceful technological people. They served other planets and sentients with their extraordinary processing prowess. It was the Idealians who found a way to replace the atmosphere of Barachi Four after a gravitic-ion storm leached the air off all the planets in the Kalila solar system. It was the Idealians who repaired the phase sheath that protected the entire world of Narsel'engri from being pounded to pieces by a passing oort cloud. It was the Idealians who helped the Humans of Terra to expand their knowledge of zero point gravity, the force that created something from nothing and that was the basis for interstellar transportation. All these things her people had accomplished, and yet they were considered no better than those odd metallic appliances known as androids.

She sighed, and when she did, she realized that the burning in her emotional core was a lava breach. It was not happiness and anticipation she felt but unarticulated fear. Of course, Rold had sensed this—as an immaculate, he would. That embarrassed her. Despite her girth and natural armor, she was weak and petty in mind.

She paused to rub the sides of her head, letting the flat side of her fingers massage the mounds of Vidun, those mechanoid temples where silica veins and carbon arteries met in tribute to a packet of delicate, high-grade circuitry. When properly functioning, the Vidun enlivened her blood with electricity by dispersing the power along her central nervous system. It should have been impossible for her to have this headache. Her internal diagnostics measured her heart rate, hormonal induction, and brain chemistry, and she had checked out in perfect condition. It could not have been from her melding with the station computer. That only enriched her life force. This pain was surely from the stress of what she was about to accomplish. If she was successful and did not die, she would be famous for centuries, because she would be able to move at right angles to forever.

Like so many worlds in the galaxy, the planet Bohdan spinning slowly below the station had once had a moon that was created through a collision from a world that had passed too closely. This crash had given this planet life by changing its composition and by giving it a large satellite to help regulate its celestial balance.

The moon had spun in Bohdan's orbit for as long as her people could remember, and the species that had risen and fallen on the planet had thought the worldlet, called Yaro, was a permanent fixture in their sky. The truth of the matter was this: Yaro's formation had not slowed the trajectory established at the time of the collision. The moon had continued to retreat from the planet at the rate of one and a half centimeters per year. Fifty standard years before, it had passed so far from Bohdan that it no longer affected the planet in a positive manner. What had once been a robust, lively world was dead now, its surface at the mercy of divergent axial tilt and irregular gravitic contractions.

Sunteel would change all this. She was about to sacrifice herself for the good of galaxy kind. If Bohdan could be balanced, then there was a fortune to be made by all, and her people would finally get the respect they so richly deserved.

Sunteel slipped her hands into the specially designed link unit before extending the organic-mechanoid interface housed in her palms. The interface was composed of a mylar nerve repository sheathing a wire formed from the integration of titanium, silica, and carbon cells. At the point of interface extension, she felt the warmth of blood as it streamed from her palms into a reservoir at the back of the link unit. There was no pain, and the leak would eventually subside with no ill effects.

This link would verify her connection into the main computer. It took only a few seconds before she became one with the instrumentation and to let herself grow large with the station. This expansive experience migrated the feeling of being huge and indestructible. Blood and electrical impulses surged through her, asserting this new reality in repeated jolts.

Once locked into the steel sinew of the Baderes Space Station, Sunteel floundered a moment until her equilibrium came on-line. Finally, she sensed a measure of stability, and then wriggled farther into the meld, waiting until the familiar burn tingled in her nerve endings. When she slid into the heat, she knew she had complete command of the station, its periphery robots as well as internal and external scanning devices. Linked so with such a marvelous machine was a humbling experience. Sunteel took a moment to move the onboard telescope, sighting down into the center of the galaxy and to the mirror of universal creation.

The station's observation equipment indicated that fluff and assorted junk littered the area, trash left behind in failed attempts to find a solution to the planet's problems. If she was not careful, the Baderes would be added to the garbage, and it would carry along her soul. Still, she had to take the risk, because she had to know what was on the other side of everything.

This desire swept memories into the spaces between the strings of scanning coordinates automatically organized by the digital neurons in her brain. These thoughts took her into the past and rubbed against her emotional core so hard, she was sure they would snap the tenuous link she had formed with the space station circuitry. Her lover, Jandel, had warned her that she trod into matters that did not concern her. His insistence that she would meet a vile end had finally driven her away from him and any life they might have had together. It had been a bitter affair without the sweetness that so many Humans attached to the word. Jandel's last words to her had been an ancient curse: *"May you know eternity amplified."* Had this not been entirely possible and something that she craved, she could have hated him for his vile rebuff. He had meant to hurt her and he had, but her own desire had polished off the pain before the words were completely out of his mouth.

For a moment, her thoughts kept her from engaging the zero-point grid that she and her team had attached to the space station's solar panel. How weak she was to miss Jandel, even if every sinew and filament in his body screamed against his envy and his greed.

Sunteel took a deep breath, filling her lungs with the warm air pumped into the station. The recirculating system would last a hundred years, but she would not need it. Once the link was complete, she would be sustained by the electric impulses fed to her by the station computer. She would have no need of food, rest, or elimination. It would be a perfect existence.

Sunteel fanned out her energy through the circuits and conveyances of the Baderes' structure. For a nanosecond, she was aware of the unrelenting cold of space pressing in on the metal skin of the station. After another nanosecond, she confirmed the life signs of her crew as they made ready to launch the shuttle toward her home world. More time slid by, and she felt the disconnect rods slinging the tiny ship out of her presence. She was utterly alone. It made her hesitate.

Instead of initializing the link, she paused to carefully scan the Baderes, telling herself it was necessary for the safety of the project, and not a stall until she built up her courage. Up, over, under, she carefully scanned the differences in the station: the roughed edges of grillwork, the cobbled feeling of the deflector units, the smooth glassiness of the cyber bonnet. Sunteel touched everything with her mind and found nothing amiss.

According to the Earthers, zero-point gravity was a natural force responsible for the creation of the universe. By applying their science of the interplanetudes, it became possible to open new doorways to other dimensional planes. If everything moved according to plan, she would slip the station into an artificially created pocket just outside the Rosch Radius of the planet she now orbited. This pocket would create the same gravitational pull on the world, and soon it would steady its axial wobble and stabilize Bohdan's weather. It would then be ready to repopulate, and the natural resources could be exploited. The people would become rich through her technological genius. She, of course, would have her name praised, and after a few hundred years, she would become a god.

That thought redoubled her commitment. Using her mind, Sunteel wove her way through the Baderes's systems until she found the core valve, a tachyon particle accelerator. She adjusted the frequency band and mentally hit the switch, sending the space station into the null space of zero-point gravity, that place of limbo between creation and noncreation. There was a momentary glitch in the balance of the inductor ratio, but she straightened it before opening the hole into space. It would be this hole that would drag down the swift orbit of the planet and restore a reasonable axial tilt. She took a deep breath, her last for eternity, and allowed the computer to completely overtake her.

Sunteel's sensibilities abandoned her as she became one with the station. It raked her insides, made her biochemicals hasten the electrical sublimation. Digital cognizance assumed its place in her thought patterns and, seconds after linking, she lost all understanding of her original life form. She had become the Baderes, existing in a state of pure energy, riding the light of dimensions right into forever.

Abruptly, Sunteel realized she was not alone. There was another who had joined her, but from her rarefied position, she couldn't be sure where or who this person was. At first, she thought it was a mirroring of her own ego, yet the energy had a dark, demonic quality to it. This power flowed into hers and melded with the Baderes.

Sunteel endeavored to reach out to this intruder, to warn him of his encroachment into eternity, but before she could, the personality swelled through the station to inundate her. It was so strong, it literally pulled her soul through the Baderes and into the frequency beam charging through creation. The assassin held her life force momentarily to mock her with its strength. It then sent her essence careening from her body and into the ocean of the space/time continuum.

2

A few months ago, my partner, Artemis Hadrien, and I had a nasty little tussle with a species known as the Waki'el. These lizardly blokes kidnapped us and implanted devices into our wrists. The devices literally turn us into Human particle accelerators and allow us to maneuver through zero-point gravity by creating a doorway into the flow. We can manually activate the implants or think it done and have it so, but unfortunately, controlling the units is a bloody hard trick in itself. There's something unnatural about conveying through the very creation energy that designed the universe and keeps the atoms from falling out of their orbits. While it might seem like a situation of grace, I can guarantee it peppers up a person's psyche with musings that makes you wonder if you lost all the grease on your steering pins. Still, the implants and our ability to function, however marginally, in zpg was the reason we were called in to work this particular murder investigation.

I walked into Baderes Space Station behind Hadrien. He was a big bloke, and even though I could take care of myself, he always insisted on being my shield when we entered new situations. In this case, Hadrien backed up slightly, practically pinning me to the bulkhead until he decided the place was safe.

I stepped away from him to take in the immensity of this orbiting station. It was ugly, the color of rust and runny egg. Titanium beams buttressed a soaring atrium roof, but the metal had lost its indigo luster under an inch of dust. Glancing toward the apex, I saw the slowly spinning planet of Bohdan through the sky portal. I paused, abruptly enchanted by the sun glinting off the rings roping in the pink planet.

My inspection was interrupted by the Senerian administrator of the station. Senerians were almost human-like, except they had these wonderful, huge hands: seven long fingers, two opposable thumbs, and a palm that was flat and full of interesting lines. The administrator paused in his entrance to raise one of his mitts in greeting. My mum would have loved to have had mallets that big. She could have batted all us kids in one well-aimed swat. I mimicked the Senerian by hoisting one of my hands in his direction. "I'm Astrologer Philipa Cyprion, and this is Investigator Artemis Hadrien."

The Senerian nodded and lowered his arm, the action stirring the air in the foyer. "I'm called Megas Telroni," he said in almost perfect British English. "We are honored that you could come on such short notice. You are highly recommended by the emperor of Earth."

I smiled. Emperor Theo felt guilty for the way he'd treated us in the whole matter of the alien implants. We'd saved his silk britches from being chewed up by the Waki'el, and now he owed us and owed us. Surely, his recommendation had buttered his backside. "We're at your disposal," I answered softly.

He nodded again, bowing slightly into it. "I assume your retainer fee arrived?"

"Yes, it did. We appreciate the speedy payment."

Hadrien stepped up and stepped into the conversation. "Please take us to the murder scene."

That was my abrupt friend. No coddly-noddly.

Telroni turned to lead us down a narrow, cramped corridor filled with blinking equipment wrapped in gold foil like Boxing Day gifts. "There really isn't much to see. No blood, nothing like that."

"Then how do you know a murder actually occurred?" Hadrien asked, running a hand through his long, shaggy blond hair.

"Well, for one thing, this great experiment didn't happen."

"That in itself is confusing," Hadrien said. "What exactly was Duriken Sunteel trying to do? The documentation we received on it was more than a bit confusing."

"I am afraid that my explanation may be just as unenlightening, but I will try. Duriken Sunteel was trying to replace the gravitic action that Bohdan's moon caused. It was our hope that she could bring the planet back into alignment. This station was built for just this express purpose."

"Who paid for the building of the station?"

"Several governments. Senerian, Idealian, Human."

"What's so special about that hunk of rock, anyway?"

"It is the home of the Bohdans," Telroni answered sharply. "What other thing can be more special? They have been turned into a species without a planet. It came upon them so quickly they were forced to enlist the help of several worlds to save their people. Bohdans are now found as itinerants, subsisting from service to Idealians, Senerians, Regerians, and quite possibly Humans. We would like to give them back their place in the galaxy.

All this sentient-rights hokum sounded like a great brass trumpet, but I didn't believe any of it.

"Correcting this problem seems a monumental task," I said. "How could Sunteel ever hope to achieve it on her own?"

He shook his head and flapped one of those big meat hooks at me. "I merely administrate the station. I am not a scientist, but as far as I understand, this station incorporates special properties not found in any orbiting plat-

form currently known. What the special properties are—
well, I have no clue." Telroni stopped to study me. "I
thought you would be the ones to tell us, especially with
your unique dispositions."

I let his comment brush by me, but Hadrien didn't
leave it alone. "You are talking about the alien implants?"

"Yes, of course. Normal Humans are helpless individuals in this case. I would think you have a special perspective on it all."

"The implants are more of a biological interdiction.
We couldn't tell you the science behind it."

Telroni began walking again. "A biological interdiction. Funny you should use those words. Duriken spoke
them to me the day before she died." He left the conversation at that, not speaking again until we reached a
command bridge crowded with equipment and people.
A large Idealian broke from the alien rainbow of crime
scene technicians. He strode over to us upon seeing Telroni's enormous hand beckon him. When he reached our
side of the room, he paused, bowed deeply, and then he
beeped.

Yes, he beeped. It was a small sound, yet loud enough
that Hadrien glanced at me with a frown.

"This is Cordous Anu," Telroni announced. "He is the
chief security progenitor of Alien Affairs for the Idealian
Central Government."

What Progenitor Anu really was fell somewhere between man and machine. He was perhaps two and a half
meters tall, but that was the end of any resemblance to
carbon-based life forms that I'd ever before encountered.
His skin was the color of steel and standing directly
under the overhead spotlights, it looked as if his barrel-
shaped torso had a metallic base to it. His hair, long and
wild, hung in deep blue ringlets to his waist, a waist, I
might add, that was concealed in ribbons of wires,

pumping blood vessels, and strange green nodules. He wore no clothes, but any privacy he might have needed from the universe was provided by a series of interlocking, bony plates that ran from pelvis to foot. This armor was decorated with rings, colored beads, and shiny baubles, many of which were snapped around twisting cartilage that arced about his body like the roots of a tree containing an old water pipe.

When he spoke, Anu's voice sounded metallic, as if he might be squeezing words through a larynx strung with copper wire. "Duriken Sunteel was murdered. From what we can deduce of her injuries, it was a most violent death."

He turned after this flat statement to lead us through the throng to the victim. She was a smaller version of Anu, the only difference in physical appearance being two fleshy breasts that popped through spaces in her natural armor. This alien sat before a computer console, her hands pressed flat on two metal touch pads. Her black eyes, strange without a halo of white, were wide open, as though she'd been surprised in her last moments. This surprise ran the length of her face, finally settling into a mouth adorned by two curvaceous, thick lips frozen in a grimace.

"Begging your pardon, sir," I said, "but I see no signs of a struggle. How do you know this was murder?"

Anu assumed an imperious attitude with me. "I've heard that Humans expect every death to have particular parameters that fit their idea of sentience."

"Now hold on a minute," Hadrien said. "You asked for our help. We just have to establish a basis for fact."

The alien scowled, and it was a mean look with all that weird hardware he sported. "I did not ask for your help. The Idealian apex asked your emperor for assistance. I do not happen to agree with this decision formulated by my government. We are quite capable of solving this problem on our own."

"And yet you don't have a clue as how to do that, do you?" I asked.

He paused and then snorted, but before he could defend himself further, Telroni spoke up. "You see, it is a delicate matter. The experiment that was proceeding from the station under Sunteel's direction has been funded by many divergent governments in this arm of the galaxy. Her death is a staggering loss for most of the investors."

I nodded, taking a moment to heighten the tension by studying the dead Idealian female. Mechanoid species had been known by Earthers for years, but none so advanced as these blokes. Hadrien and I hadn't had time for a proper briefing and had to admit that we were flying with our bloomers flapping open in the sweet, Brighton Beach breeze. "So how did she die?"

"She had her life force ripped from her containment unit."

It was my turn to shake my head. "So, just how *do* you determine that her life force was ripped from her containment unit?"

He moved to the corpse to demonstrate. Flipping her hair gently back, he revealed a hole just below her right ear. "This is a biotap. There is one on the other side of her throat. Internal imbalances caused by severe pressure forced it to burst. When it did, it released the life force."

"You actually have a containment unit for the soul?"

"Soul? We prefer to think of it as essence. But, yes, we do."

I stared at the ragged spot on her neck until what he had said made sense. Duriken Sunteel's persona had literally popped her valves and, like steam, had escaped into the ether. The question was this: Had she been straddled in a bad place between dimensions when it had happened?

Before I could ask the question, the space station rumbled, shaking so violently that it knocked me flat on my keister.

3

The vibration stopped after a few seconds, but it had been enough of a shake to dislodge a few interior hull panels in the station. Hadrien hoisted me to my feet before demanding an explanation.

"I beg your pardon," Telroni said. "We have been having difficulties since Duriken attempted the experiment. There are Human engineers here studying the problem. Your Emperor Theo has been generous with the experts."

It was hard to tell if he was being a sarcastic twit, so I let it go. "Who are we going to interview first?"

Telroni turned and stalked off down the corridor, throwing words over his shoulder. "An Idealian who had every opportunity to make the project go bad."

Our makeshift interrogation room was so far off the beaten path it was as difficult to find as the toilet tissue roll in a dark loo.

When we arrived, we found Immaculate Rold waiting like some hulking metal tree. He didn't exactly look sneaky, it was just the bloody weird feeling of malevolence that blew off his gears. Rold sat at the table, studying us intently, wetting his lips often and leaving a filmy residue that reminded me of motor oil.

Hadrien decided to play the mean old clamper by pacing the length of the cubby and giving Rold the silent, suspicious treatment, while I opened up my logos calculator to run an astrological profile on the Idealian.

According to information supplied by Progenitor Anu's office, Rold was born, created, or switched on during the second month of winter on the fiftieth day at the third hour to dusk in an Idealian city known as Guuet. It took me twenty minutes to convert the birth data, but I finally came upon a date and time I could use: January 6, 2254. Firmly set in the midst of the twelfth house of Capricorn, Rold was born in the morning with his moon in Scorpio, his ascending sign of Virgo and his midheaven in Capricorn. Any way you looked at it, Rold was a mechanoid in search of easy money, but he gained his riches through secretive ways. It was probably a sound supposition that truth was not on his plate at teatime.

Hadrien finally glanced at me. "Are you ready, Philipa?"

I nodded before taking a deep breath and focusing on this strange being seated before me. "You had every opportunity to murder Duriken Sunteel. You felt threatened by her. You wanted the glory all to yourself, didn't you, me mate?"

"No," he barked. "Obscurity has always been fine by me. I am immaculate. It can be no other way."

Hadrien barged into the conversation. "What exactly does it mean to be an immaculate as opposed to a progenitor?"

Rold shook his head slowly, and I found myself listening for the sound of a stone rubbing against a boulder. It didn't happen. "Your species is woefully ill informed, yet you compliment each other with your ideas of superiority."

"Yep, that's us," I answered. "Humans—the last great horde to overtake the galaxy."

"Well, your kind is certainly doing that."

"Answer Investigator Hadrien's question."

He snorted. "Think of it this way, Astrologer Cyprion.

Progenitors make things happen. Immaculates are those who the things happen to."

"So, you are in some sort of subservient role to someone like Progenitor Anu?"

"No. I am not anyone's servant. Anu is on a different social course. That is all."

I couldn't even begin to extract what that different social course might be, so I moved on. "You have a great desire for wealth. It's difficult to be wealthy and live an obscure life. One day, someone is going to notice you."

"I do not crave wealth," Rold growled. The pinging quality of his voice grew louder, just like someone drawing deep, wheezing breaths.

Hadrien jumped into the game before I could fill my mouth with words. "You played a big part in the implementation of the seven quar-monagra. What exactly is the seven quar-monagra?"

"It is the seventh law of the interplanetudes. Why do you not know this? Your species invented the science."

Rold was right about that, but from the time of inception to this moment's breath, four thousand alien species used the interplanetudes within the confines of their particular languages. As an astrologer making her greengages by jaunting around the known galaxy to give readings on this and that, it was getting a might hard to translate all the terms a species might use.

I dropped my calculator stylus on the table and sat back to eyeball this crude-looking life form. Unlike the polished points that marked Progenitor Anu's natural armor, this Idealian seemed to wear a cloak of worn, secondhand duds. There were dark spots where it probably should have been shiny, and the smooth places were nicked and scarred.

"How could the seventh law assist you in this experiment?" I asked.

"Duriken Sunteel was going to effect a change in the space/time continuum with thought—pure thought," he answered wistfully. "Once she had control of the station, she would have become the Baderes—powerful enough to maintain the planet's axial tilt by using the creation force." He paused, took a deep, pinging sigh, and glanced at Hadrien while he addressed me. "I would have gladly traded places with her."

Hadrien ignored this obvious try at sensitivity by sitting down at the table. "Explain how you were going to accomplish this. The creation energy is uncontrollable."

"We had managed to harness the unpredictable nature of the force," he said.

That answer made Hadrien sit back and look at me. I, on the other hand, leaned forward to check out Rold's black eyes. They were demon pies, all right, and the lack of white surrounding the iris just made them more so.

Hadrien glanced at me and shook his head. There was a sad expression outlining his chiseled face, as well as a bit of a droop in the color of his usually bright, blue eyes. He suffered from the same stresses that I did because of these alien implants, and he looked like he was already weary of the daily battle. "Is it possible to control the creation force?" he asked me.

"I suppose anything is possible," I answered.

Hadrien turned his attention back to Rold. "I take it that correcting the planet's drift was a one-way ticket into the null space of zero-point gravity."

"It could not be accomplished any other way," he answered. "Someone had to maintain the balance in the space station."

"How do you suppose Duriken Sunteel was murdered?"

"I would assume someone plugged into the system and tore her life force from her."

"She popped a valve. Wouldn't that suggest a great deal of internal pressure or something?"

"That is what it would suggest. But you must remember, she was part of the station when it happened."

"Part of the station?"

"She'd become one with the unit surrounding us."

"How did she do that?"

"We have the power to interface with purely mechanical equipment the same way we can interface with purely organic beings. We are superior in that respect."

"That created a value-added tax, so to speak."

He stared at me, confused, just like Hadrien got when I fell into my East London slang, so I clarified myself. "The stress of maintaining control of the internal operations of the station was overwhelming enough. Fighting off an interloper was too much to handle."

"Yes. That is exactly right." Rold stopped to stare at the metallic banding across his knuckles. "I wonder one thing about her death."

"And that would be?"

"We were all shipped off the Baderes before Duriken pulled the switch. There may have been a stowaway, but I really doubt it. The last time I checked, all personnel had been evacuated from the station. There was only a single life sign as we jettisoned off. At least, that is what the scanners indicated."

I finished for him, seeing where he was going with his determination. "In other words, you think the person or entity that killed Sunteel was from another dimension."

He nodded, but his only audible response was a beeping sigh.

4

Rold kept tight as a tin clam, refusing to implicate anyone, refusing to talk about anyone, refusing to give us any more clues than we'd already gotten.

I have to be honest; I suspected from the start that we might not be looking for a bloke on this side of the dimensional curtain. As Hadrien and I had found out with the little experimentation that we'd done with the alien implants, there were a goodly measure of creepy entities greasing the engine of cosmic interdimensionality.

When it looked like we were throwing a ball against a soft wall, we let Rold return to his quarters on the station and invited a female Idealian into our cubby for a little polite conversation as well as a few well-placed innuendoes. Hadrien seemed nervous, like he was uncomfortable with the whole subject, so I decided to sit back and play with this mechanical hussy's horoscope in an attempt to shed some metaphysical light upon the situation at hand. Mostly, though, I stared at her fleshy titties, marveling how ingenious life could be. If those breasts held milk, then it would have to flow out on the snapping energy of electricity. They were lightly carved with blue veins that looked suspiciously of wiring and made me wonder about such things as personal schematics.

"You're called Gasba, and you're the team physician," Hadrien said. "Are you progenitor or immaculate?"

Mechanical noise added static to her voice, accentuating the imperious tone of her words. "I am progenitor. Immaculates are not doctors. They are not even nurses."

"How was Duriken Sunteel's health?" Hadrien asked. "Oil flowing to all the right parts? Gears turning like they should?"

Gasba tossed him a look that had a death threat attached. "You mock my species."

"Yeah, I do," he said. "I suppose you've never mocked a Human?"

She lost her snarling expression, and it was as if her face receded into a valley surrounded by peaks of metallic cheekbone coils. "Sunteel passed every test. She was in excellent physical condition. All the oil flowed to the right parts."

"What about mentally?"

"Mentally, she was as close to perfect as could be achieved."

"What gauge do you use to determine perfect?"

She shook her head. "Having Humans trying to discover a mechanoid killer is a useless application of time and energy. You know nothing of my species. Your Emperor Theo meddles in situations that he should avoid. Our apex stupidly listens to his murmurings when he should be eradicating his interference."

"We never said we were looking for an Idealian," I interrupted.

"That is your focus, nonetheless."

Hadrien growled back into the conversation. "By what gauges do you measure mental fitness, Doctor?"

She snorted, and it sounded like it was composed of loose gravel spinning in a trap. "Our brains are a combination of organic and mechanoid systems. For instance, we have brain chemicals, but the release of these agents is determined by silica-based, nanoprocessors found within the nucleus of neurons. You, as a totally organic-carbon creature, rely upon brain chemicals being expertly timed by your body's rhythmic actions. When it is time for your brain to send thyroxine to your thyroid glands, it simply does it. But with us, we can inhibit the flow of any brain chemical simply by willing it so. We, therefore, take an active part in balancing our emotional and physical states. Sunteel was a powerful Idealian. She scored consistently high on the tests for mental stability."

"And yet she was willing to commit suicide to see this planet pulled back into alignment."

"We do not use this concept of suicide. It was her duty if she were to expand at an evolutionary level. She was a favorite in the apex's court. He granted her this opportunity. It was a gift."

"Some gift," Hadrien muttered.

The doctor shrugged. "If the experiment had been successful, Sunteel would have been placed among the pantheon of levern." She paused, and it looked like she sneered, but a second later the expression disappeared. "Levern are like Human saints, except that their families are treated in great reverence and their progeny enjoy several political and social benefits."

"How do immaculates feel about such things?"

"I do not know. I would suggest that you ask one of them. They do not make obligations to the levern. They have their own pantheon to observe and serve."

"Do progenitors and immaculates get along peacefully in your society?"

She weighed the question for at least twenty seconds. "No, we do not. We have our differences just like the peoples on your home world. As Earthers you must understand that domestic difficulties arise easily. We are not a species without passion."

Hadrien leaned back in his chair, his movement sending a squeal into the room. He studied the Idealian silently and gave me time to pull up Duriken Sunteel's chart.

From what I could tell, Sunteel was heavy into Neptune energy. Neptune represents one of the subprinciples of the interplanetudes known as the tenet of instrumentation. A person so heavily weighted in this force tends to surrender his personal will to serve the universe. This alignment increases the need to make a statement of humanitarian pleasure. A Neptunian influence will find a way to release powerful urges that express spiritual understanding or upheaval. If Neptune is negatively aspected, then the upheaval can turn dark and evil, and for Sunteel, this was a major consideration. Neptune squared Uranus, a planet devoted to creative outreach—meaning she fought grandiose egotism in her desire to produce a legacy. Dr. Gasba, like Rold, probably thought of Sunteel as a visionary with a mean streak, but a visionary, nonetheless, and she would go to any lengths to protect her memory.

"What do you think happened to Sunteel?" Hadrien asked quietly.

Gasba burned a moment before answering. "I think she was murdered by her mate."

Hadrien flipped through the manila paper folder he'd put together for the case. "You are talking about Progenitor Jandel Sajan?"

"Yes. A thoroughly despicable creature."

"Why? Was he more organic that mechanoid?"

"He was a disgusting ooze of miscalculation. What Sunteel saw in him was beyond my understanding."

"Money, power, influence, perhaps?"

"Money? We have a social government. We are paid in stipends, and our sustenance is provided."

"But power and influence do make a difference, huh?"

"Yes. Always."

"Why would Sajan want to see her dead?"

"Because she represented everything he wasn't: courage, determination, self-will. No matter what he did, he could not find the same balance that she had."

"Why do you think that was?"

"Because he was born with about half the nanoprocessors that she had."

"In other words, he was stupid."

"Not stupid—slow. It takes him too much time to process things. He is like an Earth lizard—a creature who must first warm himself in the sun before becoming alive."

"He had an issue about coming on-line, mechanoidly speaking."

"Yes. That is a serious flaw in my species. Much talent and determination goes unrecognized by this limitation."

"If he wasn't in Sunteel's league, then how could he have possibly murdered her?"

Gasba adjusted her weight in the chair. "He wasn't unintelligent. He could have figured out something."

"Like what?"

"I do not know. Many things. Maybe he possessed the ability to negotiate interdimensional vibrations."

"Went in the back door on the zero-point gravity induction."

"Maybe."

The moment after the doctor replied, her assertion gained a little value, because there was a decided shift to the feeling of our surroundings. I knew without a doubt that an electronic mooring wire had broken free of the Baderes, allowing the station to drift into the flowing frequency of creation energy.

5

Existence became creamy. Like hot butter in a cool churn, it flowed through me to congeal heavily into places like my lungs, joints, and stomach. I sat back in the chair, but it felt as though I kept going, floating through the object until I was nearly prone. Hadrien hadn't moved; he'd simply closed his eyes, experiencing this rarefied atmosphere while soaking in a pervasive feeling of joy tinged with abject terror.

It was as if we could never get past the fear once we activated the studs on the alien implants and stepped into creation energy. We'd tried for weeks on end to analyze the reason for this unsettling emotion. There never seemed to be anything to be frightened of when standing in this bright energy, but something was never right. I kept thinking that it had to do with a lack of boundaries. I just couldn't recover my equilibrium without a comfort zone to zoom to.

Sound, sight, and thought functioned fine in this vibrational frequency, and a loud snap abruptly drew my interest to the Idealian. Gasba wore a panicked mask, her indigo eyes had grown large and round in her wire-bundled head. Then, much to my surprise, dark fluid oozed from her mouth; she took a ragged breath; and then she slumped backward, hanging dead in space and time.

Alarms sounded throughout the station, and suddenly, someone turned off the creation spigot, stanching the

flow of the universal vibration. Dr. Gasba slammed the
deck with a heavy thunk. Hadrien and I shook off the
lethargy and went to her aid. Unfortunately, it was too
late.

We knelt before her, seeing for the first time that the
pop valve on her neck had broken open like an exploding egg. Black blood and dark mucus bubbled from the
wound as did a sickly sweet scent. Hadrien came to a
slow stand and took three long steps to reach the wall
communicator. He slammed the speaker button with
the flat of his hand, and when someone finally answered, he sighed in response, "We need a medic in
here. Dr. Gasba is down. From all appearances, she
seems to be dead."

It was Telroni who answered. "We're endeavoring to
send assistance, Investigator Hadrien. There are several
other injured Idealians, too."

"What happened?" Hadrien demanded.

"Unknown." With that, the Senerian cut the communication, leaving Hadrien and me with the corpse and
more questions.

"This station is a can of bolts ready to fly apart,"
Hadrien muttered.

"Yes," I answered, sitting back on my bum. "But
where are the bolts going to fly—through this dimension
or into another?"

He shook his head and returned to hunker down beside me. "Tell me you saw this coming in our horo-
scopes,"

"I didn't have a clue, Artie."

He sighed again. "We're not going to get the truth out
of anyone here." He paused, took a deep draw of air,
and then changed the subject. "This jump into zero-point
gravity was different."

"I agree, but I can't seem to find words to express
what was different about it." I crawled to a stand, feeling

grit beneath my hands when I pushed off the deck.

"It was as if it was out of phase just slightly," he added quietly.

I nodded, but the corpse unsettled me, so I turned away deliberately to stare out of the viewing porthole. The window was large, and the glittering rings of Bohdan were enchanting; diamonds and rubies with sparkling topaz and emeralds. The planet had a strange mix for an atmosphere but was mostly pink ammonia. How weird that a poison to Humans could create a pastel paradise for another species.

My interest in the murder case momentarily fled as the scene out the porthole stirred my imagination, and I considered universal possibilities. While the interplanetudes gave balance to the way the dimensions or causal planes worked, it was not by any means a complete science.

"Having seen this happen," Hadrien said, "I'm wondering if Duriken Sunteel merely tripped and fell while in zero-point gravity."

I turned. He'd abandoned the body to stand behind me at the porthole. "They use interstellar modes of travel, including zpg. If there was a specific problem, it would have arisen in the beginning, don't you think?"

"I think lots of things," he murmured. "These folks give me the willies. I don't like people who beep."

I shivered. "I don't like dead blokes, whether they beep or not."

He nodded and placed an arm comfortingly around my shoulder. "Do you have a zpg headache?"

Our forays into the creation via the door provided by the implants occasionally left us with noggin bangers. "No. I feel all right. Outstanding, as a matter of fact."

"Yeah, full of life, huh?"

Now that he said it, yes. I was reenergized like never before.

Three Idealian males stormed into the small room like an avalanche of gray steel boulders. They ignored us to rush to Gasba's body, communicating in clicks, wheezes, beeps, and flutters, while they pulled on tubes, pop rivets, fingers, and hair. One of the medics paused to back away before confronting us. He was a Goliath, but his words were spoken low. "What happened to her?"

"We don't know," I answered. "One minute she was fine, the next minute the Baderes apparently launched into a phased inconsequence, and she couldn't take it."

He nodded and spun on his studded heel to fling an order at the duo working frantically over Gasba. "Stop. Call for a body bag. There is no hope for this one."

The others halted immediately, stood, bowed, and charged from the room. Their leader waited for the hatch to close behind them before he transferred his attention onto us. "I'm Dr. Drer. I was Gasba's counterpart."

"Counterpart? Do you mean you were married?"

"Married? Yes, that is how it would translate to Humans. We were married for many Earth years. We were partners." Then, without prelude, he blurted out the reason for her death and the noise and fierce power in which he did it made us both back away. "Gasba did not possess an IDT node. Blast, that Duriken!"

"What the hell is an IDT node?" Hadrien asked.

Drer hesitated a moment, and when he answered, he'd resumed his calm, soft manner. "It is a protuberance at the ends of our brain stems. It enables Idealians to balance the conflicting vibrations within zero-point gravity. Duriken's had gone bad. My mate had donated her own so that the experiment could commence under Duriken's direction. When the shift happened, Gasba couldn't sustain the influence. Her death must have been excruciating."

6

*We decided to call it an evening with the inter-*views to give the staff a chance to bring the station back into balance. To be honest, we needed a little help ourselves to recover our own footing, and Hadrien was the first to escape our interrogation cubbyhole. He led me down dark corridors to our temporary quarters in another lonely sector of the Baderes. Once inside, he did a paranoid thing by changing the locking sequence on the hatch.

"They've given us room and board as far from the main population as they could," he said, turning back to me. "I don't like it. Keep your ears and eyes open, Philipa. There are so many aliens and so many things going on that I have a feeling that we are being kept sequestered for a bad reason."

I shook my head and checked out the room. It was dingy, dirty, and greasy. A small heater embedded in the bulkhead looked like it was the only environmental control in the whole room. "God, I've stayed in better fleabags on Earth."

Hadrien managed a grin. "I've got a feeling that you may find more than Earthers' fleas bedded down in this space. Watch where you put your bare ass, okay?"

I smiled, nodded, and it took a step toward the crooked metal counter that comprised the galley. "The next few days are going to be hard ones."

"Meaning?"

"Meaning that Saturn is easing in on Uranus—constricted freedom of action."

"Us?"

"And them."

Hadrien grunted, but beyond that, he didn't reply. I checked the old-fashioned fusion cooker on the counter, and I saw his reflection in the glass door when I opened it.

Hadrien was a former lieutenant with Earth's Terrapol, a galactic police force, but after we'd had our noses pushed into the dirt by the government of our home world, he'd decided to leave his career behind and become a private flatfoot. I'd gone with him, saying goodbye to a planet that didn't seem to merit my interest anymore. Our collaboration had made my days a confusing confrontation of feelings mixed up with undefined guilt because I'd recently come off the nastiness of losing my husband, Eric. I worked through the abundance of emotion about him on a daily basis simply because I could no longer avoid it. Being treated with such respect and love by Hadrien had made me realize how thoughtless a bastard Eric had been.

"What do you think is on that planet below us that is so valuable as to try an interdimensional stunt like this?"

He shrugged. "I suppose it could be anything."

"Anything? No. I checked out the almanac on Bohdan. It's composed of a small iron core, has very little water, and air that smells like a fresh wank in the heat of the summer. There is nothing remarkable about this planet."

"Well, there is something going on beyond experimental interest. Did you finish reading the background on this project?"

"Yes. Over a trillion Earth credits to finance the operation, and that's just what Theo spent. All for a ball of rock with fewer natural minerals than a standard meteor?"

I walked into the bedroom and smelled urine. Checking the accommodations, I found general filth. "Well, it would seem that the money did not go toward housekeeping. This station looks like it's seen better days. Maybe it killed Sunteel. You know, choked her to death with a bit of loose rust."

Hadrien laughed but didn't answer. I stomped back into the main room, where I found him with his face stuck in front of an open refrigeration unit. He shook his head. "They've stowed the ice box with Senerian cold dinners. That crap is worse than eating dirt." Hadrien slammed the door, shaking the odd little knick-knacks on the counter above it. He swung about and headed for our travel trunk to dig into the dried food provisions we always transported with us. Selecting a large package of dehydrated carrots, he threw the moisture bag into a small cooker. He was about to continue his observation about non-Human species when a tentative tapping at the hatch interrupted his domestic duties.

Now, I've roved all over the galactic outback, but the bloke on the other side of the entrance was as weird as it could get. It had gray skin similar to the Idealian hide, but that was as far as the similarities went. I counted four eyes, each one a bauble set high atop a quivering, fleshy stalk. Soft, black hair ran in streamers between these appendages, stopping just above its thick-lipped mouth. The alien had four arms, four hands, sixteen fingers, each mounted with slate-colored sucker pads. It wasn't a big capper—in fact, it was only about a meter and a quarter tall—but all those eyes set atop its head made me feel like it had the power to stare right through me.

Hadrien remained outwardly uninspired, yet the catch

in his question told me otherwise. "Who are you?"

The creature bowed and answered in a surprisingly rich, deep baritone voice. "I am Va-qua-nua."

"And I ask again: Who are you?"

"I am a Bohdan. I was here during the experiment."

Hadrien glanced at me before shrugging. I pointed to the stained red couch decorating the far wall of our quarters. The alien slunk to the seat, squatting slightly before settling onto the lumpy settee.

It took him only a moment to bring stillness to his many appendages. Once accomplished, he explained his reasons for seeking us out. "I am an Idealian servicer."

"A servicer?" I asked, joining Hadrien and him in the sitting area. "What's a servicer? A servant, perhaps?"

"In a manner of speaking, yes, a servant is what I would be known as on Earth. I was here to take care of the team members' personal hygiene."

"You're the bath boy?" Hadrien asked.

Va-qua-nua nodded, and his eyeballs shook. "They do not bathe as many species do. It would affect them adversely to do so."

"Oh, they fight a bit of rust," I answered.

"It is not rust, but a fair analogy. Certain elements do not mix well with their mechanoid physiology. Also, it is difficult for them to tend to their needs because they have a limited range of movement. They are stiff."

"How did you become a servicer?" I asked.

He sighed, making a little popping noise. "My people are homeless because of the disaster that our planet befell. We were forced to rely upon the generosity of other species." He stopped speaking and let his gaze nip along his suction cups. Glancing up, he blew a hard breath through delicate-looking nostrils. "I used to be a teacher, a professor of Bohdan literature. Unfortunately, the Idealians have no use for our culture or art. I found employment where I could."

"Just how old are you?" I asked.

"In Earther terms? I am approximately three hundred years old."

Hadrien whistled. "So you were there when the moon rode away."

"Yes, I was there. The devastation started slowly at first. Ice mantles shifting, polar decay, weather changes. It did not take long, though, before the effects were irreversible. We could no longer live on the planet that had supported my kind for millions of years."

"It must have been difficult to leave."

"Yes. Families were torn apart by the exodus. Some people migrated to Istos, some to the Regerian home world of Carnova, some to Seneria, and even some went to Paltoni-ga. The Idealians needed our domestic capabilities, and so they provided sanctuary in return for our service support." He stopped speaking again, but instead of aiming his gaze at his fingers, he looked out the porthole. "Such a beautiful world, so hostile, so unique, so unattainable. I do miss it."

"Why have you come to us?" Hadrien demanded. He leaned forward in the high-backed chair he'd claimed and stared at this runt of an alien as if he could see something that wasn't obvious.

"To warn you that there is treachery afoot," Va-qua-nua answered. "Administrator Telroni is not who he claims to be."

"Who is he?"

Va-qua-nua angled his body toward Hadrien as though he were meeting him halfway. "He is a Shimbang."

"And what is a Shimbang?" I asked quietly.

He shivered slightly as he answered. "A Shimbang is a ghost who has been induced into corporeality from another causal plane. This station is haunted with them, and they are very dangerous."

7

I know that words and meanings between interga-lactic species can prove to be trouble and strife. I've learned to keep my jelly-bits into myself over the years, but after hearing this creature's assertion, I couldn't help it. I smiled.

Seeing it, Va-qua-nua assumed the wrong reason. "You don't believe me."

"On the contrary, I do." Eric was still a night visitor for me, though I lay soft and comfortable in Hadrien's embrace. Leaks in the space/time continuum seemed to be more frequent with me now. Ghostly apparitions, creepy feelings, and strange smells invaded my sleep every day. It was like I was locked partially into the creation energy and the doors to other dimensions were always slightly ajar. "I suppose I'm trying to get a handle on what kind of creature a Shimbang is."

"They are evil. You never know when they will appear to take over the bodies of the innocent."

"Well, I'm confused," Hadrien said. "Is Telroni dead, animated by this life force, or is he some kind of host?"

Va-qua-nua shook his eye stalks. "Death is a matter of perspective, is it not?"

"And exactly what perspective do the Shimbang come from?"

"The Shimbang are an old species. They have affected many planets in this galaxy, including, I'm sure, your own home world of Earth."

"Where is their home world?" I asked.

"I do not know. Legend says it is beyond the stars at the place where time begins."

"Beyond the stars? Do you mean they are from the next dimension?"

"I cannot say. All I can say for sure is Telroni is a Shimbang. To answer your previous question, there is one thing I know to be true about this species. When the Shimbang exits Administrator Telroni's body, he will die. The exodus of the Shimbang life force will take his with it."

Hadrien sat back in the chair, sighed, and ran a hand through his long hair. "How can you tell Telroni is a Shimbang? He's got a pair of meat hooks that would make any Senerian jealous."

Va-qua-nua pursed his thick lips and whipped a hand through his own hair. "You must understand. A Shimbang can be anything it wants to be for whatever reason."

"So can you see the differences with your eyes?" I asked.

"No. I sense the difference with my hide."

"Your skin is sensitive to perceiving life forces that are naked to the normal sight range?"

"Yes. That is correct. I am a visual creature. You might think of me as a walking ocular sheath. I can see at the molecular level. When I increase my perceptive level, I can detect motion at an atomic level."

Suddenly, I felt jaybird naked. "What else do you know about the Shimbang?"

"These beings fill out the corporeal visage, but they lack the ability to complete the form at the atomic level. If they could, they would be trapped in the shape they assume. I think such a situation might be hideous to these beings."

I nodded. When traveling within the midst of the creation energy, I have passed through solid walls, a trick that always fills me with trepidation. Should something go wrong, I would be trapped, my atomic particles mixing with those of the wall. I could understand why the Shimbang might find this a repulsive situation. "Is there an imposed time limit on them?"

"I do not know."

"Why would the Shimbang be interested in your world?" Hadrien asked.

"They are not. They are interested in the space that contains it."

"What does that mean?"

He shrugged. "There is something about the nature of resident vibrations surrounding Bohdan. I do not know what it is."

"Do the Idealians know?"

Again he shrugged. "I cannot say."

I glanced at Hadrien and saw a small frown litter his features. Turning my attention back to Va-qua-nua, I burned a moment studying him. "Are your people happy as servicers?"

"Happiness is a Human emotion. I am neither unhappy nor happy. I simply am. It is enough."

Alien philosophy turned smoke screen. That kind of crap never made sense to me, so I used a little perspective of my own. The Bohdans would desire to have their home world returned to them at all costs. It would eventually become an obsession. "There are several Idealians here. Did they bring their servicers?"

"No. I am the only one."

"Were you going to stay with Sunteel once she'd activated the zero-point gravity device?"

He wet his lips with a long, black tongue. "No. I was to return home to enter into another's service. She'd sold her personal property, intent upon not returning. My services transferred."

"Who is your new employer?"

"Jandel Sajan. He is her former mate."

"We understand that they had some kind of falling out," I said.

Va-qua-nua shook his head. "I do not understand."

"Did they part on amicable terms?"

"All Idealians are amicable. I do not know the specific circumstances between them."

Hadrien pushed past this to return to the Shimbang. "You said Telroni is posing as a Senerian."

"That is correct."

"What happened to the real Senerian who was the station operator?"

"I do not know. Telroni, the Shimbang, was here when the Idealian team arrived."

"Who else was with him?"

"Several other Senerians, Humans, many Idealians, and a few Regerians. All beings who were what they claimed to be."

"Are you certain?"

"Yes."

"What was the relationship between Sunteel and Telroni?"

"Mild antagonism. He is a rather impetuous creature."

"What does that mean?"

"That means he wanted to launch the final phase of the project before the research was examined and verified."

"Why?"

"It was money, so he said. This project was costing the Senerians a great deal."

"But if he's Shimbang, why would he care?"

"Shimbang have their own agendas. I do not know what this specific one requires."

"And so they are using the Idealians as a means to the end," I said. "But why?"

"The Idealians are the only species that I am aware of who can expand their life force to appreciable sizes."

"What does that mean?" Hadrien barked.

Va-qua-nua swiveled his head and his eyeballs shivered on their stalks. "They are the essence of zero-point gravity."

"Explain that. We're a couple of laymen."

The creature rose and took two shuffling steps before spinning about to face us again. "The nature of zero-point gravity is this: It is a force that creates something from nothing. It is how this universe was formed. Do you agree?"

"Yes."

"When most creatures are formed, they contain the elements of zero-point gravity. It is the force that creates them, that brings them from nothing into something. Humans call this the life force, essence, or soul. It animates and generates. It fills the shell of corporeality."

"So?"

"So, that is all that it does. My life force is contained within my body, as is yours. It doesn't leak out unless there is death. It does not transmute, diffuse, or disappear. Once brought into a state of something, it remains as something. Energy can only be converted."

"And mass can only be converted relative to mass," I said.

"Exactly. At least for you and every other being known in this galaxy, even the Shimbang. The ghost cannot animate into something that contains more mass than the essence it has to fill it."

"But the Idealians can," I answered.

"That is correct. When Sunteel melded with the space station, she increased her force and matched the mass of the Baderes. She literally expanded her life force to fill it."

"Can all Idealians do this?"

"No," he said. "Only those who are born correctly. They must have the proper parameters of the IDT node."

8

*Va-qua-nua left us with more questions than an-*swers, but we were so tired from the day's travel and ensuing problems that we ate our reconstituted veggies in silence before retiring.

As we lay in the narrow bunk, Hadrien wrapped his arms around me like I was the last hot buttered crossbun left on the shelf. It was partly a sign of affection, but more than anything else, it was a worry that I might disappear into the night, hop-skipping into the nether regions of the next dimension. His days spent with the implant had left him more open to the sorrow that underpinned the material realm. While packed inside the creation energy, this sense of disappointment could be overwhelming—so overwhelming that he'd not ventured into zero-point gravity in many weeks.

My gaze was drawn to the porthole and the glittering rings of the planet. The world was a useless ball of dust, yet it was mystifyingly beautiful. It was as if it held a resonance of its own that most planets didn't have. Earth was a rock with such power, but it was also full of life energy, and this verdancy carried its own signature throughout creation. What was it that haunted Bohdan?

I flipped over and snuggled closer to my lover, but before I could close my eyes, it happened again. As I said before, life moves through me, and it did so at that very moment. I could see snicks and snacks of other dimensions, not in their full splendor, but as floaters and zippers. They coalesced in sparkling colors, all strange creatures that didn't resemble Humans in any way. Rest period after rest period, they would come without fail as if I were more awake psychically when I was almost asleep. Whatever the reason, it was starting to drive me billi-bonkers. This evening, the beings came and went in varied procession—hundreds of them.

"Visitors?" Hadrien whispered.

I turned my head slightly to see him studying me, a look of understanding and compassion giving testimony to his concern. "Yes. There are so many tonight. I've never encountered this number of beings before. Maybe it has something to do with the Baderes. I don't know."

"A dimensional vortex of sorts?"

"Might be. Then again, it may have nothing to do with it."

He kissed me lightly upon the neck, nuzzling, unable to do more than that. For some blessed reason, he couldn't see or feel these night travelers, and I envied him. I felt like a peeper taking in a storefront show down in the alien red light district of interdimensionality.

I sat up, swinging my bare legs over the edge of the bunk and feeling the cold blast of filtered air from a semiclogged environments register. A flicker of red caught my attention, and I glanced toward the sticky galley counter. Standing there was an odd, shimmering being. He came, he went, and I put him out of my mind.

"What's wrong?" he asked.

"Nothing. I just have to hit the Jimmy Riddle." With that, I padded to the bathroom, where I rinsed my eyes with stale water dribbling from a tiny sink spigot. It did little to refresh me, but at the moment I dried my cheeks, my attention faltered at the dusty mirror. I could see faces and people staring at me. They changed like some flicking cartoon, so fast I had to look away to keep dizziness from swamping me.

This place was so active that I couldn't sleep, even though my eyes hurt from the changes in pressure, atmosphere, and close work at the calculator. So, instead of going back to bed, I decided to take another look at this strange case of Duriken Sunteel. I glanced at Hadrien as I stepped back into the bedroom. He slept peacefully, his bulk spread across the bunk.

I walked into the main suite, poured a fruit drink from our valise supplies, and decided to have a look at a few of the documents the Senerian government had passed to us. Plopping down at the table, I pulled the overhead lamp close to the hard paper facsimiles. It wasn't that I was much interested in the documents themselves; it was the signature at the bottom of each that excited the divvy in me.

An astrologer must use whatever scientific or arcane methods support her cause. I had no problem breaking the backs on a new set of astro-cards any more than I did reading palms. In this case, I'd figured that any personal information translated to us about the suspects would be false or wrong, so any logos I prepared would stink like little bunny farts. The episode with Gasba proved me right in my prudence, and I was glad I'd thought to get a signature of each team member. The Senerian government had balked at the price of sending actual paper to me, but in the end, a courier had left them in our quarters while we'd been interviewing Immaculate Rold.

I picked up the top document and found Sunteel's scrawling hand. She made the first letters of each of her names large and flowing, which indicated that she was a person who contained a lot of water energy. Translated into astro-speak, Sunteel could identify a problem and find a flowing solution to it. It also indicated that she might have difficulties thinking for herself and listening to her own guidance—both concepts falling in the house

of Virgo. A small *l* pulling up her last name told me
that she suffered from the effects of a transiting Saturn,
and if a project lasted too long or the conflicts were too
fierce, she might lose her self-confidence in most ven-
tures. Had this happened to her here at Baderes? Had
the trouble with her mate made Sunteel careless? Had
she been plagued by low self-esteem because the challenges of the experiment had been too great?

I dropped her document and scrabbled through a stack
looking for one signed by Rold. His handwriting was a
series of hard, angular strokes and deep lines. There was
a passle-full of Mars energy pushing out of that signature. I moved on from Rold to Dr. Gasba, finding a person who had a more nurturing attitude than I'd given
her credit for when we'd met. A nurturer, yes, but she
also had a strong Gemini pull, one that made her conceal
her soft side.

Flipping through the stack, I stopped at a document
signed by Dr. Drer. It was a medical release form for a
Senerian named Ulan Malu. The signature was shaky,
tight, and by no means legible. This tin can had what
looked like a case of the nerves.

My study was abruptly interrupted by the buzzing of
the intercom. I reached around the hatch and banged the
button with the flat of my hand. "What?" I demanded.

"This is Cordous Anu. I am sorry to bother you, Astrologer Cyprion, but we have a rather remarkable situation of which you should be in attendance."

"What's happened?" Hadrien called out from the
other room.

"We've discovered a body in one of the ventilation
shafts," Anu answered. "We do not recognize the species."

9

We rushed to the designated location and did indeed find a creature who looked like it should have been the mix for steak and kidney pie.

Hadrien crawled into the vent before me, making room for me to squeeze into the conduit beside him so I could better study this strange-looking alien.

It was orange, bright and brilliant, like my mum's St. Patrick's Day glad rags. The thing had two skinny little legs that ended in stumpy paws, little hands with blunt fingers, and a bubble head that carried one enormous, round eyeball. Though it was as naked as the day it came into this dimension, I couldn't tell if it had titties or a Hamstead wick and so there was no way to decide if it was female or male.

The smell filling the shaft reminded me of rubbing alcohol, and there was no outward sign of death: no feces, no urine, no blood.

"What do you make of it?" Anu called out.

I glanced back to see him standing a ways beyond the vent opening, holding his hand over his nose. Obviously, his mechanoid sniffer had some sort of natural device to enhance odors. "It's a regular mystery, mate. When was this station last swept?"

"A day ago. I had my unit check all traps and shafts. It was not here then."

Telroni's face appeared at the end of the vent. "Do you have any idea what it is?"

"Not a clue," Hadrien said.

"Well, it certainly stinks," he answered.

I swiveled a private look at Hadrien, who shook his head slowly. "What exactly do you people smell?"

"It is foul," the mechanoid answered. "Can you not ascertain that for yourself?"

"Let's drag it out of here and get it to sick bay for a once-over," I ordered.

"I will get a crew on it immediately," Telroni said before disappearing from view.

I backed out of the vent, and Hadrien crawled after me. Once standing in the corridor, we discovered that we each had sticky, orange fairy dust all over our nice, clean, dark blue jumpsuits.

"Ah, this is a real pony trap, it is," I whined, wiping some of the sparkles from my pants. "I suppose we need to get this analyzed."

Anu studied our clothes before shutting his eyes. He stood there for a minute whirring to himself. Opening his eyes again, he shook his head. "I receive no vibratory evidence out of the ordinary from the dust upon your uniforms. To be honest, though, I think you need to incinerate your apparel."

"It doesn't stink that bad," Hadrien snapped.

"Maybe not to you, but my nose is going numb." Anu took several steps away from us. Before we could reply, he barked a command into the small, square communicator resting upon his shoulder. He then strode away.

"Weird-ass aliens," Hadrien grumbled. Then, settling his attention onto me, he cocked his head toward the creature in the vent. "I've never seen anything like this fellow, even during my vacations into the next dimension."

"It may not be from the next dimension," I said. "Or the dimension beyond that." I paused to lean on the lip of the shaft. "What if it were accidentally scooped up when the space station shifted into the creation flow?"

"You're suggesting that it was in the process of interdimensional travel when it smacked into the Baderes?"

"Why not?"

He grunted. "Now, that would cause an interdimensional incident, wouldn't it?"

His words made something tickle the back of my brain, but I couldn't pull up the thought to scratch it. I turned away and took a few steps down the hallway toward sick bay. Hadrien followed, and we passed Dr. Drer as the Idealian stomped by with a cleanup crew. He turned up his nose at us, frowning at this smell that eluded us. We'd only walked a few meters more before he barked a question in our direction.

"Is this not the vent in which the dead creature was found?"

We stopped and spun around to stare at him. He stood at the end of the shaft, glaring at us.

"Yes," I said. "What's the matter? Can't you smell it?"

"I can neither smell it nor see it."

"I didn't know Idealians had a sense of humor," Hadrien said.

"I am not trying to be humorous. This vent is empty."

I couldn't hide a scowl of displeasure and barely kept a civil tongue in my head during the trot back to the shaft. We wheeled up beside Drer and, gazing up the cut, we found that the mechanoid did not lie. The little alien was gone.

"Well, this doesn't make any sense," Hadrien muttered. "It was here a minute ago."

"Perhaps it was not dead," Drer offered. "Of course, if the smell you wear was from its fluids, then I would say that it was in the final stages of decay."

I spun away from the shaft. The second I did, I ex-

perienced an attack of nausea and a strike of dizziness.
I reeled against the bulkhead, slamming hard into it as
I fought for my balance. Hadrien was right there to support me, but I slid down the wall and landed with a plop
on my arse. Everything faded on me, the scene in the
corridor turned fuzzy, and the face of my lover swam
out of view. I panicked, realizing that I had been drawn
into an interdimensional twist of some sort. I could feel
night visitors passing through me, tugging on my life
force while they moved on by. In my mind, I screamed
for them to hear me, but each time they trod upon my
soul, I lost a bit more of my grounding in corporeality.
It was then that I saw the strange creature who a moment
before had lain dead in the ventilation shaft.

I reached out with my thoughts, trying to communicate my discomfort and fear, but it shook its head and
pointed beyond me. I followed its stubby hand to see
that this alien was not alone. On the periphery of understanding, I was presented to millions of little orange
souls, all crying out in pain and dismay.

The sound was deafening, a roar like I'd never heard
in the material plane. I struggled to escape this torture,
but before I managed to slide back into my own continuum, I fell down one of those long, dark, interdimensional rabbit holes.

10

I awoke to the harsh lights of the Baderes's sick bay and to the concerned expression worn by Hadrien. He stood over me, gently massaging my forehead as if this would chase the bloody-assed demons from my mind. If only it could.

"How do you feel?" Hadrien whispered.

I struggled to sit up, but he pushed gently against my collarbone, and I realized I was as weak as fiddlesticks. My throat was like the deserts of Moran-ee, but it didn't stop me from squeezing words through the grit. "What happened?"

"You collapsed," he answered. Before he could continue, he was joined by Drer, who touched the crook of my elbow to take my pulse.

"Your blood pressure was greatly elevated," he said. "That is quite a shortcoming of your species."

"I suppose you've got that problem licked," Hadrien muttered.

Drer glanced at him and then quickly tapped a small beadlike stud at his temple. His eyes rolled back in his head, but instead of seeing a white surface, the underside was a luminous green. It was a chilling surprise, and I shivered while he gave me a once-over as if he were a walking MRI machine. He explained while he checked my innards. "Idealian internal blood pressure is regulated by the presence of nanocells contained within our plasma. They are like tiny, natural computers. These cells regenerate constantly."

"Then how come your mate and Duriken Sunteel popped their corks?" Hadrien asked.

Drer paused, clicked, and then continued with his examination before replying. "That was purely an electrical reaction. At least, I believe it to be so."

"Like a battery exploding?"

"You might equate it with that." He turned silent, intent upon his duties.

I flipped my attention to Hadrien. "Did I phase out of this realm or something?"

He shook his head. "No. As far as I could tell, you stayed in this dimension."

"My awareness didn't."

"What did you experience?"

I didn't answer but waited for Drer to finish his examination. "Can I have some water?"

The Idealian pinged an answer and stomped away to the sink to pour off a tumbler of liquid. I wiggled to a sitting position, despite a wave of dizziness fighting me for my balance. Once up, I felt in a bit more control of the situation. Drer returned and handed me the smudgy, plastic glass. I slugged the tepid water like it was the very blood of Christ, and when my throat felt better, I was able to ask the question that hung onto my frontal lobe. "What do you know about Human physiology?"

Drer rolled his eyeballs back before answering. "Quite a lot, actually. I spent ten Earth standard years as a physician for the mining colony on Traxes Moon. Please do not let my glowing eyeballs fool you." He smiled, and though it didn't make him any prettier, it suddenly made him less formidable.

"Are you all born with the ability to roll back your eyes?" Hadrien asked.

"No. Only some of us have diagnostic talents. We

become doctors, technicians, and mechanics."

Hadrien snorted. "From surgeon to grease monkey."

Drer nodded. "Yes. We are greatly respected for our abilities. It is a hereditary trait in my family."

Heredity? How could something like scanning equipment come down the familial line?

He stopped talking to return the glass to the sink. Then, turning, he studied me. "For our edification, please explain what happened to you. It may help in deducing facts about Duriken Sunteel's murder."

I blew a hard breath, suddenly weary of trying to explain the unexplainable. "I can feel the life forces of species in crossover dimensions. They move through me as if our souls share the same living space. This time, I felt that orange critter we found lying in the vent."

"If it were dead, then it should have remained in the shaft," Drer said. "We can presume that it is alive on some level or was never dead at all."

"You saw more, didn't you?" Hadrien asked.

I stopped talking to touch him gently upon the face. "Yes. There were thousands of these creatures all reaching out like they were in misery." I inserted another pause, almost afraid to admit to the last piece of the puzzle, but finally, I announced my shortcomings. "It scared me into senselessness, I suppose. There were thousands of them, hands and bodies pressing toward me. And the wail was like the damned standing knee deep in the hot coals of Hell."

Drer pinged slightly, and I glanced at him. His expression mirrored Hadrien's, so I changed the subject. "Did you happen to do a scan on the fairy dust we got all over our britches? Anu did a quick check but came up empty. Perhaps it had something to do with me dizzy spell."

"I did analyze it, but I know of no substance like it. There are several configurations. Unfortunately, I could not find a match. It might be sensible to remove those soiled clothes and take them to the station incinerator."

"Is it radioactive or anything?" Hadrien asked.

"Not that I can tell." Drer stood there and in the silence, I heard the whirring sound behind each breath he drew.

"What else?" I asked him as I tried to slide off the table again. Drer stopped me with a hand to my chest. "Please, lie quietly. You need to know what I have found in my examination of your body."

His words caged Hadrien's attention. "Is something wrong?"

Drer shrugged. It was a mechanical movement, almost like a piston rising from the block of an engine. "What I can tell you is this: You are undergoing a change at the molecular level."

"What?" I croaked. "What kind of change?"

"This we know for certain: Zero-point gravity reorients the Human by changing the natural function of the guest cells."

"Guest cells?" Hadrien growled. "What the hell are those?"

"Apparently, in Human prehistory, these cells were, how shall we say, free rangers? They existed as specialized entities. At some point, they melded with the basic cell structures and copied their own DNA sequencing, bringing on cellular regeneration in the person where they reside."

"So, they can be found in every cell in me body?" I asked.

"They exist in most of your cells. Your brain cells are different. I've never encountered them in this portion of the Human body."

Hadrien slipped his hand around my fingers and squeezed reassuringly. "What are you saying, Dr. Drer?"

"I am saying that Astrologer Cyprion now has independent guest cells present in her brain. It is advancing the function of the neuronic activity. This may be why she can see beyond this causal plane."

11

Blast those Waki'el straight to bloody Hell. Their
implant in my wrist had been a success; it had turned
me from Human into something that was betwixt and
between.

Upon hearing Drer's diagnosis, I wanted to shout out
to Hadrien to kill me and to end my misery, but what
good would it have done? The probability was that when
I crossed over into the land of the dead, I would be just
as I was now, unable to even seek comfort in a realm
where people existed as pure energy until the time they
decided to reincarnate.

The consternation must have rung out like the bells
at Westminster Abbey on a quiet Sunday morning, because the Idealian stepped back and stared at Hadrien.
"Perhaps I should leave you alone." With that, he disappeared into the other room and I was forced to finish
this conversation with Hadrien.

"I'm sorry."

Hadrien shook his head. "Philipa, did these dizzy
spells just start?"

"Yes," I answered. "I'm not hiding a dirty dingy from
you, Artie. Since I climbed aboard this rattletrap, I've
been swamped. Maybe Va-qua-nua was right; there's
some sort of spatial anomaly in this sector of the woods,
and I'm being affected by it."

"And why isn't it happening to me?"

I crawled from the bunk and drew out the silence a

minute before replying. Standing there, I fought that
punchy feeling that grabs you after you've come off a
long drunk—only it wasn't from a good saucing. In my
heart I knew that I stood precariously at the edge of
some sort of transformative experience. I was afraid to
take that step, frightened that I might dump over the
precipice into some fiery volcano of afterlife. Could Drer
have been right? Was my brain fat with extra cells that
rampaged around my gray matter like mustangs on a
wild run? "Women have different brain structures than
men. You know that. Besides, the Waki'el didn't know
what they were doing when they linked our bodies to
their equipment. Your implant may not function exactly
the same way mine does."

He growled. "God, I wish I could rip this piece of
shit out of my arm!"

The medics back on Earth hadn't thought it a smart
thing to do. When they checked us, they'd noticed that
the contraptions had made connections on their own,
fusing with our nervous systems and braiding through
ligament, bone, and blood vessels to firmly establish
themselves within the bodies of their unwilling hosts.

"Bastard Waki'el," he said. "If there is a Hell, I hope
their whole goddamned species burns there."

"You've got no protest from me."

Hadrien didn't answer. Instead, he held his hand out
for me to take. After I did, he spoke. "I love you, Philipa. I will be with you as far as I can go."

It was supposed to comfort me, but it did just the
opposite. Rather than show my irritation, I merely nodded, slipped my hand from his, and wobbled to the
hatch. "Let's go talk to Telroni before Va-qua-nua's pre-
diction of his death happens."

"Don't you think you should get some rest?"

"I'm tired. And I'm half afraid to close me eyes."

"Philipa, it's the middle of the sleep period."

"Yes, but now I'm wondering if Va-qua-nua might not be right. Maybe Telroni is really possessed by a Shimbang, and little orange blokes in air vents have no place in their alien agenda."

"So, was this something you gleaned from the creation energy or is a little female intuition cutting in?"

I grinned. "Intuition. That's me bread and treacle. Without it, I'm nothing."

We walked along the corridor in silence after that, and I couldn't help wondering where Hadrien's thoughts led him. There was no indication on his face.

We found Telroni's quarters at a busy intersection near the Baderes's main hub. I pressed the alert bell, joining Hadrien to eyeball all the different species of folks aboard this station.

"There are a lot of people here who aren't here because of the murder investigation," Hadrien said. "It's like the place is an open market for every itinerant trader on his way to some alien mecca."

After a minute, Telroni appeared, looking sharp-eyed and angry at the interruption. It was true that his species were great hibernators, taking every opportunity to sleep, but this bloke looked fresh and ready to attack. He proved it by snapping at me. "What is so important that you come here? Have there been more sightings that Progenitor Anu has not seen fit to inform me of?"

"No," I said. "No more sightings. Hadrien and I are here to visit with you."

"I really do not have time for small talk."

"We've had someone express concerns about you, Administrator Telroni," Hadrien said. "Perhaps you would like to take this opportunity to defend yourself."

His eyes grew large and round, and he stepped back to allow us to enter his quarters. Inside, we found a Spartan cubicle fitted with a single bunk. A small desk sat in one corner, strewn with papers, and two straight-backed chairs completed the furnishings. I didn't sit down but went right to his desk to take a peek at his papers. Telroni seemed not to notice my interest.

"Who has spoken against me?" he demanded.

"We didn't say anyone spoke against you," Hadrien answered, taking a seat. "We only said they had concerns. Tell us, sir, what you think about these orange creatures."

I twisted around to see the expression on this bug's face, but he gave no indication that he was put off by the question.

"I have no idea what they are. The sentient was not invited aboard this station. I can only assume it was aboard one of the ships passing through recently."

"But you swept the station, and he didn't come to light."

Telroni shrugged. "I do not have an answer."

"You don't act very concerned about this invasion."

Telroni grunted. "I am concerned, and I have just finished reading the report. Unfortunately, I am in no position to comment on any of it, much less do anything about it."

"Why not?"

"Because any authority that I once had has been revoked by my government. I received the transmission earlier today. I am to return home as soon as the investigation is complete, where I will be reassigned—to an outpost that will undoubtedly be an unpleasant experience. At this point, I simply do not have the power or authority to do anything about the situation."

I turned from the desk and the papers because everything I saw was written in a language I didn't understand. Stepping to the bunk, I sat down heavily before patting the space beside me. "Join me, Administrator. I'd like to look at your hands."

His face changed then, going from bland to mean. "Excuse me?"

Since the earliest times in Human history, palmistry, or chieromancy, as it was often known, has had a direct connection to astrology, but for centuries both arts were considered merely mumbo jumbo. Fortunately, at the turn of the early twenty-first century, more and more people became enlightened about the intelligence and understanding that ancient mystical practitioners held. They discovered proof that changes in the brain were almost immediately detectable in the changing lines of the hands, something that true arcane scientists have known all along. Thoughts are the builders of transformative experience, and evidence of new mentality can be mapped throughout the Human anatomy. Senerians were like Humans when it came to reading the past, present, and future in their palms.

"I'm an astrologer, Administrator. Allow me to do my job. This interpretation of your palm could clear you of any suspicion."

"Suspicion?" he squeaked. "I believe I have a right to know who has spoken concerns about me."

"Yes, you do, but we were asked not to say anything just yet," Hadrien lied. "Don't worry. If you're innocent, then everything will be all right."

Telroni hesitated, licking his lips with a dark tongue. Finally, he swung into the space next to me and presented me with one of his butcher blocks.

The size of his hand in my lap was a surprise. Yes, it was a big meat chopper, but it had to have weighed a good kilo and a half. It must have hurt his delicate-looking shoulder.

Many alien species contained the same types of elements that Human hands did. This fellow had a couple more fingers, but he had all the appropriate lines and astrological mounts necessary to read. I checked one of his two thumbs first, finding that it was overly long and set high on the hand, indicating determination as well as deep thinking. Moving on to his other digits, I deduced an individual who spent time in deep thought yet who avoided the outward expression of his ideas. He had a small first finger and, unlike his thumb, it was set low on his hand, indicating a person who lacked leadership, strength, and any sort of expertise. This was an odd combination, given the fact that he'd been in charge of this space station for a number of months.

"Well?" Telroni asked.

"I'm not done yet, mate. Give me a few more minutes."

He snuffled but remained silent in his protests, an action that confirmed his inability to express himself.

Before he could find his voice, I checked those little pads on the palm of his hand. These bumps were known as mounts, and they represented the interplay of Jupiter, Saturn, Mercury, Mars, Venus, the Moon, and the Sun. From what I could tell, he showed off a bubbly mount of Saturn and, combined with the conical shape of his fingers, I figured him for a careful, methodical being who leaned toward morbidness. Morbidity was classic with his species, so again, he fit the slot.

He had no mount of Jupiter, which indicated luck and pride, and his mount of the Sun spoke of a creature who was clever but not truly gifted in matters of life. The upper mount of Mars spoke of an individual who had the courage of a soldier, while the mount of the Moon told me he had an absence of common sense. In other words, he could take orders well, because he had a hard time thinking for himself. So, who was calling in the commands for this fife and drum?

I continued on to check Telroni's palm lines, specifically his life line, which jammed right into his rascette, those lines that form on the underside of the wrist. It

told me that he would die while on a long voyage, and
though interdimensional travel was done in the blink of
an eye, it was considered the longest of trips. Seeing this
made me grunt out loud, and this noise brought down
the Senerian's concern.

"What is wrong?" he asked.

"Nothing," I said. "I was clearing me throat."

He squinted at me but didn't question my answer.

The greatest telling sign of a person's overall makeup
was in the shape of the hand. There were several types—
fire hand, air hand, earth hand, water hand, artistic hand,
useful hand, psychic hand—but when I flipped over this
meat hook I was in for another surprise. The coloring
was a slightly tarnished red, and the skin was thick, with
very little elasticity. His fingers were short in compari-
son to the size of his hand, with nails that were under-
developed.

This was the hand of a murderer.

12

*I am nothing if not a fancy dancer, and I side-*stepped my shock by hiding it. A murderer's hand is a rare occurrence indeed. It's more often that the reader sees an idiot's hand.

"Well, what have you formulated by counting the lines upon my hand?" Telroni asked.

"That you are an honest person," I lied.

"Of course," he said, taking his meat chop back. "It is the reason I was assigned to this station for this project. I earned my rank because I have integrity. It was not bestowed upon me through privilege."

"Then perhaps you'll be so honest as to tell us the true intent of this mission," I said flatly.

He studied me for a moment like he was sizing me up for a body bag. Finally, he spoke. "Did you glean a hidden intent from my hand?"

"I gleaned many things, most of which I will keep to meself. Please answer."

"You must realize that the rank of administrator is not that great in the scheme of my government. I am basically a bureaucrat. I route traffic in and out of Baderes, fill out time sheets, write general reports. When the Idealians came, I was given very little information about their experiment. It was need to know and I did not need to know, obviously."

"You had to be aware of something," Hadrien said, slipping from the chair to take a turn around this ugly little cubicle. "Come on, Telroni, you had to be privy to a few transmissions. Spill, and we won't bother you anymore."

That last part was a porky if I ever heard one, but I didn't dispute the fact. Instead, I snapped into Hadrien's badgering. "For instance, why are there so many people here now?"

Telroni shook his head and held his hands wide in surrender. "My government opened up the service routes for my own people as well as the Regerians, Idealians, and Humans. We will probably have visits from the Corrigadaires, too, before it is all over."

"Why did they do that? It's bloody hard to carry on a murder investigation with so many people around."

He shrugged. "I am sure it had to do with money. We are losing funds as each day goes by. Contracts were not honored when Sunteel died. The success of the experiment would have funneled credits into my government coffers. Now that there is no success, we have been forced to find operating capital by extending a welcome to travelers and planetary shippers."

I nodded and then hit him with an off-the-wall question that brought him up short. "What's so important about the space around Bohdan?"

He hesitated before shaking his head. "I have only gathered bits and pieces."

"Of what?" Hadrien growled impatiently.

Telroni stood, wrung his meat hooks together, and then explained in a soft voice. "This part of space has quantum anomalies."

"Such as?" I asked.

He glanced at me. "I am not sure, but I have scanned Idealian reports that talk about the presence of black holes the size of atomic particles."

Hadrien jabbed a look my way. "Mini–black holes?"

"They're only theory," I said.

"Yes, and if they do exist, why have they not affected the planet and this space station? I am not a scientist and so I cannot answer this question. I did recently read a document, though, where Duriken Sunteel claimed to have measured one such anomaly."

"So combine zero-point gravity applications and mini–black holes and you get what?" Hadrien asked.

Telroni grunted. "You get disaster—more than likely."

"Well, now," he answered. "Such a thing would cause concern, wouldn't it?"

"You are suggesting that someone had a vested interest in stopping this experiment because of mini–black holes?"

It was my turn to stand and march toward the hatch. "All things are possible." After motioning to Hadrien to follow, I sequenced the lock. "Thank you for your time, Administrator."

"Am I cleared of suspicion?" he called.

"For now," I answered.

Once outside in the corridor and several meters from Telroni's quarters, Hadrien stopped me. "You seemed awfully fast about getting out of there. What gives, Philipa?"

"A few things," I said. "One of which is that Telroni, whoever he is, has the hand of a murderer. That makes everything he says suspect to me."

Hadrien frowned. "You could actually see that? I really thought all that palm reading stuff was a load of bullshit and you were trying to shake him up for some news."

I shook my head. "I saw it as clear as a pimple on your arse." With that, I continued down the hallway, passing several Idealians as they worked at correcting parallel regulator currents that flowed hot along the bulkhead. Pausing, I studied them for a moment, not surprised when I saw one of them pass his fingers through the streaming bank of ionized crystals. The red line arced like a small sun exploding, but the mechanoid ignored the flash to place a tube in the juncture box beyond the flux.

Hadrien leaned over to whisper in my ear. "What's going on in that brain of yours?"

I reached up to massage his cheek. "Something that I don't hardly believe meself. Come on. You'll know for certain as soon as I do. Let's visit Progenitor Anu."

We didn't find the Idealian at home, but instead, alone on the Baderes's command bridge. He sat in the chair where Sunteel's body had been found, staring at the planet through the observation porthole. When he saw us, he dampened the view by reaching down to the console to snap on the light inhibitors, making it possible for Human eyes to look out the window and not be burned by the glow of the system's sun just beyond the planet.

"Any scorchingly astute ideas?" I asked casually, sliding into a chair opposite him.

He smiled, but his mouth had a mechanical quality that caused me to shoot my gaze away for a second. I pretended to enjoy the scene beyond the glass.

"It's a beautiful world, isn't it?"

"Not especially," he answered.

"Have your people found evidence of the orange creature?" Hadrien asked.

"No, nothing. It is as if it has vanished into another dimension."

Hadrien didn't reply but pulled out a plastic chair to mount it pony style. He stared at Anu, and his serious expression leaked into one that screamed distrust. Even the mechanoid could read it.

"What is wrong?" he demanded. "Do you secretly accuse the Idealians of some devious complicity?"

Hadrien took a deep breath before answering. "Why do you ask? Feel guilty?"

"Idealians do not often express feelings of guilt."

"How jolly for you. Are you sure you have any feelings at all?"

"Our subarchitecture contains the structure, but we do not have to employ the nanocells if we so choose." He paused to glare at me. "This has nothing to do with Idealian physiology, and this line of questioning wastes my time. What do you really want?"

"I want to know the truth," I answered. "We have discovered that this area apparently contains mini–black holes."

"So?"

I shook my head and clucked my tongue. "Come now, Anu, it's time to be up front with the stupid Humans."

"I do not know what you are talking about. I am a criminal investigator; not an astronomer."

"Your species is equipped with something called an IDT that allows you to access zero-point gravity without any major problems."

"That is correct."

"Do you have something that will allow you to access twists in the space-time continuum?"

His glare turned to a hooded look. "Why do you ask?"

I sat back and sighed. "You forget who discovered the existence of zero-point gravity, my Idealian friend. Humans. Combine zpg and mini–black holes, and you've got a theoretical way to travel back in time."

13

Like a choreographed interruption, Anu averted the answer when alert sirens suddenly rang through the station. I automatically braced myself for a dump into interdimensionality, but thankfully, we remained soundly fixed within our own causal plane. Instead, the communications console burst to life, and the Idealian looked as though he was having a hard time operating the computer. His fingers fumbled over buttons and switches until he found the right link to answer his officer.

"What is it, Chargu?" he demanded.

The answer came in the clicking, mechanical tongue of the Idealians, and as it was delivered, Anu shook his head. "I have the humans here. Please speak Intergalactic."

There was a minute where chatter interfered with the broadcast, but Chargu pushed through the noise. "Progenitor, it is the orange creature we discovered in the shaft. It is alive and evading capture."

"Where was its last position?"

"Deck seven. I have fanned soldiers out, but we cannot find him."

"I will attempt to do a remote scan of the Baderes," Anu answered. "Please stand by."

He looked much more confident this time fiddling with the knobs. After a few seconds, he spoke. "I am reading an odd energy flux on deck thirteen. It is stationary."

Deck thirteen. That's where our quarters were located. I swiveled my chair to glance at Hadrien, but he was already through the hatch running like a demon trying to avoid a vicar packing holy water. I immediately scrambled after him, followed by Anu's heavy footsteps. We met him at the lift where Hadrien waited impatiently by bouncing on the balls of his feet.

We jumped into the chute just as the doors opened. Hadrien banged the button, and down we dropped, each of us silent in our own contemplation of the creature's surprise appearance. When we were halfway to our destination, the elevator came to a bone-jarring halt.

Hadrien cursed. "This place is falling apart."

"No, it is not," Anu answered. "The internal computers and mechanics are in good working order, according to my team of engineers. These odd occurrences should not be happening."

Hadrien started punching buttons on the panel as if his impatience would somehow start the motor again.

"Have these incidents increased?" I asked.

"Yes. Problems have been logged every hour in the last two standard days. The equipment checks out as being in satisfactory working order."

I was about to answer him, but another wail interrupted me. I couldn't tell if it was mechanical or organic, but the screeching moan raised the hair on my hackles and made me think of banshees. The car abruptly started with a jolt, dropping to deck thirteen. Hadrien yanked me out of the lift before the doors had opened all the way.

He muttered something but was gone before I could get my piggies in motion. I pulled up the horse's tail to see a unit of steel gray Idealians pointing nasty, sharp weapons at the alien. It stood right outside our quarters, its skin rippling kaleidoscope colors and its one huge eyeball wide and shiny.

"At ease!" Anu snapped. Like my mum's old Dilby motorcar, I heard pops, cracks, and squeaks as the team obeyed the order. They held their positions though. Sighting beyond the Idealians, I noticed the creature blink slowly, a single dark tear tracing down its cheek.

"What do you make of this boy?" Hadrien asked no one in particular.

"I have met many species, but this one is strange to me," Anu answered.

He pushed by one of his team members to stand within the half circle they formed. The creature stopped his colorful rippling to study the Idealians. If this beast could relate disgust within his features, I'm sure that it did. Anu glanced around as several more troops arrived on the scene, followed by Telroni.

"Will someone delete that Klaxon?" he barked. "You can hear it in the next dimension."

Telroni scrabbled at the bulkhead, activating a small trapdoor that swung down and out. He pressed in a code on a keypad, and the irritating squeal stopped.

The new unit moved forward, crowding the corridor and pushing us from behind. It caused the creature to cower against the bulkhead and edge away from Anu.

"Can you understand me?" the Idealian demanded in Intergalactic.

The alien nodded, a movement that caught me off guard. Were some things not only universal but interuniversal as well?

"Who are you and where do you come from?" Anu asked.

It didn't reply, instead cocking its chinless head upward to study Hadrien and me.

"Begging the commander's pardon," Telroni ventured, "but it may be dangerous. Perhaps this is the alien who killed Duriken Sunteel."

Telroni's words instantly bothered me, but I couldn't tell if he was blowing raspberries hoping to move the suspicion from himself onto this quivering, orange bloke.

Anu made the next mistake. He stepped toward the alien. His action scared the skitter out of the runt, and it suddenly phased, fading like a ghost on holiday. When it next appeared, it had stepped outside the confines of the unit to stand at the end of the corridor.

I don't know whether Idealian processors are slower than Human brains, but whatever it was, they stared at the creature for several seconds. No one moved until Hadrien took off at a sprint to catch the critter. I ran after my partner, skidding to a stop just as I rounded the corner. Anu and his teams finally got off their mechanical derrieres to follow pursuit, but they clanked to a halt behind me.

Hadrien had rounded up the creature by pushing him into a dead end in the corridor. He stood only a meter or two from the creature, his hands up to signify harmlessness.

"Can you communicate?" he asked.

It bubbled and squeaked just like a pot of my granny's cabbage. Suddenly, the alien raised its arm, phasing again. As it did, Hadrien grabbed it by the paw and faded with the alien until there was no sign of my lover left in the hallway.

14

You would have thought that someone had cut my heart by the way I screamed. It was true, too, at least on an emotional level. Hadrien had become part of my soul, and now the essence by which I'd come to define myself was gone, faded into oblivion. If I had wanted to follow, I couldn't, even though I had the interdimensional power given me by the alien implant.

I've never been one of those sappy birds who fall out for the attention. No, I get mean, and then I get randy. The first thing I did after seeing my beloved whisked away was to spin on my heel, grab Telroni by his skinny neck, and sling the Senerian onto deck. I pitched myself atop him and, using my knees to hold those butcher's hooks to the floor, I demanded the truth.

"It's time to stop your lying, Telroni! You know who those creatures are and where they've gone."

His pasty-white skin grew red at the collar of his shirt and then crept up to his face. "Get off me!" he screeched. "I had nothing to do with that."

"You must no longer deceive this female."

The words were spoken with no inflection at all, and I whipped around to see Va-qua-nua standing there. It was time for Anu to join the melee.

"Servicer, you have no right to interfere," he bellowed, the mechanical edge in his voice sending spikes of anger up my spine. "You are dismissed."

I smacked Telroni but aimed my response at the Idealian. "Shut up! Your servicer here has been enlightening. Let him speak."

Va-qua-nua approached slowly. He paused to study Telroni, who wiggled like a pig, but I kept those murderer's hands in control with my surge of enraged strength.

"You know about the creatures," Va-qua-nua said. "They are your enemies, are they not?"

"I am Senerian," Telroni growled. "I will not stand for this kind of treatment. Unhand me, Astrologer Cyprion."

"No," I barked. "Right now, I've got a bug in me bonnet about you. Those hands of yours reveal more than you think. And I don't like what I see. Who and what are you?"

Anu put a stop to my impromptu interrogation. My hands had moved up to Telroni's neck, and I was choking the ghost out of him because he refused to cooperate. I can't be sure of how I came to this point, because my actions were all a blur—just like Hadrien when he disappeared into the well of the universe.

It took three Idealians to remove me from the Telroni. When they pulled us apart, the Senerian leveled his own threat at me.

"How dare you? You are here at the request of my government. There will be an investigation into your actions. This you can be sure of."

"Enough!" Anu shouted.

I struggled from the grasp of the Idealian soldiers to face Telroni. "You and your government know more than you're beefing out. I'm going to find out what it is."

"But that will not return your companion," Anu said.

I charged a look in his direction. "Don't go playing with the subject. I'm an astrologer, an expert in the interplanetudes. I don't make these statements lightly. This being is hiding something."

He shook his head and then closed his eyes. The expression upon his face made me think he communicated with someone. Opening his eyes once more, he studied me. "Dr. Drer will be here momentarily. He will do a spatial scan on Administrator Telroni to determine his species origin. Will that satisfy you?"

Telroni crawled to a stand. "It will not satisfy me. You have no right to subject me to your scans."

"When an investigator makes a pointed statement such as Astrologer Cyprion did, it gives me every right," Anu answered. "You will comply, or my government shall have words with your government, and you do not want that to happen."

More threats and more bureaucratic rhetoric. Idealians and Senerians were worse than the imperial gov back on Earth, and understanding this only fueled my doubts about both species. Politicians and the vermin who worked for them made my head hurt—always had.

I sighed, more from the anguish over my lost partner then the posturings, and leaned against the bulkhead to wait for Drer. The Idealian doctor soon appeared, stalking around the bend of the corridor with several of his medics with him.

He neither looked at me or even acknowledged my presence. In fact, Anu must have told him everything during his Idealian communication because he spoke not a word but went immediately to the Senerian. He rolled his eyeballs back into that tin head of his and craned his neck like a Sunday plucker at the pony races.

Telroni tried to move out of his scan, but two of the Idealians stomped in to contain him. He thrashed about for a moment until they stalled him with their hulking bodies. "You cannot do this! I will lodge a formal complaint!"

"Lodge away," I muttered.

Five minutes rode by, and during that time, I fought the ever-growing tightness in my tum. Where was Hadrien right now? Was he even alive? Would I ever see him again on this side of the dimensional veil?

Another five minutes transpired before Drer rolled his eyeballs back into place. Instead of silently communicating his findings to Anu, he spoke directly to me. "According to the energy configuration of this person, he is telling the truth. He is a Senerian."

"Yet, his essence is not," Va-qua-nua announced.

Drer pursed his lips. "It is said that Bohdans can sense such things. But I highly doubt it. Whatever his essence may be, his physical orientation is Senerian."

"I told you," Telroni spat. "You have overstepped your bounds of influence." He stopped slathering to cast a mean eye my way. "All of you." Upon that accusation, he stomped away, leaving me to face Anu and Drer.

Drer was the first to comfort my ideas. "He could, indeed, be an impostor. Cellular duplication has been an active science for years. It is the method that makes the difference. The Bohdan could be correct that what drives Telroni is not Senerian. Unfortunately, I have no way to tell for certain."

He tramped off, dragging his medics with him. Anu dismissed his own soldiers before glancing at me. "I did not have the opportunity to reply to your question," he said quietly. "The answer is yes. Idealians do have a complementary node that permits us to travel through time, but this part of our physiology has lain dormant for millennia." With that, he marched away, leaving me alone with my misery.

15

According to the interplanetudes and confirmed by the science of astrology, there are only four minutes available for an event to be determined, to occur, and to complete. We call this an orb, and some astrologers will extend this time zone for their own use, especially if they want to get something to fit their prophesies of the future. I have never been one to push the gears on Mother Nature, and now, standing alone in the hallway outside of my quarters, I wondered if I should have seen this thing coming. The only reason I had missed it is because I was a flaming coward. I was afraid to see anything bad in the trap, and I always paid for it.

It seemed that the mechanoids had blown me off for being a hysterical bird and, therefore, unworthy of answering my probing questions both about the murder and their time machine capabilities.

I dragged myself back to my quarters, determined that I wouldn't lose my composure again, but when I glanced at the rumpled sheet on the bed, I flopped down in the chair to nurse my agony and pain. Not that it did a bloody bit of good.

After a few hours of railing against the universe and its injustices, I decided that blubbering about it wouldn't bring Hadrien back to me. It was time to do something— anything.

I have learned over the months while saddled with this alien implant that if the planets are set in a correct path, I can open a window into the great beyond. I am able to gaze through the interdimensional portal to study other dimensions. Interestingly, the beasts and critters who plague me during my attempts at sleep don't seem to be there. It's a form of zero point space travel where I stay in one place, but the universe ripples around me. The problem, of course, is that I can only open these windows for the span of a single orb. The Waki'el had based their implants on the interplanetudes, and I was constrained by the physical measurements placed within the unit.

Rising from the hard plastic chair, I went first to the loo to splash my face with cold water. The tears had dried upon my cheeks, just like I was salted herring. I was such a bim over Hadrien. When had my emotions drawn me so deeply into love that I'd forgotten to keep my defenses up? Now, left alone to fend for myself, I'd taken a step into blithering idiocy. Well, it had to stop. I hiked my knickers and determined to find some clue of Hadrien's continued existence in the material realm. I returned to the table, fired up my calculator, and checked the alignment of planets in my chart.

It was a festival of squares, that point of one's chart when challenges manifest between the planets. Squares also represent opportunities to change the hardships into useful learning situations, but once in while there are so many negative values that it's hard to manifest the change through action. Unfortunately, I didn't have the luxury of sitting around on my bum waiting for Hadrien to come back. I had to look for him, which meant I had to keep believing he was alive. That need would drive away any desire I might have to take a peek at his horoscope and the last day of his current incarnation. I simply couldn't give up on this kind of relationship without fumbling about trying to find a solution to rectify it.

The one planetary configuration I needed—the one that always seemed to work for me—was that of Saturn conjunct Neptune in my Sun. In this case, the worlds had lined up according to my need, but this balance would only last a few minutes before it would wind around to a square. When that happened, the window would close.

I have a feeling this phenomenon has something to do with a quantum arrangement of atoms and Saturn conjunct Neptune is the signpost that tells me this has occurred. It may be the exact same circumstance that affects a person at the minute of his death, releasing his soul from the bonds of corporeality.

Abandoning the chair, I came to stand in the center of the room, closing my eyes for a moment as I prepared myself mentally to take on the universe. It was like trying to pull a cosmic string. In the science of the interplanetudes, the planes touched, separated by a thin layer of atomic structure known as a dimensional skin. I had found, in recent months, that not only was there the dimension we thought of as the Human afterlife, but the causal planes continued on like bubbles building atop one another. It was impossible to know where the creation flow had taken Hadrien.

All I could do was hope to get a message from him that I might recognize. Of course, the real danger would be to pick up a bunch of nonsense and then go charging away into failure and disappointment.

I pulled off the leather wristband I wore to protect the alien implant from the occasional hard knock. It was positioned just beneath my skin, the dark color of the unit making me look as though I had a bruise. I used my thumb to press it soundly, and the second I did, I experienced what I've come to call a Delphic moment.

In ancient Greece, Delphi was a temple honoring Apollo, the god of wisdom and light. At Delphi, seekers would ask the priestess, known as the oracle, to decipher the mysteries of life and to utter the truth of a person's destiny. It was said she could see far into the future through a single moment in time.

Though I didn't gaze into the future, I nonetheless rolled an eyeball toward eternity.

Dizziness invaded me, along with an odd sensation of buzzing. The feeling traipsed down my spine and into my extremities until I vibrated. My surroundings rippled like someone had thrown a rock into the pool and breathing became something I seemed to think about doing. I must have taken in air, but I could not feel it hit my lungs.

I opened the hatchway into another universe. It grew as if it were a flower opening right before me—I'd been told it resembled a Hawking-Hershog vortex—but understanding that was not in my bailiwick. I do know that if someone had entered the quarters, they would have detected a yoke of incandescent mist, sparkling with a lovely light. There seemed to be no way to enter this phenomenon, and it didn't take much to maintain the doorway.

Squinting into the quantum opening, I saw through the haze to take in swirling gold stars. I could hear voices—chattering, snickering sounds—noise that made me flinch and my skin crawl like a bounty of army ants walked across my torso. It was hard to concentrate because the room was small, the heat grew intense, and my fear blossomed exponentially as I worried that I'd created a gap into a strange causal plane of non-Human existence that I might not be able to close.

I stood there for several moments just like the oracle

at Delphi, doing everything I could to conjure up the vision of my lost lover. The planets moved swiftly in the logos, and my window of opportunity slid by before I cleared out the mutterings and murmurings. The inter-dimensional hatch squeezed to a singularity, but before it did, I heard one word clearly: Argos.

16

*As the window shut into the beyond, a quiet tap-*ping came at the hatch. I paused to swipe at the perspiration on my forehead before cycling the door and opening it. Drer stood there, an imposing hulk of bony armor, filaments, and tubing, yet considering him, I'd have to say that he had a gentle look on his face.

"Yes?" I asked. "What is it?"

"I came to see how you were faring," he said quietly.

I stepped back so he could march inside, shutting the hatch firmly before speaking. "Me soul is buggered, if that's what you want to know."

He frowned and the movement contained a mechanical movement. I pointed to the hard chair.

"Why do you care?" I said after he seated himself.

Drer sighed, and the sound had a ping to it. "You may recall that I just lost my mate."

His words pushed irritation into my answer, despite my understanding of what he tried to do. "Well, Hadrien isn't lost to me. Not yet."

"Is that something you have read in your astrological charts?"

I sat down on the foot of the bed. "No, it's not something I've read in the stars."

He shook his head and when he did, I saw a bit of golden liquid sloshing about in one of the tubes encircling his head. "Everything in your universe moves by chance."

"What's that supposed to mean? We are governed by the same universal laws as every creature in this dimension."

"Yes, I realize that, but we come at it from different directions."

"How so, mate?"

"You are a species who uses intuition, are you not?"

"Yes. If you've worked with Humans, then you know this."

"You try to look into the future by using your feelings as a gauge."

"Yes."

"Does it work?"

"Sometimes. Unfortunately, external factors cloud the issue. We end up buying into the vision that's the prettiest, most of the time."

"Is that what you are doing now?"

I nodded, snorting softly. "It sure is, Doc."

"My people do not use our emotions in the same way. We work from a subarchitecture that responds with appropriate subjectivity."

I stared at him. Just what was this bloke saying? "Do you mean, you have a subjectivity scale that slides up and down based on the stimuli?"

"It is more complicated than that, but essentially you are correct."

"It sounds boring."

"Perhaps it is." He smiled. "I cannot say one way or the other."

"So when your mate died, what was your subjectivity setting?"

His smile disappeared. "I had no subjectivity. I was at zero for many hours."

"How did the meter rise?"

"We are irrevocably locked into the moment. It took

a thought from me. That is all, but I did not wish to think."

"But that indicates grief."

"Yes. Grief on a subjective scale.'

These blokes really were machines, despite the fact that they walked, talked, and ate. "Tell me something, Doc."

"If I can."

"Your comrade, Progenitor Anu, told me that you have a mechanoid device within you that allows you to travel through time. Is it true?"

Drer snorted and pinged. "He is not my comrade. He is an overleader in our government. One does not consider him a friend or even an acquaintance."

"I detect a bit of dislike on your side."

"Not dislike. Suspicion on the high end of the subjective scale."

"So, you don't trust Anu?"

"No, I do not."

"Why? What has he done?"

"I know none of this personally, but he has a reputation for being a corrupt, ruthless administrator. He is not favored among the people. Still, the apex must find him trustworthy to have sent him on this project.

"So, what you are saying is that he can tip a lie as fast as he can tip the truth."

Drer leaned forward in the chair and clasped his hands. The second he did, I was reminded of Hadrien. He assumed the stance often when he tilled his thoughts for answers to murder investigations. "I would think that Human intuition would prevent the tipping of a lie."

I grunted, unable to tell if he was being facetious or not. "Well, most Human intuition is unreliable—at least, I've found it to be so on more than one occasion. Do you think Anu is actively seeking to cover up mistakes made by the Idealian government?"

His face transformed and, despite the biowires and feeder canals circulating around his head, I saw true, unadorned sadness. I knew how he felt at that moment. "My mate thought so. We are far from perfect, Astrologer Cyprion. We are closer to Humans in our fallibility than most would claim, and fear drives us. But then, fear drives every species, does it not?"

"What do Idealians have to fear?"

He sat back, sighed, and shook his head. "Many things, but mostly it is the knowledge that we are a dying species and, unless we find answers soon, we will become extinct."

"Is that what drove Duriken Sunteel? Is that what she was trying to discover?"

"I do not know. I was not in the loop of information. I came after her death was discovered at my mate's request. Yet I suspect it had something to do with it. Why else would you be asking about our time travel capabilities?"

I rose from the bed and, so he wouldn't check the surprise on my mug, I turned toward the porthole to study the planet spinning slowly below the station. When I was sure I could speak without flipping my hand by displaying my ignorance, I twisted back to study him before demanding the answer in a flat, noncommittal voice. "Tell me about your time travel abilities."

"We have, for lack of a better description, a piece of cosmic string encased in every cell of our bodies."

Cosmic strings? Even after the discovery of zero-point gravity and interstellar travel, the theory of cosmic strings had remained in the realm of theory. A black hole contained an infinitely small point in the space-time continuum known as a one-dimensional singularity. Anything that fell into one of these objects would likely be squeezed into the singularity atom by atom. If a traveler could survive the squeezing process, he might emerge in another universe if all his atoms could find a way to recombine after being squashed by the immense gravity.

A cosmic string, though, was considered to be a two-dimensional singularity that was thought to be an infinitely long, thin line. If what Drer said was true and differences in semantics weren't interfering, then Humans had miscalculated on a theoretical basis.

"Do these embedded cosmic strings work?"

"By that I am assuming you want to know if we are able to travel back into time."

I took a deep breath and paused in my reply, because a hundred desperate thoughts twittered in my gray matter. Stepping to the bunk, I sat down heavily, ran a hand over my mouth, and commanded my noodle to stop quivering with ideas about how to use this to get Hadrien safely home. "Can you?"

"It is possible. I have heard that a few of my kind have done so."

"How?"

He held his hands out in supplication, and for the first time I noticed that Idealians' palms contained no lines. "It was accomplished centuries ago and had to do with a genetic alteration that changed the subarchitecture so that the strings worked in cohesion. Separated by cellular resistance, they cannot be activated. Of course, I understand that the experiments were plagued by the usual paradoxes consistent with time travel."

I rose again and stalked to the porthole. "What kind of paradoxes?"

"I do not have specifics, Astrologer Cyprion. This is not my field of expertise."

"Tell me what you have heard," I growled.

"Well, the travelers could not access a time before they existed."

"What about the many worlds theory?" I snapped.

"Many worlds? I am unfamiliar with that term."

I flipped around to face him. "Parallel words created by changes in a specific time line. If you went back into time and killed your grandmother, would it prevent you from being born? The hypothesis states that a new divergence or another dimensionality would come into being because you could not undo the time of your birth."

"If that were true, then how would the traveler find his way back to his point of origin?"

"I suspect he couldn't."

Drer didn't answer, so I turned back to the view of Bohdan. Va-qua-nua said the space around the planet was littered with mini–black holes. By bringing a cosmic string and a black hole together, it was possible, according to theory, to create closed, timelike curves. Add another factor of zero-point gravity, and it might be possible to look down the avenue into the past and the future. Was that what Duriken Sunteel ultimately had in mind?

17

Hadrien and I had requested an interview with Jan-
del Sajan when he'd arrived aboard the station, and
shortly after my conversation with Drer, the request was
granted. I made the Idealian wait until I'd eaten, taken
a shower, and changed my cammies before venturing out
into the station. As I did my walkabout, I noticed that
the Baderes had emptied out. Had the mechanical difficulties scattered visitors who were afraid of being slung
to every part of the universe while they slept in their
hammocks? It was so quiet, this place was practically a
mustard-colored mausoleum. The rubber soles of my
shoes smacked purposefully against the linoleum lining
the central catwalk, and the hum of the environmentals
provided me a concerto of white noise. I stopped before
the lift, glancing down the corridor for any signs of life,
but the lights had been dimmed and the hallway was
dark and silent. Taking a deep breath, I dragged my gaze
back to the shiny steel doors of the elevator. It's then
that I saw it.

A face stared at me from this mirrored surface. It was
Idealian, but it was hard to tell if it was male or female
from the angle at which it appeared. Black eyes studied
me, reflecting a yellow light for which I could find no
source. I looked boldly back at this night visitor, suddenly pissed off at the intrusion. These blasted interdimensional shadows were starting to plague me at all
hours now, and I couldn't think of a way to escape them.

Finally, the lift answered my call, the doors popped open, and the apparition disappeared. I stepped inside the box, ready to cast the visitor from my mind, but when the car started toward the appointed deck, the ghost turned up on the wall beside me. It blinked at me and then popped off like a genie back into some interdimensional bottle. I'd not seen that kind of trick before.

The lift plopped me out somewhere in the guts of the station. Power had been shunted elsewhere on the Baderes, and this deck was dark and chilly enough for me to see my breath. At one point in my travels, I was forced to duck at the waist to avoid low-slung steam pipes. A bloody Idealian would have to be as greasy as a side of bacon to squeeze through this tunnel.

I followed directions over a steel bridge and through the metal woods until I came to the facilities maintenance chamber and there, half buried by station wiring, I found Jandel Sajan.

He didn't acknowledge my entrance but instead calmly continued working on an electrical panel.

"Jandel Sajan, I'm Astrologer Cyprion."

He still didn't turn. "I apologize for not meeting with you sooner. I have been trying to bring the station back on-line."

"What's wrong with it?"

"I do not know. All sectors report perfect or near perfect working order. Any bugs in the system are so minor that they would normally be neutralized by the computer's nanosweepers."

"Maybe the computer has a virus," I said.

"I cannot find anything."

"Maybe it's an interdimensional contagion."

My words finally drew enough attention from him that he twisted slowly so he could regard me better. He spent a minute studying me with black eyes very similar to those that had ratted me in the elevator. "I have considered it."

"And?"

"And I have found nothing."

This bloke was already testing the fire with porkies. "Come on. It's like someone is punching raisins into the rising bread dough."

My analogy had enough strength behind it to make him struggle clear of the piles of wiring to approach me. He pointed to a hard-backed chair and a smudgy metal table, and after I'd slipped into the squeaky seat, he spoke.

"Yes. It is like punching raisins into bread dough. Many electrical blockages are occurring, and the power equivalents are fluctuating. But how did you know?"

"Could it be caused by the mini–black holes scattered through the area?"

"I have a team working on that. We can find no new anomalous properties in this sector of space." He paused and held out his hand to shake. "You did not come here to discuss the failure of this apparatus."

I shook his mitt, feeling the restrained power behind his stubby fingers. "There are a few people aboard the station who do not like you."

"True, I am sure."

"Why?"

"Why? Because I intercede in matters specifically for the apex."

"What kinds of matters?"

"I am responsible for social integration on Istos."

"Social integration. What's that?"

He took a deep, pinging breath and situated a golden bauble decorating his torso. "The apex issues a decree, and I am sworn to carry it out. My duties encompass such things as population control and environmental health."

"Population control? What kind of population control?"

"What do you think? We specify certain parameters for procreation."

"Do people listen to you?"

"We have always obeyed, Astrologer Cyprion. That has never been a point of rebellion in our society."

"Why didn't you return to Istos? You could have escaped this conversation, at least."

"My apex has commanded me to remain until the investigation is complete. Duriken Sunteel was a member of his court and my former mate." He pointed to the jumble of wiring. "I am obligated to repair the damage she has done." Sajan headed back to his fix-it job, a pinging sigh upon his lips.

"You didn't like Sunteel much, did you?"

He shook his head. "We do not deal in like or dislike if we do not allow ourselves to. I am above that. Unfortunately, I had allowed myself to become impassioned about her deceit."

"What kind of deceit?"

He frowned but then hid the expression by picking up a laser driver and tinkering on the box.

I slashed an insistent edge onto my voice. "What kind of deceit?"

"It is none of your business," he answered flatly.

"Well, let's see. You were mad enough to curse her. You could have been mad enough to kill her."

He spun on me. "I have never killed anyone."

Standing there, he looked too hulking to be believed. How could a steel tank not kill?

Sajan answered me before I could press my luck asking him again. "Sunteel was not above manipulating people. She manipulated me by using my position to force her hand with the apex."

"I thought she was a favorite of the apex."

"She was very bright; she had many more processing cells than the average Idealian. The apex kept her at court because he wanted to keep expansive talent from escaping his grasp. With her at court, he could restrain her flamboyance and channel her intellect to his needs."

"So let me guess. You had an arranged marriage with her."

He nodded. "Of course. All responsible relationships are arranged."

"Are there irresponsible relationships on your world?"

"Yes. There are those who refuse to follow the status quo. Sunteel was one of those people."

"What did she do?"

"She stole the progeny of others."

I squinted at him. "Progeny? You mean children?"

"No, I mean ideas, concepts, visualizations."

"So, a progenitor is a person with ideas?"

"Yes."

"What's an immaculate?"

He snorted, a mechanical clinking accenting his reaction. "An immaculate is a person without ideas. At least, I have always found them to be so."

"Well, if you are telling me the truth, then who do you think killed Duriken Sunteel?"

"I do not know the individual, but I am certain of one thing."

"And that would be?"

"Your murderer is an Idealian."

"Why is that?"

"We are the only ones who can understand this—how do you say—bloody space station? Sunteel's murderer was familiar with the Baderes's systems, which tells me that he or she acted prior to the zpg launch sequence."

"How do you figure that?"

He pulled on a wire and sparks flew, but Sajan ignored them to answer me. "Once Sunteel had entered into link with the station, she would have been able to control and vanquish any intruder."

18

Sajan started out with answers, but after a few more minutes, he shut right down like the screw lid on a pickle jar. The station quaked again during our conversation and rather than stay in the bowels of the station surrounded by pipes, sharp metal grating, and electrical arcs, I decided to go back to my quarters. I was so beat by this time that any night visitors who might wish to rouse me would find themselves facing my zombielike, drooling persona.

The last thing I remember was climbing into the bunk and smelling Hadrien's scent on the bed sheets. Yearning struck up hard inside of me, but exhaustion and worry quelled the flames before they ignited into an emotional bonfire.

Once the long rest period was finally over, I got up, showered again, and ate. Yes, in space, two showers in so short a span might be considered compulsive behavior, but I was practically alone among aliens. All the metal-skinned, big-handed, one-eyed bug aliens made my skin crawl, and water, no matter how brackish, piddling, and cold, brought on a bit of comfort and a reminder of life spent among Humans. Why that had suddenly become important, I couldn't guess. I'd roved clear across the galaxy and spent time giving astrological readings to species who were a hundred times more exotic than the characters aboard the Baderes.

After my ritual bath, I sat in the center of the living

room on a hard plastic chair, staring at the wondrous rings of Bohdan. The environmentals had cycled, and the quarters was silent. I have always run away from moments of such sublime reflection. Eric's death had sent me on an unending escape from my own thoughts, and until I'd met Hadrien, I'd followed the curling road through the galaxy. Now, having lost Hadrien in the mists of interdimensionality, I craved the solitude and the silence. Much of this newfound desire had to do with the fact that the Waki'el devices had expanded my understanding of the way the universe worked. Creation was a big, crowded place, and when you lost people, they usually stayed lost.

Instead of resuming interrogations in the cubbyhole allotted us, I stayed in my quarters and invited interviewees in one at a time for short discussions. The first person on my list was an Idealian named Fay-et. She came stomping into my space with a snarl upon her steel-colored lips, but her indignant air gave me a private giggle. This was a mechanoid who was familiar with the emotions that rode on the same bandwidth as arrogance and snootiness. I could tell right off Fay-et was all suckers and mash, and I knew that given half the chance, she would feed me porkies as a matter of course. I decided to end the lies before they started.

"Please do me the favor of not trying to conceal the truth," I began. Pointing to my logos calculator sitting on the table, I fed her raw meat. "That computer confirms me intuition, and that intuition, especially about aliens such as Idealians, is uncanny."

Fay-et slowly lost the curl to her lip but remained silent, so I sat down and checked my calculator in the interim, drawing out the quiet just like Hadrien had taught me to do. What was he fond of saying? *Get them to fidget, and you can read the Book of Job in their movements.*

According to the information coming up, Fay-et was born under a grand water trine, a configuration that meant that most everything in her life flowed evenly. She was rarely put off by circumstances around her, and if something of an upsetting nature rocked her boat, she could bring herself back onto an even keel with little trouble. Still, Fay-et had a bunch of big, mean old squares influenced by Saturn. They opposed her flow by making everything come slowly: success, relationships, understanding, and action. She was perfectly content to sit by and watch the universe move away in all directions. Her handwriting sample—a tight, straight print—seemed to confirm the planetary alignment.

I glanced up from my tabulations to study her. Fay-et, as Idealians went, was no great beauty. In fact, the more she sat in my space, the more oppressive became the atmosphere. "You are an engineer who has not gotten the respect she deserves," I said flatly.

She shrugged, one of those movements that made me certain she was mechanically driven.

"In fact, I'll wager you lost a few promotions in your time because you lack the steely energy to produce imaginative engineering applications. As absorbed as your people are, they value imagination because it's not a standard among your species." I sat back and crossed my arms, as much to keep her energy at bay as to rest my elbows. "Imagination is what I think would be of great value on this team."

"So you would think."

"Why is it not true, then? Why were you placed on the crew?"

Fay-et suddenly smiled, and it transformed her from ugly to hideous. It was all I could do not to shiver. "Your star charts do not show you the reality of Idealian society. It is because I have the touch."

"The touch? And that would be?"

"My DNA strands are mutable. I can conform to many different mechanical and computer components made from silica to extravagant metals that your species has never even heard of."

"You mean you can link with the station in the same manner as Duriken Sunteel?"

"Yes. That, Astrologer Cyprion, is more important than imagination for an engineer."

"But you find it distasteful."

Fay-et lost her unattractive smile and glanced down at the deck. Her gaze lingered on her big, booted feet before she lifted her chin to stare at me.

This female was going to go doggers with me, this I could tell, so I popped the question with more force behind my words. "You find it distasteful. Correct?"

"I have never told anyone that."

"I told you, I'm intuitive. I sense these things. Why do you find it distasteful?"

"Once, long ago, I bonded with an accretion accelerator."

"What's that?"

"It is a chamber that simulates the activity of the accretion disk at the center of our galaxy."

I studied her, trying to figure out if I was the victim of some cultural miscommunication. An accretion disk is a flattened ring of gas orbiting a black hole, and this material is pulled into the object. In the sun-dense center of the Milky Way, there's a gigantic black hole that sucks the life out of neighboring systems by slowly gobbling them up.

"Who built the accelerator?" I asked.

"My people. Long ago, it was a ritual machine."

"A ritual machine?"

"Yes. It had spiritual significance for us because we believed for millennia that we were spawned from the disk. We had never had contact with completely organic life forms until about two thousand standard Earth years ago. We did not realize that we are a blend of machine and living components. We thought we were the only beings in the galaxy, and that our origins were not engineered."

"Well, taking it to the finer points, all species are engineered, whether by direct intervention or random evolution."

"Yes, but we had no clue that we were different than most species beyond our initial thoughts of supremacy."

"It was a tough time for your species, then?"

"The Day of Knowledge was not tough, Astrologer Cyprion, it was a time of self-emulation of the Idealian soul." Fay-et grunted. "We have no idea of our true origins, and we never will. Most species we have contacted think of us as walking computers and nothing more. We have no respect, yet we are often looked toward to provide the answers."

"Like the Senerians and the Bohdans have."

"Precisely."

"Please tell me more about why you bonded with the accretion accelerator," I said.

"It was a form of protest as much as it was a confirmation of my mechanoid strength."

I uncrossed my arms and leaned forward. "Was it illegal to do so?"

"To bond? Yes. As I said, we had created the units as a ritual application, and when we discovered through science and understanding that we were not what we had thought we were, the government outlawed their use. They felt that it unnecessarily hindered the truth and our evolutionary growth. Something beautiful and mysterious was taken away from us."

"When did this happen?"

"In Earth reckoning, one thousand two hundred years ago." Fay-et shifted in the chair and the little plastic thing squealed under her weight. "It might have been all right had the government replaced the ritual with something else."

"So the use of the accelerators moved underground."

She studied me for a moment and then nodded. "Do you still perform a ceremony on your world known as a baptism?"

"Some religions still do."

"Well, that is what bonding with an accretion accelerator is like. It opens up the awareness to possibilities that have been denied collectively and individually."

"What happened to you when you experienced the bonding?"

"I became one with the quantum world. I gleaned a true understanding of physicality. I crossed a dimensional threshold that I could never deny. It made me aware that no matter what I do, I am mortal and I will someday be reduced to rusty parts and gelatinous slime."

"Did you touch your soul?"

"I was made aware of it and it changed me forever. I stopped striving for those things that could never be mine. I believe this change was the whole point of the ritual when it was done openly and joyously. But our government obviously felt that we were a second-rate citizenry when compared to the achievements of other species."

"So, along came the Humans, zero-point gravity, and another chance at a ritual that might be condoned."

Fay-et stared at me, and I found myself wondering if she saw through eyes replete with feedback figures like the computer readouts on gun scopes. "You are bright for your species. Brighter than most."

"What did zero-point gravity offer the Idealians?"

"A chance to gain access to other universes, to experience in reality what our imaginations had offered us."

"But not all could access zero-point gravity."

"None of us could."

Now that surprised me. "Why? I thought you were born with the IDT that allowed for this."

"No. That was a technological invention doled out sparingly. You have to be a certain rank to receive one. When you do, it places you in a brotherhood of sorts."

"So not everyone has access to this device. Was this decision political or economic?"

"Economic."

"Why?"

"The IDT node must be fabricated in zero-point gravity. For many years we had a contract with a community of people living inside a zero-p pocket."

Balloon heads. Folks born in colony ships suspended within the creation force. "Did something happen to end this relationship?"

"They were destroyed. I do not know the circumstances."

"Personally, what do you believe Duriken Sunteel was trying to do?"

"She was trying to correct the orbit and axial oscillation of the planet Bohdan."

"Why?"

"I believe it was being done so that my people could evacuate our home world."

"What's wrong with your home world?"

"Mini–black holes."

"I beg your pardon."

"Mini–black holes. The fabric of space in the region is popping open like pimples upon an adolescent's face. It has become very unstable."

How I wished Hadrien were here! His questions were penetrating and to the point. He could suck the marrow out of a bone like my grandmum at Sunday dinner. "Tell me, Engineer Fay-et, who do you think killed Duriken Sunteel?"

She frowned and then reached up to swipe a hand through the tangle of wire and filament that passed for hair in her species. "I should not say because I do not know for certain."

"I didn't ask you to be certain. I asked your opinion."

Fay-et hesitated again, squinted, and then choked up the goods. "In my opinion, I would say that Dr. Gasba killed her."

Great. Just when I thought she would point me to a live person, she tossed in the busted cork. "Why would she kill Sunteel? She gave up her IDT node for her."

"Well, she did not have much choice in that."

"Gasba was forced to submit to Sunteel's needs with parts from her own body?"

"Yes."

"Is this customary on your world?"

"Many people are born to sacrifice themselves in this way."

I studied her, trying to work my way around her ambiguous answer. "People are born specifically as vessels containing spare parts for other folks?"

"That is what I said."

"I'm surprised they are educated and allowed to become doctors. It seems an awful waste of manpower."

Fay-et frowned. "Educated?"

"Schooled?"

"I know what the term means, Astrologer Cyprion," she growled and pinged. "We are born with race memory and fully developed consciousness. I could think and speak at one day old."

"So, Dr. Gasba was destined to be a parts supply house, but she still had the opportunity to self-actualize?"

"Yes. It was an unfortunate accident that her node had

been harvested and she was trapped in the zero-point gravity shift."

"Her mate was quite upset."

Fay-et snorted. "I would assume so. I heard that he had talked her into giving up her IDT when it became apparent that Sunteel's unit had gone bad."

19

I had just finished interviewing Engineer Fay-et when the Baderes exploded with activity. An incoming transport docked to spit out wagon loads of Senerian sulters, big-pawed blokes who made runs to outposts with the express reason of selling their wares. It riled me down to my knickers, because all these extra folks would spoil the crime scene even more and hinder my chances of recovering Hadrien.

When the announcement was made about the sulters, I immediately went to see Anu, but I was further boiled up by the fact that he and his crew were gathered down on the maintenance deck buying from the merchants. I approached him as he stuffed some puffed treat into his thick-lipped mouth.

"I thought you characters ate motor oil and battery acid," I said.

My irritation was not lost on him. "We eat Humans every chance we get, too."

I was in no bloody mood to play with him. "These people are going to interfere with the investigation. There are too many variables being introduced."

He took another bite of his pastry before pointing at a clot of Senerian sulters engaging in an argument over the freshness of some three-eyed fish. "They were here just before Duriken Sunteel's death. I invited them back so that you might have a chance to discuss a few things with the captain and first mate."

I squinted at him. This news changed everything and further tinkled on my barley cake. "Why weren't we told about this?"

"Because I did not know until I had a talk with Telroni. Many ships had stopped here while the experiment was being set up. I am trying to narrow down possibilities for you." He paused. "Believe it or not, I am endeavoring to be of assistance to you. Besides, the Baderes has a provisioning problem."

"No food?"

"Exactly. My crew cannot subsist on motor oil alone." He smiled. "You may interview those Senerians at your convenience. I will make certain they are available."

"How can you do that?"

"By disabling their ship. I have one of my engineers accomplishing the matter as we speak."

There was more to this clamper than met the electronic eye. "Can one of your crew grab their ship's log?"

"Already done. It has been downloaded to the Baderes's main file. You may pull it up in your quarters."

I nodded and headed away, hurrying around the growing number of Senerians working their way into the upper decks of the space station. It felt a bit weird to be among them, and that concerned me. I have lived half my life around aliens. Why then did these bloody anvil hands bother me so much?

I returned to my quarters, praying that Hadrien had somehow returned from the beyond, but the cramped cubby was empty except for our personal junk.

It took several minutes and Fay-et's help before I could access the *Zanru*'s log. When I finally did, I realized that one of the Idealians had done a quick interpreting job, changing the phonetic squeaks and clicks of the Senerian language into Intergalactic. The words were odd, the meanings ambiguous, and the sentence structure absurd to the point of laughable, but I slowly worked my way through, hoping to find something I could use.

The captain's name was Marctori. He used the log as if it were a personal diary, giving his thoughts about the people he'd encountered along the way. From his words, I gathered that he was a species bigot and a being who was not inclined to trust anyone, even Senerians. He hated Telroni, finding him to be somewhat of a pompous ass, which he considered odd for his people. They were money grubbers, thieves, loan sharks, and all around wanks, but pomposity was usually not a mark of the species.

That particular paragraph made me sit back in my seat. Had Va-qua-nua spoken the truth about Telroni? Could his pretentious displays be a signal that he was not what he seemed?

I leaned forward again, wishing beyond hope that Hadrien was here. He was so good at finding the sneaky suspicion, the blatant miscalculation, and the twisted metaphor that led to significant discovery.

Marctori's log was divided into several significant sections, so I decided to focus on the days preceding Duriken Sunteel's death. The sulters had been outbound from Tinavor, a planet in the Galactic Cusp, a sector of space that was close but still at a marginally safe distance to the Milky Way's accretion disk. It was an area defined with star nurseries and budding adolescent suns, a place where deploying any zero-point gravity method of interstellar travel was not only considered dangerous but foolhardy. Overshoot your rocket's reentry, and your ride might materialize in the nuclear furnace of one of the tightly packed stars. So, to avoid this kind of disaster, species who navigated along the Cusp used a method of time dilation. Earth scientists found this mode of travel to be as randy as trying to punch out of zpg in the midst of an asteroid belt, but the Senerians had apparently felt that they'd perfected the mechanics necessary to sling them past the globular clusters and into empty regions of space.

I paused again. Marctori talked of how well he'd flown his vessel and how quickly they'd made the trip from Tinavor. They'd even had time to stop at Puushu, Nagoni and Argos.

Argos. That was the word that had come across the dimensions to me. What could the sulters have needed or wanted from Argos?

For Humans, this planet might well have been legend. It was unattainable with zero-point gravity because it was a world that sat at the juncture of time and eternity.

According to the theoretical physicists, entering this zone was like trying to capture an atom's shadow. Eternity is consolidated in every moment as it moves time, but as it does move time, it does so at right angles to it. Argos was considered unapproachable even by immersion in the creation flow because the fifth dimension of eternity was always entering the fourth dimension of time. This planet was considered the counterbalance, the world that kept our space-time continuum in perfect check. How then could Marctori and his bands of merchants approach Argos without disappearing into forever?

20

I decided to start off the sulter interviews by talk-ing to the *Zanru*'s second-in-command, Manya Krosani. She was actually the first female Senerian I'd ever encountered, and one look at those big pie plates she called hands, I realized that her species had built their culture around them. As she slid into the plastic chair in my quarters, I noted that each of her fingers was decorated with baubles, her long nails were painted ruby red, and swirling tattoos covered her palms. My mum would have said she had twitter hands, because Krosani fidgeted, strummed, and picked nervously.

I didn't have a bit of information on Krosani, so I was out of luck with my calculator. Instead, I flipped cards while I prepared to talk to her. My occasional grunt must have given her a case of alien heartburn, and so she spoke up.

"You waste my time with such tricks of divination. Please ask me your questions so that I may return to my duties. I have several sales pending."

I dropped the ace of wands, a card denoting the rising power of spirit force. "What kind of sales?" I asked.

"I do not see where that is any business of yours," she snapped.

I let my fingers flick off two more cards—two of disks and Mother Earth—change and manifestation. "You're embarrassed about what you sell. Your life experience has transformed the way you feel about the creation of this product. Why? What has happened that has brought you to this point in time?"

She studied me, her big hands suddenly stilled. After a minute of digesting some funky thought, she nodded. "You are truly able to see the truth. I have heard that about you."

"About me? Now how would you have heard about me?"

She sat back and plopped her meat hooks into her lap. "You have an earned reputation through this part of the galaxy. Some people say you don't exist; others say that to sit in your light is to know something special."

It was my turn to sit back and study her. Was this some sort of sulting maneuver, a gentle prod from a lifelong salesperson? "You're lying."

"Am I? You have the power to dictate to the emperor of Earth, and through that, you have set the course of galactic history for several species. Is it not known to you that your leader is one of the most powerful beings in the galaxy?"

"Theo is what's left over after you burn the blivet."

"Blivet?"

"Yeah. That would be five liters of shit in a four-liter bag."

She stared at me with a confused look on her long face.

"You're just trashing me mind right now. I can't be going on with this knickknack that you're talking. Let's get back to the matter at hand. What do you sell?"

"Will your cards not tell you?"

"I'm not a bleedin' mind reader."

"And yet you know intuitively how I feel. Amazing." She let her gaze scud across the cards, and then her attention diverted to my wrist gauntlet. "Earth leather. Very expensive. Gold stitching—even more costly. Is that where you harbor the Waki'el implant?"

Did everyone really know about us? "To coin a familiar phrase: That is none of your business." Then, buttressing my sentence with a growl, I made my demand. "What do you sell?"

Her hands started going again, but Korsani finally answered. "I am a prostitute of time."

Intergalactic dialect. "I don't know what a prostitute of time is. You will have to be more specific. Do you have physical relations with males? You know—sex?"

"I only have sex with my own species."

"Is that how you earn your money—from having sex?"

"No. I am a prostitute of time. I can give you more time than you have."

"How?"

"An exchange of light. I carry threads of time DNA in my body."

It was all I could do not to pinch up my lips and squint my eyes. What was this loony blabbering about? "Explain this. What is a time DNA?"

Korsani's gaze slid from my wrist and toward the distance. I had a nasty feeling she was about to tell me a porky that would be big enough to feed a whole country. "It is a natural occurrence in many species. It creates time/light material."

"Subatomic material?"

"Yes."

"How does it do that?"

She shrugged.

"How do you transfer the material?"

"Through saliva. I am one who is known as a charm among my people."

"Not everyone can transfer this material, then?"

"No. Very few." She leaned forward. "I have been a charm for far too long, and I wish to stop this manner of living. I want to sell something else."

"But Marctori won't let you stop."

She frowned. "He has nothing to do with this decision. He is simply a miserable Senerian who owns a collapsing space freighter. I have been given this gift to use, and it would be considered reprehensible not to pass time to those who need it." Sitting back, she studied me for a few moments. "You, for one, need time to find your partner."

"How did you know about that?"

"It was the first story told as I boarded the Baderes."

"We didn't come together to discuss me. I need answers to questions about the death of Duriken Sunteel."

Korsani rose, twiddled the rings on her fingers and thumbs, and took a couple of steps around the small room. "I do not know much about Duriken Sunteel except that she shopped regularly with Captain Marctori. We'd made three runs to the Baderes delivering supplies to her."

"What kind of supplies?"

"Fuel cells, energy packets, linkage manipulators."

"Linkage manipulators?"

"Yes. They keep zpg bandwidth within acceptable parameters. Argos technology."

Argos. "You've been to this planet and dealt with its people."

"Many times. They are mavens of interdimensional travel."

"Mavens, huh? What makes them such experts?"

"They live at the center of the universe."

"What does that mean?"

"I do not know exactly. I know that it has to do with the varying causal planes. I am sorry, but I am not a time engineer, only a carrier."

"What was Marctori's relationship with Sunteel?"

"It was peaceable for the most part, except for that last run."

"What happened?"

"Sunteel was not happy with the product. She claimed it was inferior."

"What product?"

She shook her head. "It was a private commission between them. Marctori complained about her obstinacy several times, but he never told me what he had sold her."

"When was the last time you saw Sunteel alive?"

"When she threw Marctori and me off the Baderes."

"It got as bad as all that?"

"Yes, it did."

"Did Marctori threaten her out loud?"

"No. That is a way to lose a future customer." Korsani stepped up to my chair. "May I go now?"

I nodded. "Stay close in case I need to talk to you about something."

She bowed slightly, using the back of my chair and the table to rest her hands upon. When she was at eye level with me, she said: "You need time to find the one called Hadrien. I admire that effort. Because I do, I give you the gift of time with no requirement for payment."

With that said, she pushed a big fat, tongue right into my mouth, holding me in her big-handed embrace while she did. Electricity passed—yes, I'm sure that's what it was. Not sexual, just filled with brilliant heat.

Korsani straightened and left, not even bothering to pop a word in parting. I, on the other hand, immediately started worrying about transmittable alien diseases.

21

After Korsani left, I brushed my teeth at least ten times before forcing myself to hydrate a packet of soup that Hadrien had whipped up during one of his cookathons. He was like my old granny sometimes, catering to me through the domestic arts and satisfying me with his love by filling my belly. Hadrien was only gone a short while, and I missed him desperately.

I ate and then fell into the bunk, exhaustion becoming my best friend of late. The dreams I had were as involved as a plodding British drama, crudded up with symbolism, images, and deep emotion. When I awoke, I had the odd feeling in the solar plexus, like I'd kept myself tense during my nocturnal feeding. I decided a shower was in order to cleanse away the stink and the hurt, but each drop of water that plipped from the pipe only served to remind me of my pain. In the end, I realized that without Hadrien, I existed in a void that not even his luscious soup could fill.

I invited in another Idealian for an interview, just to keep my mind off my travails. Her name was Yuncol Nemer, and she was a Progenitor as well as the team's regulator. Maybe I was getting used to the bum-faced mechanoids, but as she slid into the chair in my quarters, she seemed to do so with a bit more grace than her counterparts. Nemer might have been pretty, too, with delicate features enhanced by delicate wiring and tubes snaking around her face. She had startling blue eyes, and of course, in my present rub, I was reminded of Hadrien and his azure orbs.

I sat down at the table, stalling tears by studying my calculator. According to the information provided me, Nemer was a classic Virgo, a being who was all work and no play. She was highly organized, meticulous, and methodical. It didn't say much for her imagination, but the one thing she had going for her was clarity. I sat back in the chair and crossed my arms, sighing loudly as I did. Nemer cocked her head slightly to regard me.

"You are grieving," she said.

"Does it show? Or did you hear about my companion, too?"

"Both." She leaned back in her own chair and mimicked me by crossing her own arms. "You should release your grief. It does not serve you. It clouds your vision. How can you hope to catch this murderer when you can think of nothing but your companion?"

"Well, that's easier said than done. I'm on me Todd, and grief or not, I've got to find this killer—if for no one other than Hadrien."

"What does 'on me Todd' mean?"

I smiled. My East London slang always gave Hadrien pause, too. "It means that I'm on me own. Rhymes with Todd Sloane."

She frowned. "Earthers have too many dialects. It is not conducive to adequate communication."

It was my turn to frown because her words forced up considerations that popped like bubbles in my brain. "What does a regulator do?"

"I report information to the apex. I regulate communications to Istos, and I make sure that supplies are brought in on a regular basis through the proper channels."

"Duriken Sunteel avoided proper channels, didn't she?"

Nemer squinted, and her response picked up a few more pings. "She felt that much of the Idealian equipment and parts were inferior to what she could purchase on the galactic black market."

"That probably didn't make her popular at home."

"I do not believe it mattered much to the people who count."

"How was the communication between Duriken Sunteel and her crew?"

Nemer's frown turned to a scowl that she tried to cover with a hand to her face, but she realized that I saw through her fingers and answered me frankly. "How do Earthers say it? Communication was lousy."

"Why?"

"Sunteel was a dictatorial leader. We are all professionals in what we do. If it had not been for our input, she would not have been able to attempt the realignment of the planet. Yet she treated us with disdain."

"Why?"

"Because she was a favorite of the apex. He would allow her to do as she pleased for the most part."

"Was there some sort of physical relationship between them?"

"Of course. They were lovers. He did not bother to keep any of it close. He was proud of Sunteel, but in my opinion, his pride was sorely misplaced.

"How did the other members of the team take to this treatment?"

"Each held his or her own counsel. I cannot speak for others."

"But you obviously observe interactions. How else can you report back to your superiors on Istos?"

She smiled. "You are quick. I have heard that you were."

Irritation threatened to trickle into my enforced calm. "Does everyone know about me?"

"Everyone."

I pulled a deep breath and turned back to the subject. "Do you think the favoritism that the apex showed Sunteel caused a bit of hard feelings among the team?"

"Hard feelings? I do not understand. Feelings are emotions, and emotions cannot be quantified as hard or soft."

"You had disagreements."

"Yes. More than there should have been."

"What was the biggest argument?"

She thought a moment before answering. "I believe there was a big row between Duriken and Rold that went on for several days."

"What was it about?"

"Rold was methodical with his zero-point calculations. He had taken his ability as a matter of pride, something that he should not have done, but immaculates can be obsessive to the point of stupid. Sunteel made him alter his work, and then she signed off on it as her own."

"What do you mean by she signed off on it as her own?"

"They were calculations that involved zpg and time dilation. The idea that zpg and time dilation could work conjointly had always been speculated but had remained theory until Rold discovered workable equations."

"So she stole his work."

"She reclassified it. Such actions are permitted in our society."

"When she reclassified it, Rold's work became hers legally?"

"Yes."

"By reclassifying his work, what did Rold lose?"

"He lost nothing. He is immaculate and, therefore, has nothing to lose, save for the effort he put behind his thoughts. Thoughts, of course, cannot be quantified or protected."

"I'll bet it tricked his dick just a bit."

She shook her head. "I do not know the meaning of your words."

"It put jelly atop his butter; it pissed him off."

"Yes. I believe it left him in a momentary rage. That would have been a logical though unnecessary response. Still, immaculates can be hard to control."

"Why?"

"Because they have many fetters on their DNA composition. They simply are not as advanced as progenitors when it comes to expressing balance."

"So, he could have gotten mad enough to punch Sunteel's ticket?"

"If you mean could he have killed her, then yes. He could have."

This confession was the first sure sign of a motive for murder, but as Hadrien often cautioned me, aliens were not Humans, and motives ascribed to them often met with failure.

"What recourse did Rold have other than killing Sunteel?"

"He had none. Sunteel was a first-level administrator with the direct support of the apex."

"Would his discoveries have shoved him past her on the administrative level?"

"If the experiment had been successful, he would have been granted a monetary stipend, but no, he is immaculate, as I have said. He could not attain administrative ranking."

"Would you say that Sunteel was jealous of Rold?"

"Jealous? I do not know."

"Did Rold do anything, or did he just bow down to her authority?"

Nemer hesitated, and in the silence of the room, I heard the metallic ting of her breath. Finally, she spoke. "He did something that he should not have done. Rold communicated with Duriken's mate, Jandel Sajan."

"How do you know this?"

"I am the one who was told to send the communication."

"Do you know Sajan?"

"Yes."

"What do you think about him?"

"He is very powerful. His appointment by the apex gives him much say in matters of our society."

"Even though many people think he is slow?"

"He is slow but efficient. His cleansing programs have been successful."

"Cleansing programs?"

"Yes."

"What are they?"

"I do not know. He deals directly with immaculates. I am not sure what is done."

"What happened after Sajan found out that Sunteel had nicked Rold's numbers?"

Nemer paused again, this time to take a deep sigh of her own. "Jandel traveled to the Baderes to confront his mate."

"Were you privy to the confrontation?"

"Yes. We all were. Jandel had not wanted Duriken to sacrifice herself to bring Bohdan back into alignment, and he scolded her for reclassifying Rold's work."

"Was that because he loved her?"

"I do not know. He was angry, though. He felt that her action about Rold's work was beneath her. She would not listen. She told him that her modifications in the equations made it a legally binding act on her part."

"What did Sajan do?"

"He cursed her."

"You mean he called her vile names?"

Nemer shook her head. "No, he spoke an ancient curse against her."

"Which was?"

"That she may know eternity amplified."

"I don't understand. Can you provide more clarity?"

"It is a curse that our ancestors used when they wished a person to die but not die. The body atrophies, but the life force continues on into eternity, unable to escape because the soul is trapped in a nebulous place that is neither the corporeal or metaphysical dimension. You Earthers refer to it as riding the creation wind."

22

In astrology, a sesquisquare is a challenge that has the possibility of turning into a trine. A trine indicates flow in any given situation, but while trapped in a sesquisquare, the person experiences irritation and ruinous thinking. I was at a point when I could have bitten through the metal bum of any Idealian who passed my way.

After discovering that Sunteel's mate had been aboard the Baderes just before it all went wrong, I found myself squirreling my distrust into a pocket of anger. I had the gnarly suspicion that Anu was stonewalling me brick by brick. Still, there was one thing I learned in the course of living a life based on the interplanetudes: Hang on, even it's by your fingernails, because eventually the law of attraction will bring you the satisfaction that you crave.

At that point, I prayed that the blasted Idealians would all pop their circuits so I could go home to grieve over my lost lover, but the sad part is, I've got way to much Sagittarius in me to give up the show before the last curtain call. I was like a chicken facing down metal-faced foxes, and I was determined to pluck out some eyeballs.

Instead of facing Anu with my questions, I chose to bring in another Idealian, a bloke named Pel Tan. He came shuffling into my quarters, and when he did, I noticed that he was smaller than his counterparts. His wires and tubes were dented, and his bony infrastructure showed deep gouges and long scratches.

"You look like you been buggered a few times," I said in way of greeting.

He stared at me with dark eyes that, despite the twisting wires around his face, looked tired. "I do not understand your statement," he answered.

I shook my head and plastered on a smile that I didn't feel. "Have a sit down, Pel Tan, and tell me what it's like to be an immaculate."

He did as I instructed, grunting as his arse hit the chair. It had that irritating, metallic ring to it, and I found myself gritting my teeth against the sound. "Are you ill?"

"No, Astrologer Cyprion, I am not. I am simply old and weary."

"How old are you?"

"In standard Earth years, I am four hundred ninety-five years old."

This clanking rock was a regular Methuselah. "How long do Idealians live?"

"As long as our parts hold up. Is that not the way it is with all species?"

"Some are more resilient than others, with an impressive life cycle. I had no idea that your species tramped around for so many years."

He grunted again but didn't offer any more clarification, so I sat down before my logos calculator to determine just who this Idealian was. According to the figures, he was a walking metal crate of Leo energy, but this excessive creative force was tempered by Piscean prudence, a situation that cut through his individual empowerment.

"I'm trying to get a handle on the differences between progenitors and immaculates. You're immaculate and a soldier. Are most soldiers immaculates?"

"No."

"Are they servants?"

"No."

"Are they low on the social scale?"

"Yes, invariably."

"Why?"

"Because we are purified by the fire of experience. Progenitors are the ones who create the experience for us."

I propped my elbow upon the table and used my hand to cradle my forehead. This apple kiss was starting to get old now. "I've had enough double-talk from you people to last me a lifetime," I growled.

He wigged his metallic eyebrow at me. "I do not understand."

I shook my head and massaged my face until my hand made a circuit around my lips and down to my chin. "Why were you chosen as security for this team?"

He was a waterfall of grunts, and I did all I could to contain a grimace. "It is because of one of those experiences that I volunteered to provide security on this experiment."

"What was the experience?"

"I was derelict in my duties. I allowed a progenitor to die when I should have taken the death blow in his place."

"How did that happen?"

"It does not matter. It is ancient history."

"From the scars you carry around, it looks like you've seen your share of battles."

He rumbled and pinged. "These scars are not from battles. They are from societal torture."

"Excuse me, gov, but I don't understand what you're saying. What is societal torture?"

"Following my court-martial, I was punished by having my cegra lobe disconnected."

"What's a cegra lobe do?"

"It directs the bodily functions. Without its intercession, an Idealian finds himself in a state similar to suspended animation."

"Similar? Either you are or you aren't in suspended animation."

"When the cegra lobe is disconnected, it affects all systems but the brain. We are quite aware of outside stimuli. We can continue to think and process incoming information. We simply become statues without proper motor functions. Once the switch is terminated, we have no need to eat or eliminate. We are simply complete in our thought processes."

"And this was done to you."

"Yes. I was then placed in a public square for all to scorn. There were many years when I was exposed to the harsh elements and to the indiscretions of bystanders. He pointed to a series of jagged scars across his chest. "Graffiti," he said.

I shivered. "You are a harsh people, you are."

"Perhaps."

"So, I take it they reactivated your cegra lobe after a while."

"Yes, once my sentence of confinement was completed."

"Didn't all this abuse make you angry?"

He glanced at me with a quizzical look and then shook his head. "Only if I had allowed it to, which I did not."

Maybe it was the increasing guest cells in my brain, but his answer just didn't make a wanking bit of sense to me. I diddled with a question, yet in the end, I let it go to concentrate on the case. "Why were you chosen to be security for this crew?"

"Because no one else volunteered."

"That's surprising. Why didn't anyone else volunteer?"

"The experiment was considered folly by many. It was speculated that it would do nothing to help our planet and was thought to be just a foolish plot hatched by a love struck apex. He is not forced to keep rein upon his emotions like everyone else."

"Why not?"

"Because it is not conducive to creative thinking. The apex is the best of us all: well-tuned, brilliant, balanced. He is the highest and most revered progenitor of all, filled with ideas and plans, and all because he is allowed to test the parameters of imbalance."

"Is that what brought him into collusion with Emperor Theo of Earth?"

Pel Tan held out his hands in submission, and my gaze was suddenly drawn to his scarred palms. He was missing his right index finger. "I cannot say. I am an immaculate. I cannot presume such things about the apex."

"What exactly is wrong with your planet?"

Pel Tan grunted again. "Everything."

"Be a trifle more specific, please."

"We have overpopulated. We have overused our natural resources. We have endangered the space around our planet."

"Endangered the space around your planet? How?"

"By attempting similar experiments with zero-point gravity. It has created farms of unstable space. I am not an engineer, so I cannot be more specific. I do know there are areas within our solar system that can no longer be accessed without mortal danger."

"How long has this experimentation been going on?"

"For the last two centuries."

I diverted the subject, intending on picking up the subject with an Idealian who could answer my questions. "Were you present when Jandel threatened Sunteel?"

"Yes. I escorted him to his ship afterward."

"Did he leave immediately?"

"No."

"Why?"

"He returned just before the crew was to embark. He claimed to have forgotten to tell Sunteel something."

"Do you know what it was?"

Pel Tan shook his head. "His anger had liberated. I assumed he was going to tell her he was sorry for his previous actions."

"Was he alone when he returned?"

"No. He was with his concubine, Zeria Tooz."

"Concubine?" I heard my voice swing up a notch, and I was forced to take a deep breath. "Is this a common practice among Idealians?"

"Yes," he said.

"How did Duriken Sunteel feel about this concubine?"

"When she allowed herself to feel anything, I would say that she hated the female."

"Why?"

He shrugged. "I do not know all of the intimate details, but I do know that Zeria Tooz was from a powerful family who opposed all zero-point gravity experimentation. I believe she is the one who convinced Jandel that what Sunteel suggested was dangerous and wrong."

23

I suppose when I think of a concubine, I've got my mind set on seeing a lithesome female who looks a lot like the storybook Scheherazade, so to see Zeria Tooz stomp into my quarters gave me a start. She was an Idealian, after all, complete with armor, tubes, and wires.

Tooz slid into the chair and studied me as I sat down at the table to check the numbers on her logos. She didn't wait for me to speak but instead launched into conversation with a feminine voice surrounded by pings and mechanical sighs.

"I feel deeply for your loss, Astrologer Cyprion. I cannot imagine how you have the courage to keep at this farce of an investigation."

"Farce? I'm bloody serious here."

"You are, but no one else is."

I abandoned my computer to stand up. "What are you talking about?"

"Your Emperor Theo is funding this operation." Tooz paused to glance at her stubby steel fingers and, apparently satisfied she didn't have a ragged nail, she let her gaze follow me back into my seat. "I am told that you foretell the future for Theo. Did you see this fiasco coming for him?"

I refused to be bullied into answering. "Theo is as genuine as any political animal can be. I'm sure he could give a fig's arse if Sunteel's murderer is found. If he's funding part of this operation, then he wants to make sure it gets back on schedule before the coffers run dry. He's not required to care. Just pay."

"You know, he is not well liked at our apex's court."

"Why not?"

"The apex thinks he is a serpent."

"A serpent? Do you mean snake?"

"Yes, that is it. My protector does not like him."

"Your protector would be Progenitor Jandel Sajan?"

"No. He is my lover. He is not my protector."

I lost ground with my impatience at the Idealian proclivity to make me rip answers from them. "Who the bloody hell is your protector?"

"Why, the apex, of course. I thought I had just made that clear."

"You didn't. What relationship do you share with the apex?"

She wrinkled her nose slightly, and it gave me the willies to see steely skin crease and pleat. "Our relationships are more complicated than Human joinings. I am at once his mate, daughter, associate, and slave."

I was really starting to hate this kind of Idealian boondoggle. My weariness wove through the sudden silence to end the subject with a grunt.

She nodded, but didn't interrupt the quiet while I read her horoscope. Tooz was the Moon in Scorpio and as far as I could tell, she was a walking death trap. She had a stellum of three planets—Mars, Saturn, and Pluto—lining up to form a hard and true flow of darkness and deceit. This one was not like Scheherazade; she was more like Mata Hari.

"So why do you continue with the farce?" Tooz abruptly said.

I glanced up, leaned back in the chair, and crossed my arms again. "I do it for clues to finding my partner."

"You admit then that you are no more interested in justice for Duriken Sunteel than is your emperor?"

I squinted at her. "Why do you care? You were busy bonking her mate. I would think that you'd be glad to see her out of the way."

An expression of sadness gilded the edges of her tubes and wires. She checked the state of her fingernails again before answering. "Duriken Sunteel was my sister. We were splice twins."

"Splice twins?"

"Yes, we replicated from the same DNA strand."

"Which strand?"

"The strand that controls our interdimensional abilities."

"Excuse me?"

"Humans seem to lack something that we refer to as a time filament. Because this essential piece of wiring does not exist in your bodies, you cannot process different angles of time/light. You have a limited range of interdimensional induction—very little, in fact. The best you can do is when your physical body dies. Something snaps on in your brain at that moment, allowing you to access another dimension. Unfortunately, you can rarely enter other causal planes until you are ready to die in the material realm. That is a sign of de-evolution. Many species have the ability to perceive different dimensions with no ill effects. We are one such species." She paused, probably looking to see if I was getting my dander up about the obvious insult to Human sentience, but I was giving her none of it.

Despite having to say it through clenched teeth, I spoke. "Go on."

"We were specially bred, Duriken and I. If my sister had not taken on this experiment, it would have fallen to me to complete. You see, our apex and your emperor have forged an alliance, one that is very nearly fifty standard years old."

"I take it that once the investigation is over, you'll be next up at the plate to play cricket."

She shook her head. "I will be called upon to complete this experiment, if that is what you are saying."

I stopped with the questions long enough to study her. According to her chart, Tooz was laying out part of the truth, but there would be a twist in the bungee when it came to her personal motivations. "You sound as though you aren't looking forward to becoming the next inter-dimensional goddess."

"It is the thing that I least desire. Though we were engineered from a splice, we were nonetheless different people. I prefer to be a shining example of cultural control in evolution."

"And since Sajan is a high muckety-muck in Idealian population management, you two look right good together. Now, don't you?"

She frowned. "I also feel deeply for Jandel."

"I thought feeling deeply was out of your Idealian purview."

"Who told you that? We feel deeply when we choose to. I choose to keep my emotions an active part of my lifestyle. Many would not agree. As the Humans are so fond of saying: Bugger them."

I laughed despite myself, but then sobered quickly to ask this next doozy of a question. "What was Duriken Sunteel really trying to do?"

"Form a spatial link between time and light."

"Can that be done?"

Tooz shook her head and glanced around the quarters. "Obviously not."

"What would the outcome of a spatial link mean for you and your world?"

"Not just our world, Astrologer Cyprion, but your world as well."

"All right. What would have happened?"

"Enhanced stability between dimensions, I should think."

"You don't know?"

"No. I have not been told yet."

"Haven't you been preparing for this your whole life?"

"I have been preparing. For what, I do not know."

Well, if that wasn't ketchup on the porky. "Do you agree with your destiny to be shot into the very fabric of a space station where you'll meld with cold metal instead of another Idealian?"

Tooz scowled. "I do not fancy it, no."

"Will you do it?"

"I will have to do it."

Blast! I was just digging around in the pie now. "Who do you think may have killed your sister?"

"I do not think she was murdered."

"You don't. Why not?"

She stood, as if ready to dismiss herself from the interrogation. "Because, despite the amassing of brilliance with the interspecies cooperation, we lack the one thing that is vital to success."

"And that is?"

Tooz smiled before answering. "We do not know what we are doing. This experiment was doomed to fail. No one needed to intercede."

24

*As an astrologer, I've come to rely upon my intu-*ition to tell me right from wrong. There was a time just before I got tight with Hadrien when I doubted this facility, but he brought it back to me through his faith in my abilities. Now, having all I could of Tooz, I sent her packing and luxuriated in the silence these secluded quarters offered. I decided to reread parts of Captain Marctori's log, and sitting in the quiet staring at this jumble of alien thoughts, I had the feeling that Argos was central to this case, and even more than that, something whined at me that this was the place where I might find my life again.

I rose, hurried to the wall communicator, and fumbled with the switches. It seemed I was all thumbs as I tried to dial Anu's personal beeper code. Finally, his metallic voice greeted my grunts.

"What is it, Astrologer Cyprion?"

"We need to have a conversation with Captain Marctori. As soon as possible."

There was a small pause and I heard murmuring before Anu answered me. "I shall have him rounded up. We will meet you in one quarter of a standard hour in the command ready room."

He flipped off without so much as a good-bye. I spun around, collected my astro-cards and my serenity, before heading away into the crowd of Senerian sulters.

These irritating little pissants were everywhere. They

plied me with wares as I walked to the Baderes's command bridge, one falling away on an answer of no with another one waiting in the wings to pounce on a possible yes. After three of these blokes tried to con me into buying love potions, purple globes of unrecognizable fruit, and bottled water that contained more grit than the Gobi Desert, I grabbed one of the makers to demand some answers. I held him firmly by one of his long fingers, knowing that if he tried to pull from my grip, he would chance cracking the delicate bones.

"What's your name?" I barked.

"I—I am Canaori," he whispered. "You are hurting me."

Good. Pain usually delivered truth. "You beggars act like you haven't sold your goods in months."

Canaori tried to pull away, but when I tightened my hold, he stopped. "I am a simple sulter. I sell hard bread. Nothing more. Would you like to buy bread from me? I bake it fresh in an electronic oven aboard my ship."

"Answer me," I growled. "Why all the hurry-scurry?"

A frown crossed his bland features when he saw I wasn't about to stop holding hands until he coughed up a little loogie of truth. "You are correct," he whispered. "We have not sold anything in months. The captain keeps bringing us here to this sector, and there are no buyers. No people. No business." He paused, then: "My bread is made of excellent quality, Biterian wheat. That is a stable, clean, produce planet. It costs me many credits to buy my supplies so my customers may enjoy good taste."

I ignored his sales pitch. "Who chooses the sales route?"

"Our government. We sell to many government employees and to those who are allied with our government. What we earn from these sales is taxed heavily. It is a hard way to make a living."

"Like Duriken Sunteel and her crew?"

"Yes. The Idealians have struck an additional bargain with my government. They are provisioned by us, but at a cheaper rate of exchange. It is not enough to live on. I have thirteen children back on my home world. They rely upon me to send funds. They are starving. You would love my bread. Honest."

I must have loosed my grip, because the wanker pulled away suddenly and hurried off up the corridor, the black bag of biscuits he carried over his shoulder bumping him along in his haste to escape me. Watching him, I felt my intuition tickle me behind the eyes, and turning, I continued on to the ready room where I found Anu, Drer, and Captain Marctori.

The Senerian sweated like a Christmas goose hanging in the butcher shop window, and he wrung his meat hooks nervously as he sat in an oversized chair that better fit one of the Idealians. Anu leaned against the bulkhead, his arms crossed over his armor-plated chest, silently studying the captain. Drer paced quietly, pausing now and again to glance out the porthole toward the glowing sun in the far distance.

"I demand to know why I have been detained," Marctori raged. "Where is Administrator Telroni? He should be here."

"We cannot seem to locate him," Anu said. "Perhaps you can enlighten us on his position."

These jokers had china saucers for eyes, and when they were trapped in a lie, their mincers grew larger by the second. I watched Marctori's reaction expand in his face. "I do not know where he is. Why would you ask me such a thing?"

I set my gear down on the desk, slid into the seat behind it, and started laying out my cards. No one else could read the symbols and understand them the way I could, which meant that I could pork it up and no one would be the wiser.

The other nice thing about flipping up the cards while interrogating someone was the amount of trepidation they entered into the picture. I'd yet to run across any species who did not understand as well as fear the diviner's powers. Marctori was true to form, and he stared hard at me as I set the spread out.

"What are you doing?" he squeaked.

"I'm gauging your responses," I said. "You might call this an astrologer's lie detector."

It was enough of a niggle to shut him up while I scanned the layout. The cards told me everything I needed to know in less than a minute, and so I cut to the chase without hesitation. "Captain Marctori has had a plan to regenerate his happiness by changing his increase."

"What does that mean?" Drer asked.

I smiled slightly. "It means that Marctori has decided to use others to turn a profit. I'm going to assume that Duriken Sunteel and her crew were targets for this plan. Perhaps you should explain, Captain."

"I am not on trial here," he said haughtily.

"In a manner of speaking," Anu answered, "you are. I am the highest representative of my government, which has an alliance with your government. I am the judge in matters of criminology, and if I were to incarcerate you on suspicion of murder, your government would give my government the benefit of the doubt. So, I would suggest that you answer Astrologer Cyprion, for she is here at the request of both our governments."

Marctori rubbed his beefers across his face, leaving a streak of dirt on his forehead that accentuated his perspiration. "It has been a lean cycle. My crew are independents. They rely upon me to find provisioning planets as well as worlds and peoples open to buying their wares. I had to do something because I faced a mutiny. That would not have been good for anyone."

"I thought you had the gov's contract for supplying the Baderes," I said.

He glanced at me, swallowed, and then shook his head. "*Had* would be the operative word."

"It was stripped from you?"

"Rescinded is a better way to explain it. I could not meet my quota. The government was going to send in a new team of sulters, and I was trying to protect my crew."

"You were trying to avert a mutiny," I said.

"It could have happened. It still might. My crew is starving. They are upset, and I am the only authority they can complain to."

"When did you get word of your dismissal?" Anu demanded.

"Just as we were en route from the Galactic Cusp to this godforsaken sector of space. It came as an interstellar transmission."

"Which you conveniently ignored?"

"I had to. It was a matter of economic survival."

"As well as a matter of your own survival," I said.

"Yes. That is true, too."

"What kind of goods did you bring to Sunteel's crew?" I asked.

"The usual: food, water, potions, computer material."

"Computer material? What are you talking about?"

"Electronics and such. This station was not well-outfitted." Marctori stopped to jut his chin toward Drer. "You were here. You bought medicine from us."

"Yes, I did," he answered. "They carried basic provisions."

"What kind of computer material did Sunteel buy?" I asked.

He hesitated. "Distillation units."

"Distillation units?" I said. "What are they?"

"They coordinate a drive engine during a time-dilation jump. It is how we maneuver out on the Cusp. If we did not, our ship would be dragged into the gravitational pull of the galactic disc." He stopped speaking to peg me with a hard look. "But I do not expect a Human female to understand this."

I snorted. "Do not assume, Senerian. You're out of your league." I decided it was a good minute to drag out his discomfort, so I drew another set of cards. Marctori studied me nervously as I played the hand. "Happiness turns to anger and cruelty in commitment of negotiation. Apparently, Sunteel was thrilled to get the units but then discovered there was a problem of such magnitude that it set her beside herself. She blamed you."

He blinked at me and then frowned. Unfortunately, I couldn't tell if I was right or wrong, and his answer could go either way. "How did you deduce this? Someone must have told you."

"No one told me. I read it in the cards. They do not lie. I've already explained this to you."

Suddenly, Drer came alive. His mechanoid actions, those movements that made him look so much like a stiff-jointed android, fell away in his swift anger. He ripped around and in one step he was on Marctori, his hands turning into the proverbial vise grips. Drer grabbed the Senerian around the neck and started squeezing.

"You are responsible for the death of my mate!" Drer cried. "You deserve to die as painfully as she did."

Marctori burbled, but no words were getting past the mechanoid's clenched hands. Anu transformed as well, shedding his lumbering stance to move quickly toward Drer. He was bigger than the doctor and obviously a great deal more powerful because with a hardy yank, he flung Drer onto the deck. The Senerian choked, his oversized paws fluttering around his injured neck.

"No," he croaked. "Not my fault."

"Yes!" Drer steamed. "If we had not had to return to this station and the units had worked properly, then my mate would be alive. Your fouled electronics caused the Baderes to phase without warning. My mate died during this interdimensional switch. You cannot deny it."

Marctori swallowed, moaning slightly before answering. "No. I had nothing to do with the inspection of the parts. I am only the captain of the transport. A middleman. A go-between. Sunteel had preordered the equipment. I took what I was given." He hacked and tried to clear his throat.

I decided it was time to interject into the melee. "Where were the parts purchased?"

Marctori coughed, spittle flying my direction. "Argos."

When he said the word, my stomach convulsed. "I thought Argos was a myth."

"It is no myth. The people of this world are supposed to be experts in time dilation. We were cheated. They did not sell us what we expected to buy."

"What do the people of Argos look like?" I demanded, my voice cracking with anticipation.

He shrugged. "How can I tell you? They are a strange species."

Anu interrupted, dragging my attention away as he pointed threateningly at Drer. "Remember your societal station, Doctor. Discontinue this violence. Immediately."

Drer grumbled but climbed to a stand slowly, using the edge of the desk to hoist himself to his feet. Anu turned away from him to approach the Senerian, who recoiled, using his hands as a shield to protect his face.

"Please," he whimpered.

"Have no fear, Captain. I intend you no harm. I am going to facilitate your answer to Astrologer Cyprion."

"How will you do this?"

"I have in my memory cells a picture of a creature who has breached this station twice since I have been here. You will tell me if it is a creature from Argos." With that said, he touched Marctori in the center of his dirty forehead. The Senerian's eyes rolled back so the yellows showed, and when Anu stepped away, he was forced to blink before replying.

"Well?" the mechanoid asked impatiently.

"Yes, that is one of them," Marctori answered. "Strange, pitiful-looking beings."

I sighed, not realizing I'd done it until the sound was out of my mouth. Anu glanced at me. "We need to go to Argos," I said flatly.

"That is impossible," Marctori said. "My ship is disabled." He cut a scowl at Anu. "But then, you might be able to repair it so that it functions adequately. I am sure that our respective governments would pay for the fuel charges."

"I cannot leave the crime scene," Anu announced.

"I can," Drer said. "I volunteer to go with Astrologer Cyprion."

"You are violent. I cannot trust that you will maintain our government's best interest."

"I am a person seeking retribution, but I am also looking for the truth."

"Your desire for revenge will cloud your judgment. Of what use could you be?"

I jumped in. "It might make him the perfect judge. Suspicion forces a person to study a situation from all angles."

Anu shook his head. "You are hoping to find your companion there. You also do not do this for the best interest of your emperor."

"My emperor would not require me to do this solely for him. Besides, Hadrien has risked his life for your people. Shouldn't you do the same for him? Or is honor something reserved only for certain species?"

The mechanoid laughed. "Your cutting words do not dissuade me, Astrologer Cyprion. But your logic does." He stepped to the communications console at the desk and flicked the unit to life. "Engineer Fay-et."

A moment later, she answered. "Yes, Progenitor?"

"Prepare the Senerian ship, *Zanru*, for launch."

25

*I collected all my gear and dragged along Had-*rien's duddy bag just in case I found him in need of a clean pair of underwear. Yes, I know this trip was indulgent, expensive behavior, but I made it all right in my mind by telling Anu to charge the costs to Theo.

The first thing I noticed when I boarded the Senerian ship was that it smelled like an overflowing yank on a hot summer's day. Strategically placed refuse bins overflowed their contents into the main corridor. The light blue carpet was stained, and the whitewashed bulkheads had been splashed with some dark substance that had been allowed to run down into a narrow gutter that ran at the curb of the deck. Glancing toward the overhead, I saw peeling paint, pitted chrome, and rusty-edged holes.

"What a tragedy," Drer said.

I swiveled my gaze to lay it on him. "That sounds just like something Hadrien would say."

"Perhaps our species are more alike than you realize," he answered.

"Judging from the way you attacked Marctori on the Baderes, I'd say we are more alike than even you realize. Why did you jump mean on him like that?"

He grunted, the sound ending with a metallic click. "I do not like to be in the presence of liars."

"Oh, and do Idealians have some special implant that conclusively identifies liars?"

"If we did, we would not need such animals as Progenitor Anu."

I tripped over a piece of loose carpet, stumbling slightly. Drer caught me by the shoulder and with the strength of his fingers alone, he kept me vertical. Pausing, I flashed him a smile as a thank-you and then kept going deep into the conversation. "Why do you call Anu an animal?"

"He kills without compassion."

"He's a bobber. That's what they do."

Drer halted to study me. "What is a bobber?"

"You know, a clamper, a cop, an investigator."

He nodded. "Still, a clamper-cop-investigator should not kill for the pleasure of it. He has a fouled activator. Of this I am positive. And yet he dares accuse me of having loose rein on my emotions. I am allowed a certain period of grieving."

"What's a fouled activator?"

Drer started walking again before answering. "Human emotions are instigated by several contributing factors. These include environment, intelligence, situation, and emotional construction. Do you agree?"

"Yes."

"Idealian physiology allows us to call up emotion when the situation demands it. We have no subarchitecture that constantly regenerates the emotional body."

It was my turn to stop. "You mean you can turn it on and off like you have a switch in your head?"

"It is in our heads, but it is not a switch. Essentially, you are correct. At this moment, I feel nothing. I am neutral. What do you feel?"

I thought a moment. "Everything," I whispered. "Fear, hurt, resignation, hopefulness, acceptance, desire."

"You feel them all at once, but the one thing that is uppermost in your emotional architecture at this minute is fear. That fear has many factors feeding into it. You fear you have lost your partner, you fear for your own life, you fear for the future, you fear what you may find when we arrive at Argos."

"That's true, every word of it."

"Idealian physiology precludes emotional values stimulated by such factors. When we become embroiled in an emotional situation, our brains send a permit pulse that activates appropriate responses. Humans suffer physical changes when emotions run unchecked. This does not happen to us. We react in the moment until the situation resolves itself and then the emotion neutralizes as a stop sequence is sent by our brain. We are not contained within the emotion as Humans are. To simplify, we do not have the range of complex perceptions that your species does. Your thoughts stimulate your reaction. With us, our reaction is stimulated by oppression of objectivity."

Somehow, I suddenly felt sorry for Drer, even though I understood precious little of what he was trying to explain to me. "Do you knowingly activate the permit pulse?"

"Yes."

"And you would willingly choose to experience grief?"

He smiled. "That is what makes us a most fascinating and unpredictable species."

I couldn't help a smile back at him, despite the fact that my Human emotions were in a stew over my lost lover. When I couldn't contain the grin, Drer glossed over my frailty by talking about Anu.

"The investigator administrator does not appear to return to neutrality. That is why I believe he has an internal problem."

"What does he return to after the stop sequence is issued?" I asked.

"Cruelty and ruthlessness. That is a foul foundation

on which to base your emotional subarchitecture."

"How can that happen? Are there different designs? Are some Idealians forced into neutrality by genetic design while others return to an emotional base?"

"It is not supposed to be that way. The return to a neutral state is our birthright, but through the intervention of disease, these things change."

"You have problems with disease?"

"Does that surprise you? Do you think we are only susceptible to graphite buildup and rust?"

I shook my head and avoided his penetrating gaze by sending my attention down the corridor. "I didn't mean to offend you, Drer."

"No offense taken." He took a few steps in silence. Then, "We are more organic than mechanic."

This time I scraped my look his way.

"I learned that from some Human. Grammatically incorrect, but nonetheless, true."

His words brought my thoughts full circle, and I was reminded about the strange process going on in my brain. Idealians must have had a telepathic chip or something, because Drer picked up on my concern.

"Guest cells in the brain may be an evolutionary advancement in your species."

"It's this bloody alien implant, Drer. It's got nothing to do with evolution."

"Oh? How do you think Idealians evolved?"

"I beg your pardon?"

"According to the old stories, we, too, were once completely organic until someone discovered a way to make us more efficient with the addition of mechanical infrastructure, and replicating silica into our DNA."

"Yes, but was the DNA diddling done against your will?"

"Probably. Organic creatures are usually opposed to the addition of nonorganic implants. You are a case in point." He paused, and I saw his dark gray tongue shoot out to wet his lips.

"You want to ask me something?"

He nodded and took a deep, tinging breath. "Knowing Human emotional architecture, I wonder how you find the courage to go on this trip to Argos."

"Why do you ask? What courage does it take?"

"Obviously, you do not understand how time dilation works."

"It works off the concept of a rotating cylinder. By harnessing extreme mass and then squeezing it together, a thin, dense cylinder is created, like a black hole passed through a hole in a colander. The ship actually travels in a spiral around the cylinder at the rate of one point two billion revolutions per second, exiting at a specific point by the interjection of a synoid wrap in the dimensional field."

He shook his head. "You are well-informed about the method of travel, but are you aware that strange things can happen at the ends of the cylinder? Time slows down, gravity increases, organic matter changes. Humans lack certain vital defenses against these occurrences."

"Do you think these things will adversely affect me?"

He shrugged and headed on down the carpet. "I would not be the least surprised if they kill you."

26

Anu sent along a contingent of Idealians whom I'd already interviewed and a few that I'd not talked with, so I could continue my probe into Sunteel's death from this side of the space-time continuum. It was hours before the *Zanru* would be ready to go, but I didn't feel much like dealing with mechanoid blokes or those buggers who fancied themselves top-flight salesmen. Instead, I sequestered in the tiny turnaround that served as guest quarters aboard this lumbering, piss-smelling ship.

I had to be honest that I was glad to be away from the Baderes and the place that I'd last seen Hadrien. My head thumped to the regular beat of the engines charging up, and moving from the fold-down table to the tiny bunk was enough to make me want to toss my lollies.

Drer's assertion that I might die didn't scare the wick out of me like it should have. I didn't know if he'd said it to make me change my mind, but when Hadrien had been snatched, it had somehow sealed my fate, and trying to fight a strong alignment of planets was a dally for which I had no energy. Let the goddamned comets, asteroids, moons, suns, and worlds beat me with their celestial power. I was a goner from beginning to end.

As the sleep period approached, a Klaxon sounded throughout the ship signaling the departure from the station. I lay on the bunk, trying to be still in mind and body because I had no idea what to expect about flying through time and space.

According to esteemed Earth scientists, time, space, matter, and energy were interchangeable when the right conditions were applied. Physicists continually expanded this relativity work and suggested that multidimensional influences produced new perspectives of understanding. In other words, when winging through space in a capsule wrapped in time, the awareness extends to encompass universal possibilities never before considered. It had to do with the blending of the forces on the brain, proving that our thoughts existed in many dimensions, though our gray matter was physically trapped in corporeality.

Yes, it was as confusing as my mum's attempt to make Italian spaghetti sauce with a Cajun roux, but now, suspended in time, I knew I was going to get a taste of this scientific mixture.

The alien implant was not the precision piece one might think it was, and I attribute this to the bloody misinformation the Waki'el had about Human physiology. Changes in bodily functions and inordinate amounts of stress caused the blasted thing to go off. It happened a lot during the first few weeks after installation, but we soon learned to keep a relaxed attitude as much as possible.

I gathered the hard pillow under my head and drew up into a fetal position on the bunk, trying to calm my jitters by using a meditation method I'd stolen from a Tibetan monk many years before. I took several deep breaths and practiced repeating the word *om*, making it as rhythmical as I could against the blaring of the ship's horn. After a bit, the siren was deleted, and all I could hear was my heavy breathing. Suddenly, my efforts proved for naught because the alien implant engaged.

My blood went crispy in my veins and crinkling pain grew through my body. The agony expanded exponentially until I cried out, the action of my scream spitting my soul into the ether. Hatred of the Waki'el, of Theo, of my own shortcomings zoomed out, too. It pushed my discontent and sadness along, fondling it like some lost child.

This emotional awareness flew from me on that last breath, and I was sure that I'd kicked the corporeal can, but instead of going the way all good ghosts went, I found myself floating through the universe.

When I say I found myself floating through the universe, it was not as if I were misting along staring at planets and stars in passing. I had become the universe, and was amplified by it, grown so large that the definition of Human no longer fit me. I was part of the creation energy, the first vibration, the frequency that held everything together—and it was exhilarating.

Humans have always been fascinated by what happens upon death. With the discovery and harnessing of zero-point gravity and the formulation of the interplanetudes, we became secure in knowing that our essence bounced into a dimension of pure thought after we turned food for worms on Earth. It was quantifiable, predictable, and with the new science, hopeful. We spent our time in this nether region, awaiting the opportunity to zing back into a new body formed in the heavy, elemental plane. This was something I could get my knackers around; I could understand and identify with it. What happened to me at this very moment was so weird that it couldn't be gauged, formulated, or even discussed because words and thoughts failed it.

I floated gently, realizing that all the mysteries of the universe were suddenly contained within me. There was nothing I did not know, though paraphrasing what I did know was impossible. I understood for the first time that all the junk scientists believed and fought for was wrong. I realized that light, the very thing we measured our existence by, was a secondary phase to something much bigger. It could not be called God. Whatever it was, it didn't have a name, didn't have a parameter, didn't have a reason. It simply was, and I was simply part of it.

This was the part of the alien implant that bumfuggled me the most. When I was caught within the creation force, I would on occasion have trouble ending the link. Hadrien had gotten to the point that he could jump back into corporeality with a thought, but I fussed and fumbled with my fear so much, I still had trouble fizzing back into the proper dimension until I calmed my willies. Fortunately, it was no problem this time.

As abruptly as it began, my union with the universe was over. I was slammed, squeezed, and flattened to a singularity, my body's atoms seeming to reintegrate one at a time until I found myself lying in the bunk, smelling the sour scent of urine and staring up at the concerned face of Dr. Drer.

"I heard you scream," he said. "Are you all right?"

I nodded, but my answer was a lie. I would never be all right again.

27

"What happened?" I croaked.

"I do not know what happened to you," Drer answered. He paused to take my wrist and, like a Human doctor, he counted my pulse. When he was done, he dropped my hand before regarding me with that steely gaze of his. "Perhaps you can tell me. I heard you screaming. Are you in pain?"

I thought about it and couldn't find one gram or trace of hurt. "No, I seem to be fine."

"It might be due to the fact that we are navigating normal space just outside of the Argos home system in this dimension."

"We're there already? It hasn't been an hour yet, has it?"

"While contained within the field generated by this ship, time moves very slowly. It has been several days in normal space."

This whole time dilation was like chasing the ponies on derby day; you could run yourself ragged, but you're never a match for a horse. That was the whole feeling here—I was mismatched.

I sat up and swung my legs over the bed. My head started thumping, growing from a tiny tingle to an eyeball-splitting pain. Were the guest cells pushing my gray matter into my ears?

"Perhaps you should rest," Drer said. "We have at

least forty-eight standard hours of in-system travel before reaching Argos."

I didn't fight him on this part. After I pulled the thin, aluminum-thread blanket up to my neck, I asked: "Do we have communication with the Argosians?"

He shook his head. "Not until we are practically on top of the planet, and then the gravitational interference from the neighboring black hole makes it difficult for standard communication."

"Standard communication?"

He tilted his head. "Yes. You do realize that Senerians have telepathic ability."

"They do?"

"The closer they are to the receiver, the better, but yes, they do. Line of sight seems to help them as well. Odd creatures."

"Why, odd?"

"Well, they have so many potential talents, but as a species, they have developed very few. For instance, why would telepathic ability require proximity and line of sight to work optimally?"

"I suppose the same thing can be said for all species. We each have our evolutionary twists to deal with." I paused to recall the Senerian kiss. "Maybe telepathy was not high on the chart of things to learn. Telroni's folks seem to be concerned with things like time cells."

Drer dragged a thoughtful look onto his ugly mug. "Time cells. Where did you hear such a thing?"

"From a Senerian time prostitute I interviewed."

He chuckled. "It is a myth, as far as Idealians can tell."

"Myth or not, she said she was doing me a favor by giving me time."

"Did she kiss you?"

"Yes, she did. Right on the mouth flappers."

Drer paced a few steps before stopping to regard me. "It's thought there is a stabilizer of some sort in their saliva."

"A stabilizer of what?"

"Of time. We deal with theories only, you understand. It is possible that she passed something to you that helped you overcome the effects of time dilation. It is also possible that by kissing your mate, you can pass this stabilizer to him." He paced again. "I should run some tests on you."

"I don't think so, Jack."

Drer scowled. "It would be a simple count to see if you had any changes in blood work, cell distribution, things such as that."

"I told you no."

"This could be a significant opportunity for your species."

"And your apex could sell the results to my emperor."

He stopped wearing down the dirty carpet to smile. "You are too bright for your own good, Astrologer Cyprion."

The insides of my ears started to throb, so I changed the subject. "You don't have anything in that medical cornucopia of yours that will smack out this whacker of a headache I have, do you?"

"Yes. It is in my quarters. I will fetch it and be back as soon as possible." He took a step toward the hatch but then turned back to me with a serious expression on his metallic-like face. "You realize that very few Humans venture this far into the center of the galaxy and live to talk about it, do you not?"

He punctuated his statement with a mechanical grunt and then marched out of my quarters. I tried to close my eyes to sleep, but when that didn't happen, I rose and wobbled about before coming to rest in front of my logos calculator.

Despite having just been introduced to the universe in a personal way, I still couldn't get a handle on the process of death—especially that of Hadrien's. I could have saved myself a lot of traveling and pain if I'd only had the chrome cobblers to interpret his check-out date. The thought of his passing was more than I could stand, but this time, the fear of not knowing seemed more oppressive, so I took a peek into Hadrien's end of days.

Many astrologers say they can accurately predict the date and time that the interdimensional switch will occur. I think that's all a load of horse pucky. Life intercedes at every juncture. Changes take place that shift the life line off center. The end-of-days numbers are indicators of a spot where it could all come crashing inward.

When I brought up the results of the calculation, I found myself squinting at the readout. Hadrien, the poor bloke, had squares, inconjuncts, and quines littering his field of play. Saturn had fallen under the crest, so to speak, meaning that its negative, dark influences had overtaken my partner. Jupiter sat on the cusp of Libra and Scorpio, and so the energies that circulated through his life were largely a matter of balancing death. Still, studying it, I couldn't see anything that shouted "transformation," and that heartened me.

I compared my logos to his and noticed that where he had squares, I had trines and sextiles, symbols of flow.

The truth presented here was clear as a diamond in a dancer's bared belly button. If I didn't help Hadrien, he was going to be the chopped meat in Sunday's pie.

Drer returned more quickly than I anticipated. He tapped on my door and showed himself in. If it could be said that Idealians could change their steel blue color, then he was definitely washed out. I could read anxiety all over his tubes and wires.

"What's the matter?" I demanded.

He shook his head. "Marctori is dead," he said.

I flew out of the chair, knocking it back as I did. "How?"

"I do not know. I am going to examine the body now. Va-qua-nua informed me of this situation via the communications link." He stopped talking to unfold his hand. Sitting in his palm was a large, white pill. He held it out. "This will ease your headache. Take it. I believe you will need it."

I grabbed the medicine and popped it, nearly choking on the size of the capsule. Once it was down, I pointed to the hatch, following him into the messy corridor and up to the bridge.

We entered the command center to a sharp scent that made my eyes wince and water, and try as I might, I could do nothing to keep the tears from tracing down my cheeks. Drer glanced at me with a confused look.

"Do you mourn his death?" he asked.

"No. This bloke stinks so bad, I can't keep me eyes from puckering."

He stared at me. "They do not appear to be puckering. Humans do have sensitive olfactory glands, but they do not work much better than the Senerian telepathy."

I was beginning to think that Drer was a species bigot. Letting this annoying thought dissipate, I shook my head and tromped over to the Senerian. The bastard leaked purple blood from a knife wound to the abdomen. To make it all the more grisly, the knife was still in him. For some reason, I was caught staring at the filigreed handle. Where had I seen that design before? When no answer came, I backed off to study the folks present on the bridge: Fay-et, Va-qua-nua, Drer, and Rold. As if he thought I expected an explanation, the Bohdan stepped forward to offer it.

"I found him thus," he said.

"Did you see anyone come or go?"

"No, I did not. He had called me upon my communication link. He wished to speak to me."

"About what?"

He hesitated by inhaling. "I am uncertain. It may have had something to do with Duriken Sunteel."

"Why would he want to speak to you about Duriken Sunteel?"

"He was concerned. I could see it in him."

"Yes, but what could you tell him?"

"Nothing more than I know."

Evasive answers always bite me in the bum, but I didn't reply. Instead, I threw an accusing glance to each person in the room. "Did anyone else see anything?"

"One of his crew members left as I came in about an hour ago," Fay-et volunteered. "But Marctori was alive then. In fact, he was in a trance state."

"Trance state?"

"Yes. I assumed he was communicating telepathically with someone, so I checked the engine flow and left the captain to his conversation."

I flipped my attention to Drer. "What is the range on these buggers?"

"Unknown. It is possible that he was communicating with someone in-system."

I paused in my interrogation to focus my gaze out the main viewing porthole. There, growing quickly in proximity was a chunky, gray moon. Its stark beauty contained my thoughts for a second until I had one of those thoughts that bus riders get when they realize the driver is dead. "Who the bloody hell is flying this trap?"

Fay-et frowned. "Autopilot was set when I last checked."

Suddenly, the Klaxon began to blow as if to confirm my intuition. We were on a collision course: squares falling into opposition and trines changing into inconjuncts.

28

*Maybe I should have checked to see if all that as-*trological flow was leading me right up to Hell's gates. I stared at the looming moon, and even though fear quickened my pulse, I was caught by the inspiring beauty of this sector in space. Star nurseries mingled with the glittering light of erupting suns. Gases—white, yellow, and magenta—threw a gauzy coverlet over this landscape. The Idealians, though, had no such appreciation of their possible final resting place. In fact, they all decided to engage their emotional reactions at the same time.

Fay-et pushed Marctori's body from the command chair and despite the gooey purple blood soaking the leather, she sat down heavily in his place to work the pilot's console. She growled, the sound laced with mechanical noise. "The computer will not respond! Marctori set this ship on a collision course."

Drer spoke up. "Delete the Klaxon before it turns my ballbearings to vibrating dust!"

Fay-et complied, but instead of silence, I could hear the whine of engines as they powered up to a greater speed. The Idealian confirmed it with a grating whine. "The swell jet has engaged. Meters indicate we are scooping accretion matter now."

"Can't you get control the ship by melding with it?" I demanded.

She glanced at me. "There is no place for me to meld.

No linkups." Returning her attention to the console, she beat on the keys. "He has input a password to prevent my override."

My heart flopped down into my tum. Marctori had committed some kind of Senerian hari-kari and in the process was going to drag us all to our deaths. How was that for manifesting anger before the great send-off? It would hold over into his next incarnation, and at that moment, I hoped it brought him back as a slug that I could squash underfoot in my new life.

Drer stepped over Marctori's body to join Fay-et, using some inborn Idealian talent to flip blank switches.

"Can you alter our course?" I asked.

"No. We are locked."

"How far are we from the moon?"

"Ninety million kilometers and closing. Approximate time of impact is twenty-nine standard minutes."

"It is still among us," Va-qua-nua announced suddenly.

I spun on him. "What the hell are you blabbering about, mate?"

"It is here. Marctori shared his body with a Shimbang, too."

I shook my head, partially aggravated and partially disgusted. All this talk of ghostly, alien possession was more than I could ever hope to cope with. Because my temper was stewing up, I grabbed the little alien by his scrawny neck and blew my breathy words into his face. "If this thing is here, you better tell him to cough up the unlock code."

"I cannot. But you can."

"What are you talking about?"

"I perceive him. My optics detect him. Yet I cannot communicate with him. You can use your alien dimensional device. Perhaps."

I couldn't help squinting at him. "That's pushing it a

far stretch there, gov. It'd have to be wallowing in the creation energy."

"It is. Maybe it waits for you to join it so it can tell you the codes."

Fay-et jumped into the conversation. "If you are going to do something, then I suggest you do it now. We are coming to a point of no return, and I cannot force the computer to re-create an access around the lock-out."

I nodded but then turned a fierce look onto Va-qua-nua. "You better be right, or I'll come back and pull your eyeball stalks off before we crash."

"I am right," he said calmly.

"Yeah, sure you are," I muttered, as I touched the stud in my wrist. Seconds later, the unit encapsulated me in zero-point gravity, and I found myself standing in the middle of the creation stream. My surroundings turned blurry, and the frantic pings, wheezes, and grunts evolved into silence. This was a ridiculous exercise. Only life-and-death coercion could have forced me into this wild-goose hunt. "Hello?" I called.

Nothing, just the far-off sound of bells. Don't ask me why my jump into forever is occasionally accompanied by this distant tinkling, but it is. Hadrien calls it the music of the spheres. Whatever it was, the sound moved gently through my awareness. "Hello?"

Nothing. I was about to cut the juice and go kill this stinky little alien when I was abruptly greeted by a thought reverberating through the vibratory flow.

"Excellent," it said. "The Bohdan is more aware than most."

"Who are you?" I asked. "Where are you?"

"I am an energy composite," it said. "I am called Clin."

"Have you been the lurker?"

"I am of the Shimbang. We assume corporeality by

filling the void places in the material realm."

"You take over people's bodies, according to the Bohdan."

"Only those who have void places in their energy."

"You fill holes in their souls, in other words."

"Yes. We exist concurrently with the host. He has no knowledge that we are there. In fact, we live communally with many species, most especially Human."

"I'm pretty bloody certain that I don't have one of you inside of me."

"If you did, you would not know."

The thoughts gave me the creeps, but I blew it off. "Well, that's all fine and good. Did you kill Marctori?"

"No. That would be foolish for such as I. We gain essence and structure by linking to those in corporeal form. Marctori was strong but corrupt. This corruption caused holes in his soul, static places that could be filled. There was room for me to evolve at a more consistent level into your dimension inside the captain. When it is a tight block of wood, I must cross the dimensional bonds to cocreate."

It made sense at the same time it didn't make sense. "Did you see who killed Marctori?"

"No. I was abruptly released when his soul was freed. Shimbang do not have eyes. We read energy signatures."

"Well, hello. Did you read an energy signature that shouldn't be there?"

"Again, no. I believe Captain Marctori committed suicide."

"How do you know this?"

"I am in league with his thoughts. He was depressed. Ideas of death attracted him."

"But you don't know for sure."

"No."

Great. Information on the great creation superhighway. "Can you at least give me the key to override the autopilot?"

"I will give this to you, but first you must be aware of something. It is the reason I have waited for you instead of melding with another corporeal form."

"What do you want to tell me?"

"The Idealians are planning to destroy the galaxy."

I almost laughed but then remembered that time was literally flying for the ship. "How can they destroy the galaxy?"

"It is what they try to do with the creation force. They are combining deadly portions of universal elements. These elements were never meant to work in unison. It will establish an entropy effect, and the galaxy will collapse upon itself. This action will have a domino effect upon other galaxies and causal planes."

"Then you somehow killed Duriken Sunteel to stop her."

"Not I. Shimbang have no power in the material realm. Still, since I shared his thoughts, something of murder should have surely arisen in Captain Marctori if he were responsible for her death. But no, they did not."

"You are a real helpful bloke, you are. How about that code now?"

If energy could sigh, I heard it. "Heed my warning, Astrologer. Only you can bring this situation to light. If you do not, the resulting implosion will destroy the causal planes touching the material dimension. Should that happen, your energy source will have no place to retire once you die."

"The code," I answered impatiently.

"Three, eighty-eight, arc seven, fourteen, arc two."

"Thank you." With that, I left the creation vibration and landed back into materiality. Dizziness nearly undid me, but Drer was there to hold me vertical.

"What is the code, Astrologer?" he demanded.

I stared at him for a moment before realizing I couldn't answer. Fighting for my memory, I could do nothing more than faint.

29

I came to life screaming the code. My vision was blurry, but I saw Fay-et enter the numbers, grimace, shake her head, and reenter them. Finally, after what seemed like an eternity to my aching head, she gained control of the *Zanru*—and not a moment too soon.

We careened to port. That's when I realized that Drer held onto me as I lay sprawled on the deck, his emotional response to this situation clear between his tubes and wires. He bared his teeth against the gravitational pull exerted by the course correction, but managed to turn his expression into a grin. Lying there, helpless, hopeless, and scared, I somehow saw Hadrien's smile in Drer's. It was bloody scary, it was.

We leveled out after a bit, and Drer helped me to sit up. Glancing by him, I saw Va-qua-nua's toadie expression. He studied me, his questions stalled behind his fat lips.

"What happened?" Drer demanded.

"What happened here?" I countered.

"You phased right before our eyes. You disappeared. I could only detect a slight shimmering in the area where you had been. Did you actually leap into another dimension?"

"No. I only leaped into the creation stream. I stayed on this causal plane. Sort of like treading water." I took a deep breath, suddenly tired.

"Was the Shimbang present as I said it was?" Va-qua-nua asked.

"Yes. It was there, and it has a name: Clin."

"How did you communicate with it?" Drer said.

"Thought."

"Why thought?"

"Because it can't be contained by the creation energy. It's the one thing free of it." Drer pulled me gently to a stand, and it surprised me. He accomplished it with tenderness and grace, something that just didn't seem to be contained within his hulking physical facade. "The Shimbang is right worried about you mechanoid folks."

"In what way?" Fay-et asked.

I wobbled to an empty chair and sat heavily into it before replying. My thoughts bounced off the inside of my skull like a coin ricocheting around the insides of a porcelain shitter. "I got me a Scotsman doing a kick and prance in me bongo drum," I muttered, rubbing my forehead.

Drer cocked his head. "I beg your pardon? The Shimbang is a Scotsman?"

I couldn't help my own smile at his question. "Never mind. He—it was there."

"What are Clin's concerns?"

"That the Idealians are going to destroy the galaxy."

Fay-et laughed. "That is ludicrous."

"Why?"

She finished inputting some code before swinging her chair in my direction. "Because we are ineffectual as a people. We are not evolving. Our science is at a standstill. We must rely upon the genius of other species, such as the Humans, before we can make new applications."

"And that gives you a crink in your pride."

She shrugged. "I do not understand the term *crink*, but I will assume that it means we are concerned with the highest order of ego emotion. Then yes, we do not like having to bow to other species."

"There is a saying on Earth: Pride goes before a fall."

"Meaning?"

"Meaning that pride will drive a person and a species to rash, stupid things that ultimately precipitate a clobbering. Species pride could be a motivating factor in Sunteel's murder."

Fay-et nodded and then cast a hard look at Drer before speaking. "We have come to the end of our genetic rope because of the prideful action of a few empowered politicians like Jandel Sajan. We are a species that is going extinct because of pride."

I sat back to check on Drer's reaction, but the movement caused a renewed ferocity in the Highland fling going on in my head.

The Idealian doctor noticed my discomfort. Without my permission, he moved behind the chair and placed the tips of his stubby forefingers upon my temples. "What are you doing?"

"I am linking with you. I am taking away your pain."

He was good to his word. Seconds later, I felt a warmth surging through my head and down into my neck. Tranquillity slathered into the heat—mental butter flowing from the churn. The ache subsided, and Drer pulled his hands away. I glanced at him to see that his eyeballs had rolled over into analysis mode. It was disconcerting, and if I'd let it, I could have gotten mean about the unauthorized examination, but for once I just let it all go. Seconds later, he pulled out of his scanning procedure.

"You should feel better. I do not detect an increase in guest cells. Perhaps you have stabilized."

"Thank you, Drer. I didn't realize that you could meld with Human life forms."

"We can link with a variety of carbon-based beings.

Humans are very easy to join with. You are an open, curious, and trusting species."

"And you love us like brothers, huh?"

He smiled, an expression I was starting to get used to. "No, we do not much care for you. Too flighty." Before I could answer, he jutted his chin toward Fay-et. "It is time to tell the astrologer what you know."

"I do not know anything."

Drer sighed and pasted in an answer. "Our planet has run low of convertible fuel."

"Convertible fuel? What kind are you using?"

"Have you ever been to our home world?"

"No."

"Our planet, Istos, is quite far from our system star. Centuries ago, we erected an extraordinary grid that encapsulates our world completely. It floats in the stratosphere and is held in place by enormous mooring stations surrounding Istos. These stations take gravitational energy from our three large moons and by converting it, they can suspend the grid."

"So, you don't see the sun or the night sky? It's like a shield overhead?"

"Yes. Most of my kind has never seen the sun rise or set upon our world. The grid collects the light and focuses it so that we can keep our temperature in an even range."

"Does it rain on Istos?"

"Yes. And the wind blows. It is all a wonderful, technological feat that we have not been able to replicate."

"That knowledge was lost during several intertribal wars," Fay-et offered. "Our hatred for each other doomed us."

"So, what's the problem? Is the grid falling apart or is your sun dying?"

Drer shook his head sadly. "One of our moons is moving out of the reach of Istos, and so the converting station will be rendered useless as will the grid."

"So, Sunteel was experimenting on the Bohdan," I said. "Why not experiment on your own world?"

"I assume it was the lack of funding," Drer answered.

Fay-et shook her head. "He does not know for certain. None of us do, but political maneuvering is probably the reason."

"Why do you say that?" I asked.

"Because the factions in the government have been feuding over this problem for years. They have yet to come up with a solution, and their bickering is placing us all in jeopardy."

"So, there are a few blokes from the nay side of the government who would have welcomed Sunteel's failure just to stick their tongues out at the yea side."

They both looked at me like my brain had gone fancy-free. I shook my head and stood. Things were clearing up fast. "We still don't know who killed the Senerian here."

Everyone glanced at Marctori's putrefying body as if they'd just remembered he was there. I added a little fire to the coal cradle. "Assuming he didn't plunge that pig sticker into his own abdomen, I'd say we have killer among us." With that, I left the bridge, followed by Va-qua-nua. I thought the alien runt was going to pester me with questions about the Shimbang, but he surprised me. Pulling up alongside, he kept pace with me before finally speaking.

"Do not trust Drer," he said in a low voice.

"Why not?"

"Because he is a member of the nay side."

Following his remark, he turned and stalked back to the bridge.

30

*I returned to my quarters and strapped on Had-*rien's holster and side arm. The leather belt was a bit big for my hips, but the weight was comforting—not so much in the fact of the protection it would offer me but of the proximity it brought my lover to me in my thoughts. When I returned to the bridge, Drer, Fay-et, and Rold were busy inspecting Marctori's decaying body.

I will occasionally get a niggle. That's the best way I can describe this feeling that is a cross between suspicion and hurt. It's a clairvoyant thing that always tends to lead me toward shutting down all trust in a situation. Walking onto the bridge, this worry frequency bopped me square in my psychic third eye.

Drer glanced at the heavy side arm I wore and then up to my face. If he could read anything in my expression, it was the fact that I wasn't playing cricket by match rules, but he didn't comment on it, so I didn't get to give him my Scotland Yard routine.

I joined the mechanoids, squatting to get a good whiff of the corpse. "What have you found out?"

"My scans indicate that he had just finished eating a hearty meal," Drer said. "And the knife is of Zubreenian origin."

"Zubreenian? I've not heard of that species."

"They live in the northern quadrant of the galaxy and are known for their modeling and metalwork." He handed me the blade to examine. "Notice how light-weight it is?"

"Yes."

"That is because it is made from pek'oh, a substance that is rare and expensive. It has a flex shaft that, when plunged into something, releases an auxiliary blade like an unfolding solar wing. This creates a circumstance that acts like a blood groove. Are you familiar with this terminology?"

I nodded. "The auxilary blade makes sure the wound is ragged enough that it's difficult to stanch blood."

"Precisely," he said. Drer paused to point at the angle of the cut. "Whoever hit him knew Senerian physiology. This stabbing wound would have inflicted several minutes of agony before Captain Marctori expired. The blade advanced through torso cartiledge and would have proved impossible for him to remove."

"Any telltale signs left behind by the murderer?" I asked.

Again he nodded. "There is a small boot print by the door. I do not know if it belongs to the attacker, but I do not believe that any of the Senerians qualify, considering their physical sizes."

"Did you check his clothing for clues?"

"I did," Rold said. "He had a money purse with eight thousand Senerian questors still in it. His jacket pockets were empty except for what appears to be a manifest tablet." He rose and reached for a small handheld computer resting on the communications console. He tossed it to me. "Perhaps you can find something. It is written in Intergalactic, which tells me that he was expecting to do business with Eastern Arm planets."

Rold said it like it was a bad thing, but I kept my trap shut and didn't remark on it, instead, tucking the tiny computer into a leather pocket on Hadrien's holster. I blipped out, then. Touching the leather brought in

charged memories and smacked me with a minute's
worth of hard worry. I found myself choking back tears.
So I wouldn't look like the princess of jerks, I popped
to a stand to turn away from the Idealians until I regained my composure. Of course, they knew what was
going on, but these beings at least had a measure of
manners and didn't pry into my pain. When I could talk
again, I turned back to ask Drer a husky-voiced question.
"Tell me, why might the Idealians want to see Marctori
dead?"

"None that I can think of," he said flatly.

"Do not skirt the facts, Drer," Fay-et said. "It could
be anyone who came aboard this ship. I noticed that Anu
was very particular about choosing the personnel for this
journey."

"So, you are suggesting that he may be behind it?" I
asked.

"Why not? He is a lord progenitor, and he probably
feels that Sunteel's work was something to be feared. I
am also certain that Tooz had much to do with such a
heinous plot."

"She seemed to be an honest person," I said inno-
cently.

"Tooz is powerful, and she is conservative. She would
think of eradicating a problem to make things easy,
smooth, and quiet."

"She's a user, is she?"

"User? A manipulator? Yes, indeed, she is."

"And Sajan is mad about her, right?"

"Mad about her?"

"He loves her."

It was Drer's turn to shrug. "I suppose he does when
he chooses to."

I shook my head, and it only spurred Drer on to
change the subject.

"Our administrators are not that closed minded," he said.

"Yes, they are," Fay-et said. "They are demanding, petulant, and cruel."

Rold hissed and then spoke to her in the Idealian language. She barked something back at him. All this dicky bird stuff got on my nerves, forcing me to chime in with an attitude. "I'm not a nig nog, you bunch of metal turds, and I demand to know what you're saying."

Drer answered. "They are cursing each other."

"Well, stop it," I snapped. This little exchange made me even more suspicious of mechanoids and their weird ways. I turned my attention onto the doctor. "What else have you discovered?"

He climbed from his knees and slid into a console chair to study me. "Something impossible," he murmured.

"What?"

"I have done a complete scan of the exterior of the body and the weapon. The knife contains fingerprints."

"Are they Senerian prints?"

"No. They are Human."

"I'm the only Human aboard."

"That is correct. You could not have done it though, because you were indisposed at the time of Marctori's death, and I was with you at the end of our journey."

I stared at him, suddenly realizing that the whole moments of the time dilation trip had turned into half moments. Like a bleary-eyed old rummy, I couldn't make my thoughts focus on the memories.

"Astrologer Cyprion?" Drer's voice seemed to come from far off. "Are you ill?"

I know I had a puckered look on my mug, but it was hard to pull out of the expression. Had I done some interdimensional traveling, surging forward in time and then back again, being somehow convinced that Captain Marctori should die by my hand? It was a Shakespearian question—that was for diddly certain.

31

We putted through space at what seemed like forty kilometers an hour, and after two days, I crawled the bulkheads like a Kafka-sized roach visiting from the filth on the edges of the Thames. Finally, we came upon Argos.

It was no wonder this place was considered by Earthers to be a planet in the realm of myth and legend. Standing at the helm on the bridge, and despite the rub-a-dub smell of blood and urine, I was enchanted by this enormous world.

Argos was surrounded by a glowing, golden sheath. The closer we drew, the more sparkling this web looked and the more diaphanous it became. I could see no evidence of satellites that anchored this structure or any kind of spacecraft bobbing about on repair duty. Old London Bridge, the pride of the Brits, had been outdone a million years before it was built.

Drer clomped up behind me. "It is quite beautiful, is it not?"

"Yes," I whispered. "What is it?"

"It is called a suspension halo," Fay-et announced as she followed Drer onto the bridge to check the navigation console. "Idealian history claims that our engineers learned the secrets to construct the halo from these beings, and then they added their own modifications to it."

"What does it do?"

"Many things," she answered. "Argos is a huge biosphere. It was terraformed from a ball of dust."

"So the Argosians are transplants from another world."

She turned to study me with a hard look. "They are known as Argos."

Her attitude boiled my nuts, but I didn't reply because it wouldn't have done any good. They needed to turn on their response mechanisms, and if they chose not to, it was like slamming sarcasm into a grav-wall. It bounced off harmlessly. "What else does this suspension halo do?"

"It keeps in the artificially created atmosphere," Drer said. "And makes it possible for them to use the radiation thrown off by the galaxy's accretion disk. It is minimal at this distance, but the halo amplifies it and directs it to keep the planetary temperature constant."

"How long ago did they build this?"

Fay-et shook her head. "The beginnings are not clear. They have been lost in the succession of time."

"But it looks new," I said. "Do they regularly maintain it?"

"Unknown. I would think they do, though."

I stepped up close to the porthole to get a better forward view of this engineering wonder. Its glittering texture caught my attention and seemed to calm me clear to my soul. I managed to turn from the window because I couldn't talk and stare at this man-made beauty at the same time. "Why aren't you blokes getting your technology from the Argos? I mean, they helped you once, why not again? Unless, of course, your politicians pissed in their tea."

Fay-et grunted. "We have done plenty of that over the centuries, and not just to the Argos." She paused to make an adjustment to the console before adding, "Our government has made it a crime to associate with Argos.

The apex has suspended collaboration with them for the past seventy years."

"So you are breaking Idealian law by coming here with me."

"Essentially, though Progenitor Anu's permission will protect us."

"Actually, as I understand it," Drer said, "your Emperor Theo has been actively trying to form a liaison with the Argos to help us reconstruct Istos's grid."

"How in the peppery hell is he doing that when most Humans die in time dilation?"

Drer held his hand out in surrender. "I do not know. Perhaps he sends an alien envoy."

Each time Theo's interference was mentioned, I experienced a blast of panic and hard suspicion. Hadrien and I had thought we'd escaped his manipulation, but I had to wonder if it was indeed so. "This kind of engineering display doesn't seem possible."

"Why?" Fay-et asked. "There are things in the galaxy of which Humans lack the mental capacity to copy. This is but a small part. Our conversation about pride might well identify your own species."

I glared at her. "What side of the tuna fish can did you crawl out of this morning?"

She laced her expression with delight. "The same one I always crawl out of. I am merely making objective observations."

"They're not that objective, believe me, sister."

"But true, nonetheless."

"You really don't like Humans, do you, Fay-et?"

"You are small, have poor eyesight, bad hearing, no strength, you stink, and you think you are the best thing since ionized bread. What is not to like?"

"You forgot to mention the one thing that you Idealians envy about us."

"What is that?"

"Our resilience. And because we have resilience, we have power. That power eludes you, and you don't even know why."

She frowned but didn't march onto the battlefield with me.

I silently studied Argos for a few more minutes until a surprising idea suddenly came to me, and I voiced it without hesitation. "Are we still in our dimension of origin?"

Fay-et slung me a sidelong glance. "Bravo," she answered quietly. "I am impressed that a Human could deduce the minute changes in her surroundings. It must be the alien shunt in your body."

When she said it, I nearly fouled my drawers. "What dimension are we in?"

"Argos appears solid to three-dimensional orientation but actually exists in NJ-45," Drer answered. "You do realize that what appears in one dimension translates through all dimensions. It is just your ability to be able to perceive it that makes it appear on this causal plane as opposed to another."

I nodded. For centuries, many religious philosophies stressed that there were ten dimensions creating the fabric of the universe of which Earth was found at the lowest most material plane and Heaven, the highest. When zero-point gravity was discovered, it was suggested that when we die, our life forces wend their way to the next level, the dimension of incorporeality or pure thought. Ghosts are thought to be citizens of this causal plane.

"Are the Argos indigenous to this planet?" I whispered.

"It is said that they traveled through the accretion disk," Drer answered. "I do not know if it is true. That would essentially be traveling via black hole transmission. If they did then, they no longer have that capability. They use a form of time dilation to transport themselves now."

"And they don't seem to need a ship to do it."

"Yes, that is correct. It is done through changes at the quantum level. For all their ugliness, they are more evolved than most species. Perhaps more evolved than all of us."

"Why didn't Anu seem to know what our little orange visitor was? He acted like he'd never seen an Argo before."

"Perhaps, he never had," Drer answered.

"Or maybe he was feeding me Sunday's leftover pork pie."

Fay-et swiveled her attention to study me. "Pork pie?"

I didn't bother to answer but instead continued to study the planet glittering in space, but my awareness swept out about me, looking for the subtle differences that Fay-et claimed were present. Aside from a slight thickening of the atmosphere, I couldn't find a bloody thing that was out of place. It was right about that time, the yeast started to rise in my bread loaf. The differences were in my personal perceptions and speed of thought. I was in an Einsteinian place as far as my brain making connections. Why was that? Was it the presence of guest cells in my oatmeal, or something to do with the Waki'el implant, or maybe a change in the overall orientation of the dimension?

I glanced at Drer, saw a sparkling reflection of the planet in the metallic-like skin of his forehead. Was it different for them, too? I didn't get a chance to ask about this boat race, because Fay-et interrupted me with a little factual information.

"The Argos are an amazing species," she said. "They draw the power for the suspension halo through several planes, beginning in our material place of origin." She paused, worked the console, and slowed the *Zanru*. "Not only are they capable of such a feat, they also use mooring rigs placed in other realms. They are truly multidimensional beings."

32

I have to honestly say, I'm not thrilled about the idea of our natural resources being sucked into other dimensions. That seems a bit heavy-handed. It wasn't any of my bloody concern, anyway, because I was here to find Hadrien, but at the moment, I wasn't even sure how to get through this sparkling mantle to the orange blokes living beneath it.

Fay-et had an idea, but instead of looking at me when she spoke, she continued to stare out of the bridge's viewing porthole. "We will need to communicate telepathically, and Idealians do not possess this talent with other species. We will need to pressure one of the sulters to help us."

"What do you mean, *pressure?*"

"I do not believe they will do it out of any loyalty to us. We are causing them to lose profit each day they are out here. Now that their captain is dead, we will have to coerce their cooperation."

As if on cue, Rold entered the bridge with a Senerian. "There is no cooperative problem, Engineer," he announced. "This being is called Ilgar. He will communicate with the Argos."

I studied the sulter by letting my gaze slide to his oversized hands. His nails were long and unkempt, and his mitts were filthy with grime and grease. Rold held him by the upper arm as if the old boy was going to scamper away.

"Well, Ilgar," I greeted. "I've got to know why you are so willing to help us."

He shook out of Rold's grip and stepped forward, bowing at the waist. "Because I wish to be on with my life. I have twenty-two children, all of whom are hungry."

"You bloomin' Senerians have never heard of birth control, have you?"

He snorted. "Birth control does not work for us. We are genetically incapable of not producing offspring."

I didn't even want to step there. "Aren't you a wee bit tiffed at the fact that your captain was murdered?"

"Tiffed?"

"Upset. Worried. Fearful that you might be next on the last hurrah."

He squinted but then finally shook his head. "That is ridiculous. I am a nobody. Marctori was earning good money with his scams. Nobody cares about the Heaven Oil I sell."

"Heaven Oil?"

"It is collected from this dimension. A process that is supposed to regenerate youth by inspiring the cells to strengthen."

"Are you saying you're not popular? You'd be swamped on Earth."

He perked up a bit. "Really? Do they have trouble getting Heaven Oil?"

"Well, yeah. I've never even heard of it."

"It does not work," Drer said.

"Yes, it does," Ilgar snapped. "I am three hundred twenty years old. I look no older than two fifty. I have used it for seventy standard years." He stopped speaking to me to murmur to himself. Finally, he straightened and nodded. "I shall find passage to Earth. Thank you for the reference."

"Now, finish telling me about Marctori."

"He was a vile being. It was necessary that he be that way, but it earned him many enemies."

"Who aboard this ship is his enemy?"

"All the sulters. I cannot say about the Idealians or about you."

"Do you know who to contact down on the planet?"

"I can contact the space docking administrator. He will open the landing bay for us."

I took a step back and waved my arm toward the porthole. "Please contact him."

"As you wish." Ilgar covered his face with his hands, mumbling incoherent words as he did. It didn't seem that he used line of sight at all, and I wondered for a minute where Drer had gotten his information. After several minutes of this, he lowered his paws and stared directly at me. "He has been expecting us. Someone already informed him of our visit."

"Who, Marctori?"

"No. It was Va-qua-nua. Do you know this name?"

"Yes." I glanced at Fay-et, who showed not one centimeter of surprise at this. Instead, she turned her attention to the navigation console.

"We are receiving coordinates to the bay doors. Thank you for your assistance, Ilgar."

The Senerian bowed again and left, taking a wide step around Rold. At that moment, I wanted to know why, but my question blew away as we approached a growing black slit in the sparkling halo. We moved toward it slowly until Fay-et positioned the *Zanru* over the expanding square.

"Changing forward stem cameras," she announced. The image at the viewing porthole shifted, and I found myself gazing straight down into darkness.

It looked like a long access tube, gargantuan in width. I could see neither one wall nor the other with any clarity, the ceiling disappeared in the darkness, and the end

of the tunnel was lost in the distance. We settled into
the locker and started to scoot through a strange landscape.

It was a contained unit, complete with robotic flyers
tending ships of all makes and origins. Cargo haulers
moved slowly through this enormous complex, tugging
rigs that could have been a quarter of a kilometer long.
Small, single-engine craft plied the tunnel, like com-
muters looking for a place to park the shuttle for the
day. A train passed beneath us, heading toward the distant wall partially obscured by purple kites floating
through the atmosphere.

"What are they?" I asked Rold.

"They are called Ziss. That is an organic element. It
moves through space without the help of metallic re-
straints."

"It doesn't need a ship, in other words."

He frowned. "That is what I said."

My next question was out before I even thought about
it. "Tell me something, Rold. Were you sleeping with
Sunteel?"

That did it. My words apparently broke a hose loose
inside that head of his. He scowled at me, a lethal look
that made me shiver. When he replied, the metallic tim-
bre in his voice grated into a growl.

"I am an immaculate. I am not permitted such a liaison in my society."

Fay-et jumped into the conversation. "That does not
stop anyone. You use it as an excuse. The truth, Astrologer Cyprion? The truth is, Rold is brilliant, but he
lacks charisma."

Charisma? These junk piles of scrapped metal and
steely blue flesh? Now that was a jolly joke. "I suppose
your tubes and filters change to bright, fluorescent colors
during mating season, do they?"

Rold arched his neck to gaze at me imperiously. "I do not understand what you are saying."

"When you mate. You turn colors or something. It's how you show off your male charisma and virility."

"No, we do not do that."

"Do you turn on your charisma gene or something?"

"Charisma is found in the islet of Langerhans near our solar centers. It is special node that activates when one comes into mating heat."

Obviously, I wasn't marching to the same flute player as he was. "Charisma means charm, sexual ferocity. Is that what it means to you?"

"No," Fay-et said, flicking buttons on the helm console. "Charisma is a chemical compound that excites the mating glands. If you have no charisma, you cannot impregnate a female. Impregnation is an important function on our world. It has become so important, in fact, that we have suffered for many a decade with decreasing resources."

I flipped a quick look toward Rold. "So what happened to your charisma?"

He must have switched on his emotional response system, because he reacted like someone had given him a sharp metal wedgie. The mechanoid stepped over to the bulkhead and leaned upon it, allowing his considerable bulk to relax under its support. "I am a carrier," he whispered.

"And that would be?"

"About a century ago, we began to realize how dire our population problems were. If we did not do something soon, we would not be able to survive on our home world." Rold ran his fingers around and under the tubes and wires decorating his face. "Certain Idealian males were chosen to accept a genetically transmitted virus. This virus would change the function of the islet of Langerhans and instead of rendering charisma chemical, it rendered whatever female you mated with sterile."

No wonder they avoided him. "You must have a lonely existence."

"Lonely, yes."

"But that's not your problem, is it?" I asked. "You're angry about what the government did to you."

He nodded. "If you want to know the truth, Astrologer Cyprion, I am angry enough to kill those responsible and anyone else who I might consider as guilty."

33

Not much more information surfaced from my mate, Rold. He slunk away as we docked, unwilling to part with any truth. A covered ramp, several meters long, swung out to hermetically seal with the *Zanru*'s main hatch, and before I knew it, Hadrien's big gun and I were heading for the welcoming committee. Drer and Fay-et accompanied me, their heavy footsteps making the metallic floor ring. Exiting into the main terminal, I was even more in awe of this spaceport.

The walls and soaring ceiling were colored in hues of majestic purples and intense forest greens. Robotic floaters bobbed in the cool, wavy atmosphere, and little apricot-colored folks dressed in magenta robes swung through the place like the queen on holiday. We were immediately noticed and approached by an orangey who grinned widely before burbling at us. Thankfully, Fay-et understood the language.

"We are to attend this one to the fountain of understanding," she said.

I followed her as she headed off behind our guide. "What's the fountain of understanding?"

"It is a well from which organic translation coders can be harvested."

I stopped. "What?"

She paused and tossed me an impatient expression. "These are perfectly harmless organisms that pass through your body once a day. While they are contained inside of you, they allow you to communicate through interface translation methods."

I did not want to know what that was all about, so I went with it, trusting that they hadn't come this far to feed me poison. We reached the well, which turned out to be a refrigerated unit sitting in a small, blue, elaborately decorated room. The Argos poured us each a plastic tumbler of yellow liquid and indicated that we should drink. It tasted like someone had used it to clean the deck, but I sucked it down anyway, always the stupid, trusting runt about things. Orangey started to speak once I swallowed the filth, and lo and behold, I could truly understand what he sputtered.

"I am Uruah."

"I'm Philipa Cyprion. This is Engineer Fay-et and Dr. Drer."

"The *Zanru* shipped out only recently. Why are you back so soon?"

Truly, time was relative. "We need to speak to someone in authority about a missing person."

The creature smiled. "I am in authority. Did this person remain on Argos after his ship departed?"

"Not exactly. He was pulled into a dimensional vortex of some sort while aboard the Baderes Space Station. Do you know about this circumstance?"

This organic translation software we'd just slugged might have given us a basic understanding of the Argos language, but it was bloody lousy at literal interpretation.

"What is a dimensional vortex?" Uruah asked.

"You blokes are supposed to be the best at skimming through the dimensions. What do you call traveling interdimensionally?"

"Traveling interdimensionally."

Does every species need to crack bad jokes? Was it a genetic fault that interfered with reasonable people? "Look, Uruah, I'm running out of time."

He studied me. "No. You have an overabundance of time. Did you receive an infusion at some point previously?"

"I had a bloody Senerian kiss me on the pucker. She said her slobber would give me time—whatever that meant."

"She may have helped your cause considerably. You are Human, correct?"

"Yes."

"You should not have been able to make the trip in a time dilation ship. Perhaps this gift of time has pushed your final hours back."

All this talk about death started to blister my patience. "Can you help us to find the person in charge who could answer my questions? My partner was taken without his permission by one of your comrades, and I'm pretty sure he came here."

"It is possible, but your friend may not have survived the trip. This is not a place for Humans or any other dual-vibration species."

"Dual-vibration?"

"Yes. You exist either in the material realm or the light/thought realm, but you have trouble adjusting your atomic structure to other causal planes. You simply do not have the bodies for it."

"And you do?"

He grunted and then shuffled over to a set of windows. We followed like lemmings until we literally stood at the edge of Argos. The view was majestic, expansive, and inviting. Bright and airy, the architecture flowed over and around colorful plazas. Step pyramids rose from a nearby commons, glittering golden in the light. The suspension halo was transparent from the inside, and I raised my gaze to enjoy the red and green streamers of a nebulonic star nursery, and that's when I had a weird thought.

"Where does the sunlight come from?"

"It is imported," he said. "From your own material realm.

"You've somehow twisted light so that it fills this space in time."

"Essentially, this planet is a hub or intersection of causal planes. Because so many frequencies pass through here, we can capture resources from all the causal planes. In essence, each plane overlaps another, and while here, you exist in the infinite number of dimensions that are possible."

"Our science of the interplanetudes says that we exist in all planes all at once," I answered.

He smiled, and it was an odd face he made. "Perhaps the science is wrong." Uruah paused, allowing me the opportunity to defend my Human theory, and when I didn't, he continued. The truth of the matter is this: You are now standing in *everywhere*. You have become a right angle to eternity and exist simultaneously into forever." He paused when I frowned and then shook his head. "It is complicated. Suffice it to say, we are not restricted in our travels, and we are not encumbered by the higher dimensions. We can live on any plane fully or partially, but even the rarefied levels are difficult to interpret from any perspective. The structures are unusual."

So the Argos had trouble maneuvering into infinity, then. "I'm looking for my lover," I said softly. "And a murderer. Maybe a whole peck of those last things."

Uruah shook his head. "I am the leeching official only. Not the constable."

Leeching official. "My lover is a tall Human with yellow hair, and if he came here, I'm sure he turned up the noise meter. Can you take us to someone who might know about a person named Artemis Hadrien?"

He took a deep breath of wavy air. "I shall check. A moment please." With that, he closed his eye, fluttered his hands, and communicated.

"Telepathy?" I asked.

"Dimensional phase," he answered.

"What does that mean?"

He held up a finger, and after a few seconds, he replied by pointing to one of the pyramids in the square. "That building sits not in this dimension."

"It appears to," Fay-et said.

"We are at an intersection of causal planes. There are many places in the universe where this occurs, and the only difference between causal planes is the speed of the vibration." He paused and jabbed a finger at me. "The one thing that is not affected by the various frequencies is your thoughts."

I studied him. He was a complicated being for all his orangeness. "You find out things by melding with the atomic structure inherent in each causal plane."

"Yes."

"How do you do it?"

"We are born that way. We are intersection people. We exist through all dimensions. You are much heavier in vibration than we are. It traps your awareness."

"Then please tell me. Is my friend on Argos?"

"I believe so, but there may be a problem."

"What's that?"

"Depending upon how long he has been here, he may have migrated into one or more dimensions. He will exist on many causal planes."

"Yes? So?"

"It would be unfortunate, because his life force would fragment to fill in the atomic structures of each causal plane. This Human called Artemis Hadrien would not be able to leave Argos—ever."

34

Upon hearing his words, I was struck down by a sudden attack of dizziness and a headache that plowed me under like a dirt farmer turning the rocks in South Wales. I staggered into Drer, who caught me effortlessly. He picked me up and carried me to a low-slung hammock chair hanging from a large, ornate hook in the overhead. When I was caught in the sinking clutches of this linen chair, he counted my pulse and studied my face. He then turned into scan mode, forcing me to watch him roll back his eyes to expose his medical hardware. In the midst of trying to focus and not faint dead away, his efforts nonetheless unsettled me. For some good reason I had started thinking of Drer as more organic than machine. His report came to me a minute later, hitting flat against my ears.

"Your blood pressure is significantly low, Astrologer Cyprion, and your temperature is above average. The presence of guest cells in your body appears to be decreasing, though. Unfortunately, I cannot ascertain if this is a positive sign of health. It may be an effect of the alien implant you wear." He paused, checked my heartbeat again. "I do believe you are suffering from the dimensional shifting in this place."

Uruah stared at me with that pop eye of his. "She has transformations occurring at the subatomic level."

"What kind of transformations?" I murmured, trying to stand.

Drer pushed me into the chair gently before Uruah came back with an answer. "You should not have come."

I roused from this strange lethargy. "Why, blast it? Stop making me snatch the explanation from you. I got through the time dilation, and I survived. Are you saying that I've got me peck of trouble right now because of the intersecting dimensions?"

My little outburst didn't faze him. "Humans are fragile. The stresses of the intersection begin to pull you apart as soon as you enter the dimensional hub. You have no defense against it. It is as if you were born lacking the crucial element of time. Still, you appear to be a Human who has more strength than most."

"A Senerian gave me the gift of time," I reminded him.

He nodded. "Yes, perhaps that's it."

"How could she do that?"

"Senerians carry a time cell. They regenerate the time/light frequency. Unfortunately, this time gift will not last with you. Your system should not be able to use it."

Had the Waki'el inadvertently given me a transmutation device while they had practiced butchery and enslavement? Could I ascribe a margin of credit to them for my continual survival?

"The longer you remain, the longer your death will take."

"Death?" Well, now, that woke me up. "I thought you said Hadrien was trapped here. You said nothing about death."

"For that lack of clarity, I apologize. It is the same thing as being trapped. Of course, even death is relative. You should leave immediately."

This time, I shrugged off the dizziness completely and ignored the head pounder and struggled to a stand. "Not on your coral-colored arse, me mate. I'm here to find

Hadrien and to find out why your comrades would transport themselves onto the Space Station Baderes uninvited."

Uruah's eyeball grew wide. "We never wish to harm anyone. We are peaceful."

I gave him the eyeball right back. "You know something, don't you? Come on, Uruah, cough it up. I haven't got time for games. Remember?"

He stepped away from me and went into communication mode, somehow descending and ascending the clausal modality until he found a response. After a minute, he shook his head slightly and stared at me. "We had not intended harm. Your partner stepped into a dimensional phase and was caught in the stream."

"Who told you that?" I demanded.

"I will take you to the one who has information." With that, Uruah trotted away, his robes flowing gently in this heavy, wavy air.

I watched him go, and right before my unbelieving eyes, he disappeared, only to return a second later, a little farther away. Had I just seen him cross through planes so rarefied that I couldn't see anything for the slant of the light?

We left the terminal and followed a snaking hallway to a gel bubble that, like a transparent lift, descended gently to the surface where I found to my momentary delight that the view through the sparkling dome was even more radiant. Unfortunately, when we reached the ground, I sensed something nasty going on.

The terminal opened out onto a wide expanse of rusty conduits. They formed a maze that was at least three or four stories high, and rushing through this odd field of pipes and T-connectors were folks who appeared and then disappeared to my eye.

"What dimension is this?"

"This is the dimension of truth," Uruah said. "It is the underpinnings of all that is."

Truth? Was it as simple as all that? "What's the next level up from truth?"

"Understanding. That is your plane of origin."

"And the level after that?"

"Enlightenment."

"Why do people keep blinking out on me?"

Uruah continued walking but called the explanation out over his shoulder. "You should not be able to perceive this. Humans are not evolved enough to view this phenomenon."

"What phenomenon?" I growled.

"Because this is the universal hub, there are slight differences in causal modalities. Your physical body is inadequate. Something does not make sense."

"She wears a creation stream harness," Drer volunteered.

This bit of gossip made Uruah stop and ogle me. "How is that possible? Obviously, the creation stream is helping to keep you stabilized."

Apparently, it was no big bloody deal to Uruah, and he turned back to hurry through the metallic labyrinth.

I stole a look at Fay-et. She held an Idealian-created service revolver in her hand and her forefinger massaged the trigger. If she had any emotion turned on, it was wariness. "I would think you'd feel comfortable here," I said.

She snorted, and her reply was laced with a sound of BBs spilling into a short shaft. "It is too dark here. What happened to all the ambient light?"

"It is here," Uruah answered. "You simply cannot perceive it."

"So we see a basement?" I asked. "How does that happen?"

He shrugged all his arms. "Truth is a harsh. There is simply no other explanation."

"Do many folks live here?" I asked.

"Yes. Many."

"Why?"

"Because they have a choice."

That pretty well shut our meat lockers. We followed our little orange guide at least a kilometer from the terminal exit. As we did, I started to recognize signs of familiar, material life. People here were solid. There was no ethereal quality extenuating from the objects of this plane, no sparkling light, no feeling of spiritual superiority. The world in this plane was a practical place filled with heavy concerns and responsibilities. Everything that I perceived here was flat with truth.

Our safari among the bottom dwellers of Argos ended at a rusty steel door. It was pitted and covered in grime, and as Uruah drew back his hand from tapping on it, I saw dirt covering his sherbet-colored knuckles. A moment later, the door was answered by a naked Argo who sported bright golden flecks in his burnt orange flesh. I stood there, mesmerized. This old Turkish delight carried his own lighting source with him. In fact, he was as sparkling as the planet's halo. Did it mean that those who filtered truth made their own light here?

He and Uruah gibbered in some language that the translation bugs in my body couldn't fathom. Finally, our guide turned to us. "This is Kiumah. He is the administrator for this causal intersection. He is in authority for this phase shift."

"Phase shift?" I asked.

"Yes. The planes move, Astrologer Cyprion. What is here at this moment will change in perspective before you can complete your talk with Kiumah. He will then be phased to a different level contained within this dimension."

"Then what?"

"Then nothing," Kiumah said. His voice was deep, rich, and resonant, and he seemed confident of himself despite his weepy eyeball. "Moving through the intra-dimensional levels is, for you, the same thing as aging. Do not be concerned." He bowed. "Please enter my home."

We tromped into his house, a metallic place of no windows and walls made of scars, dings, and curls of water pipe and grill vents. Inside, I found three other Argos illuminating the space with their own incandescent properties. Together, they cast the place in golden light, and I found that this frequency color range satisfied and calmed me.

The mechanoids, though, were a different matter. They whirred and sputtered, clinked and pinged as they adjusted their visual receptors. One of the beings in the room surged with brightness and I watched, fascinated, as a milky membrane snapped down over Drer's eyes.

We were invited to sit upon metal boxes surrounding a floor hearth that contained boiling water instead of fire. The moment my hiney contacted the box, I realized I was chilled, and the steam rising from the artificial pond felt good.

Kiumah moved on to a small metal container placed against one of the walls. When he pulled open the top drawer, ambient light glistened into the shadows. He brought out a crystal bottle filled with dark liquid and returned to the water hearth. Uncorking the container, he took a good pull of the plink-plonk before passing it on to Drer. The mechanoid hesitated a moment but then took a tiny sip. He quickly pushed the flask into my hand.

I smelled the brew, and I could tell this stout was hardy stuff that would straighten up the perspective and the attitude. Taking a big tifter of it, I luxuriated in the burn of the liquid. It was pure battery acid, and I liked it.

Passing the tot on to Fay-et, I let her fiddle with the offering as I began the questioning. "I have a feeling that you, Kiumah, interfere in many matters of my celestial realm."

He smiled. "You understand that, do you?"

"Well, I don't rightly know if I understand it, but it seems to make sense based on what I've experienced recently."

Fay-et interrupted to hand Kiumah the bottle. "Were your associates involved in the death of Duriken Sunteel?"

"That would be impossible due to the fact that Duriken Sunteel is still alive."

"No, she was found dead aboard the Baderes Space Station."

"Her physical container may no longer function, but her life force wafts on the creation energy through the dimensional planes. I suppose to creatures bounded by the heavy atmospheres, this is a concept that is hard to accept."

"She is lost to us, no matter where her life force resides," Drer said flatly.

"That is correct. From your limited perspective."

"You hedged the question," I said. "Did you or your associates have anything to do with Duriken Sunteel's death?"

"No."

"Were you there aboard the station when she activated the zero-point gravity sequences?" Fay-et asked.

"Yes. We felt it prudent to have an agent aboard in case the action caused reciprocal effects throughout the universe. Someone with experience needed to curtail it."

"What happened to that person?"

"He came home after it was apparent that Duriken Sunteel had met with opposition."

I couldn't keep from asking the question that sat on the front tip of my brain. "Who are the Argos, anyway? What is your agenda?"

Kiumah snapped the cork back into the bottle and placed it in a small puddle forming by his bare feet. "We are a species who maintains the balance between causal planes. We will modify any situation that needs rebuilding to preserve the sanctity of dimensional unity. We take this responsibility seriously."

"So you stick your eyebalis in where they don't belong."

"We stick our entire body in, Astrologer."

"What gives you the right to interfere with the balance or imbalance of the universe?"

"Can you think of an entity more prepared to be of service?"

"Do you consider yourselves divine?"

"No. Divinity is a concept that speaks more toward the ultimate inception of the universe. We are unaware of the root causes for the establishment of time and space. We are simply a species who can access the different causal planes without difficulty."

"How can you do that, by the way?"

"Our DNA is multiatomic. We fit all causal parameters. In other words, we are capable of blending with the new dimension by taking on its properties. You might call us dimensional mimics."

My understanding had a hard time wrapping around his words, and I sat there blaming it on the translation critters befouling my thought processes. "You're Shimbang, aren't you?" I blurted.

He scowled, and it was a right weird look what with that big mince pie he called an eye filling out his face. "The Shimbang are the enemies of Argos."

"Enemies?"

"Yes. They are of the same DNA structure as the Argos, but they have enhanced their life forces with technology. When they did that, they broke all ties with our kind."

"Why?"

"Because we do not advocate their methods. It restricted them to the point that they cannot function unless they have a host body to provide an encapsulating shell. Fear imprisoned them in their evolutionary choices."

Fay-et frowned but didn't go there, instead, turning her ugly mug onto Kiumah. "So you are saying that your efforts of balance may be occasionally unhinged by the Shimbang?"

"Not occasionally. All of the time. It is their way to interfere when self-gain is the objective."

"Did the Shimbang kill Duriken?"

"No, I do not think so. What she did would promote their greed because they were planning on abusing the outcome."

"Then, your bloke did it?" I pressed.

"No. My bloke did not. He would not interfere unless a particular point in the experiment was reached, and there was no evidence that Duriken Sunteel would have met the criteria."

"Kiumah, please tell me why you're the guy in the know about this whole situation."

"Because any dimensional configurations that can possibly have a wide-ranging, disastrous effect upon the galaxy and the material dimension is my responsibility. We have watched over our parts of the universe with vigilance. The thing that Duriken Sunteel would have created could have placed us all in danger. In fact, we are still in danger because I gather from others that the Idealian, Human, and the Senerian governments are planning to resurrect this project. If I could offer an opinion, I would say that Progenitor Sunteel was in the physical way of a lot of people."

I paused, squinted, and then peeled the skin off the onion. "Or is it that the Argos are all hot raspberries blown a summer's day? Your stink outweighs your perfume. Greed runs your motors, too."

"I do not deny it. Argos has much at stake. Unfortunately, I am not at liberty to tell you what it is. I can assure you, though, it doesn't involve conquering Humans or Idealians. Decisions have been put in place millions of years ago concerning local current events. You cannot change them, so there is no need to discuss them."

"If you can shield yourselves from our normal range of perception, why did the little orange fellow show to pop in and out of the Baderes? Certainly you know about that. My partner was caught in his phasing."

He nodded but then shook his head. "I apologize for that. We were experiencing unknown technical difficulties."

35

*My response broke the silence in the room, sound-*ing like a drop of water in an expansive, dimensional lake. "Your agent was hiding inside Telroni, wasn't he? You operate just like the Shimbang and can fill up those null spaces in the being's essence. Va-qua-nua really saw an Argo. He introduced himself to me as Clin."

Kiumah dropped his gaze. "Yes. The Bohdan has certain powers of insight. The unfortunate thing is that they lack any deep introspection, and instead of using these natural talents to promote their possibilities, they immediately retreat into barbaric attitudes. With them, everything they sense but do not understand is the cause of demons."

"What happened when your guy bugged out?"

"He had difficulty crossing through the shell of the station."

"Why?"

"Unknown. We believe it is the dark matter present in that part of your dimensional frequency."

"Dark matter screws you up?"

Kiumah seemed to consider my sentence. "Dark matter screws us up."

I rose from my metal milk carton and took a short spin around the room. There was no artwork glued to the walls, no soft beds or chairs; just a lot of rust and collapsed plumbing tied up with rags and protected with cardboard. "Why do you live like this?"

He managed to pull on a confused look into that one moon pie eye of his. "How else should I live?"

"Well, it seems to me, you've got the power to piddle in the universal puddle. You could live with riches and light and yet you live in the desiccated remains of an old boiler room. Are the Argos so unconcerned with self that they wouldn't gladly use the loo topside and let the shit filter down onto the head of someone else?"

He smiled. "Ah, yes. Shit. Merde. Turd. Feces. Wank and pooh-pooh."

I couldn't help crossing his smile with a grin of my own. "Well, at least that concept translated."

"The one fact that holds true for you holds true for me."

"And that would be?"

He motioned for me to sit again, and after I obliged him, he reached over to pat my knee tenderly. "I like living here."

Fay-et spoiled this quiet moment. "Why are you so open and honest about your activities? Are you not afraid of raising the anger of other governments?"

Kiumah shook his head. "There is nothing anyone can do to us that would be successful."

"What about the Shimbang?"

"Not the Shimbang, not the Regerians, not the Senerians, not the Idealians, and especially not the Humans."

As if to prove how powerless I was against the everyday dimensional forces of Argos, I suddenly swooned again. The faint came onto me in a blister of stars and heat. This was getting bloody old, it was.

I toppled off my crate and landed on the damp metal floor. Something made me concentrate on this cold moisture leaking through my cammies, and it seemed the more I focused on the sensation, the less bad the dizzies were.

Kiumah helped me to sit up, grabbing me by the wrist

as he did. I was grateful for his help, but his strong grasp
was ill-placed, because it activated the Waki'el device.
It's then that I saw Hadrien.

He appeared in the room with me, wearing a halo of
gentle blue light. I thought for certain I was hallucinat-
ing, but he spoke to me—though I heard it as a voice
inside of my head.

"I've been looking for you for days," he whispered.
"I need your help."

"Artie? Is it really you, or am I imagining this?"

"It's me, Philipa. Please listen to me. I need your
help."

It took me a moment more to process the fact that he
was alive—at least in some form. "Yes," I finally murmured. "We have to get away from the dimensional hub.
Our atomic structure is breaking down." I paused to
study him while I argued with myself about hallucina-
tions. It was too good to be true. "How have you survived, Artie?"

He grinned, and my heart pumped out an exhale that
I neglected to retrieve again. "I figured that the creation
force might be the safest place to stay for a while."

"So you ducked into zero-point gravity?"

"Yeah. You're here with me. Weird, isn't it?"

Yes, it was bloody unreal. We'd never tripped the
light fantastic like this before. The creation energy was
milky and thick, a place of calm, gelatinous consistency.
A nice place to float. Dreamy, easy, joyous. Why did I
ever leave when I came here?

Hadrien must have grown used to this marvelous feeling, because he grabbed me by my tranced-out awareness and snatched me straight into good old-fashioned
sensibility. "I'm trapped, Philipa. I've been skimming
through dimensionally now for days. I've swung up,
down, and around. Do you know how many universes
are contained within eternity? Do you?"

"I have no idea."

"There are billions and billions, all layered like felt, one atop the other. They're like bubbles in the causal planes—whole biospheres of galaxies, stars, dead space, planets, and life. Too damned much life." He looked at me, and despite the ethereal quality surrounding him, I could tell he was tired. "I want to go home, Philipa. Back to the material realm and that one universal bubble where we belong. I've got to have your help."

"How?"

"I can't control the speed with which I access the bands between the causal planes. I can actually pinpoint a landing place, but the action of the creation force drives me right through before I can activate my stud."

"That's never happened before."

"It's the action of the dimensional hub, I think. Here the planes converge, and it seems to have a reciprocal effect on zero-point gravity. The longer you remain in the creation force, the harder it is to disengage—even with a thought."

"Well, how can I help you?"

"I need you to try to break the rust off the lock. Open the door for me."

I was about to say something else but I was abruptly jolted out of the creation stream. Whatever it was, I found myself staring into Kiumah's ugly, one-eyed mug.

"Damnit!" I barked. "He was here."

He backed away like my tongue had snapped out of my loaf and had whacked him in his nose. Drer helped me to sit up.

"Did you see Hadrien?" he asked quietly.

His question brought me back into myself all the way. "Did you?"

"Yes." His voice sounded husky under its mantle of gravel and ping. "At first I only sensed his presence. By moving into scan mode, it enhanced my perspective, and

I saw his reflection in my mirroring optics."

"We saw him, too," Kiumah said. "He travels the river of manifestation."

I couldn't even begin to fathom his words, but I didn't care. "Did you hear what he was telling me?"

"No."

I turned my attention onto Drer. "We have to get back to the ship and away from here as soon as possible."

"Why?"

"Because it's the only way to save Hadrien." I turned to Kiumah. "Thank you, old bloke. You inadvertently solved one of me problems."

"Ahh," he said with a knowing shake of his head. "Mars opposes Jupiter."

I couldn't help a grin before running off toward the spaceport. If there is ever a chance of success taking place, Mars, the planet of bold action, and Jupiter, the planet of benevolence and good luck, have to come together in a precise configuration.

The dirty streets of truth's reality met us at every turn as we headed back toward the terminal exit. Orange folks wagged fingers at us, cooing something about our hasty travel through the dimensional bypasses. We finally reached the lift that would carry us through the tendrils of crisscrossing dimensions and back to the ship.

Since the day the Waki'el invaded our bodies and our humanity, Hadrien and I had been exploring the breadth and depth of the alien implants. We had discovered that the units worked on a constrained frequency and when both were activated, I knew exactly where in the creation force Hadrien was and he knew where I lurked.

I could only think that the dizzy spells were caused by his skimming through the dimensions as he tried to keep his atoms on the string. Pretty bloody smart of that boy. Still, what I'd planned might work, and then again, it might not, so that last part nearly had me peeing my britches by the time we entered the bridge of the Senerian ship.

"Our crew is deficient," Fay-et announced. "Several of the sulters are not aboard."

"Leave them," I growled. "They were told not to debark for any reason."

"You realize that we did not get the information we require," Drer said calmly. I glanced at him as he wandered over to the communication console to flip a switch and a study a readout. "We still do not know exactly what goods Marctori bought here and then delivered to Duriken Sunteel."

Rold entered the bridge at the moment Drer spoke. His expression told me he was an angry Arthur J. Biddle, a fellow who was tired of being diddled. "You cannot leave until Va-qua-nua returns. I have sent him on an errand. Wait another hour, please."

He sat down at the helm control. "I do not see what good this information will do, but on that last run, Marctori sold Duriken gravity annealers."

I stared at him for a minute, mainly because my thoughts were garbled over Hadrien, the delay, and now this bit of information. Gravity annealers were devices that regulated the flow of the creation force, channeling it like a whirlpool vortex. Earth scientists had been experimenting with these contraptions for interstellar travel, but the species who had invented them, the Jimto'ok, had built some fail-safe into the design that didn't allow a Human to use this method efficiently.

Sitting down heavily in a swivel chair by the navigation console, I burned another minute to get my brain molecules into marching order. "Do the Argos manufacture them?"

He shrugged. "I am assuming so."

"What was she planning to do with the annealers?"

"She wanted to funnel the zero-point gravity energy by smoothing it."

"Smoothing it?"

"Yes. The annealers would have melded the creation force to the physical dimension."

"Creating an open doorway," I said.

"Precisely. With this doorway, it would not have necessitated her stay in the space between the dimensions. She could have come and gone as she pleased, and the space station would continue to operate."

"But why all this to save a planet that has little to offer in resources?"

"Why, indeed?" Drer piped up. "We gain nothing and have lost everything."

Rold shook his head. "I do as I am told, and when told nothing at all, I do not ask questions."

"That is your downfall," Fay-et said. "You should ask questions."

"Who would listen to me? I am half a person in the eyes of most of my people, when, in fact, I should be a hero. The government shall learn one day of everything that I have done to protect Istos."

With that, he clomped off the bridge, giving me the opportunity to once more concentrate on snagging Hadrien. "I'll be in me quarters. Please inform me when Va-qua-nua is back on board and we leave. I also need to know the exact moment when we switch into time dilation mode. Can you do that?"

"Of course," Fay-et answered. "I will do so." I turned to go, but she called me back. "Will this endeavor bring your partner soundly into the material plane?"

I signed off cryptically. "I don't know."

36

More was going on under the bed than between the sheets with the Idealians. Rold had violence seeping through those tubes of his, pissed off to the pixel that he'd had his load of old cobblers taken from him by a fierce decree at population control. He blamed everyone he could, and I was certain that Sajan received the brunt of his hatred since he was the one who had enforced the cultural culling. Fay-et wanted to be an Idealian messiah, the bringer of truth and justice, tinged with the attitude of a metallic Amazonian warrior. When I thought about it though, I found her an anachronism. As much as she said she wanted the truth, she was the one waving the gun around when we entered the dimensional plane where it manifested.

Then there was Drer, a being I couldn't put the touch on, but his presence was a persistent nibble at my sensitivities. Hadrien was better than I at buttering the crumpet. When I got him back to the absolute dimension of terra firma, he would help me.

Hope. For the first time in days, I had possibilities.

I had just closed and sealed the door to my quarters when Fay-et beeped my intercom. "Va-qua-nua is back aboard, and we are T minus one minute to cleared departure. Time outbound to dilation is twenty-two Earth standard minutes."

I nodded at the bulkhead but didn't respond, my thoughts suddenly off on a walkabout twenty-two minutes from now. The last time they'd kicked up the juice, I'd come away spacesick. This time I had to maintain control.

Sliding into the creaky little chair by the creaky little table, I laid out my astro-cards just so I wouldn't lose my gourd in the next nineteen minutes. The spreads kept coming up losers: boxcars and craps. The transformation card perched side by side with the liberating sun. It could mean that Hadrien might make it or he might not. Whatever intuitive sense I had flew away with my worries.

The worst part of this whole weird episode was that I realized I was chained to Hadrien. I loved him, and no matter what I tried to tell myself, life in the corporeal realm would have been rotters without him. If I couldn't get him through, then I would join him to spread my atoms across the dimensions. It was better than being a widow of the spirit.

Then there was the worry that I'd done some unspeakable act of murder while I was out trudging about during the last blast off into time. How had that happened? How had my fingerprints gotten onto the knife? The matter seemed simple enough when I considered it logically. Drer had simply lied, but if so, why?

Fay-et dialed in again. "Five minutes to switch-over, Astrologer Cyprion."

This time I reached for the wall unit and beeped my readiness. "Let me know when we're thirty seconds from dilation."

"Aye. I will contact you." She paused and then beeped me again. "Good luck."

With that simple acknowledgment, I left my life and that of my partner's in the hands of people who were more like calculating Humans than calculating machines.

I stripped off all my clothes and sat on the deck in the middle of the room, breathing deeply and calming myself with words from an old prayer that I rarely even thought about. Not that it would do any good, even though it made me feel better. I was at the mercy of the universe, held firmly by the laws of the interplanetudes.

"One minute to time dilation entry point," Fay-et announced over the intercom. "We will remain in force for only a short time, Astrologer Cyprion. You must hurry."

"How much time do I have?"

"In actuality, you have infinite time, but in practicality, we will remain in this configuration for no more than two minutes on our side of the equation."

"Check. I'll get in and get out."

"How will you judge time in the creation energy?"

I shrugged as if she could see me. "I'll count the seconds."

"As you wish."

I took a final deep breath and let my finger wave over the stud in my wrist.

"Fifteen seconds," Fay-et said.

I swallowed, ended the stupid prayer with a mental demand for success, and placed the tip of my thumb on the stud.

The engineer came back on-line. "Five, four, three, two, one. Ignition."

I pressed the button and felt the fire shoot through my nerves until it rolled into my brain. Sweat beads popped on my forehead, and the dizziness returned. I tried to take another deep breath, but my awareness charged into the creation energy, so I didn't know if I was successful or not. In fact, I wasn't even sure the combination of time dilation and zero-point gravity hadn't punched a hole straight through my brain. My physical body wheezed into oblivion, and my life force roved free in eternity.

I did sense things differently than my normal jaunts into the universe. This place was sluggish and full of

odd, creaking noises that came from different angles. It
was dark—so black that I couldn't make out a hand held
before my face. I had no sensation of touching hard
ground, no point of reference to keep me from spinning
off gently into this otherworldly realm.

Panic pulled in on me at that point, and claustrophobia
threatened to erupt, but I stalled it all in the nick of time.
A few thoughts later, I seriously considered returning to
the husk of my material self. The notion lingered with
me, despite my feverish desire to be reunited with my
lover. I stayed, fighting down my guilt and fear, counting off Mississippi seconds until a greenish haze developed at the periphery of my perspective. It pushed away
the black emptiness and my trepidation with it, filling
me with a new resignation. I was a creature on a mission.

Stepping through this mist, I found myself in the Ber-
muda Triangle of space. Here, I was surrounded by min-
ions from all different species and all different times.
They floated about aimlessly, their thoughts passing
through me like gelatin through a sieve. It was an uncomfortable feeling to be connected with time and light
in this manner, and so linked, I could sense a strong
feeling of apprehension. This was not a good place to
linger.

I swam into their midst and bobbled gently, calling
out Hadrien's name. Moments later, I was taken by surprise, because I was yanked roughly by the ankle. I
fought my invisible assailant, but I couldn't escape the
grip on my leg. I was dragged into a vortex that spun
me out of the mist and into the blackness before dump-
ing me back in the physical dimension. Hadrien landed
square on top of me, wearing nothing more than the skin
God had given him.

37

Hadrien immediately wrapped me in his arms and kissed me, muttering thank-yous in between his passionate greeting. I was swamped by the dizziness, but so happy to have him back that I decided it would be okay to faint away at the touch of his lips. That would have probably happened, too, but I was interrupted in my fall to bliss by Drer's pinging voice.

"I am glad to see you have returned to us, Investigator Hadrien," he said.

The surprise was enough to disengage my lover's attention, and he rolled onto the floor to sit up beside me. His hand never left my arm. As he answered Drer, he massaged my wrist that held the alien implant, assuring himself that I was locked firmly into my dimension of origin. I sat up slowly.

"Yes," Hadrien husked. "I'm safe, thanks to your help."

Drer tipped a short bow toward him. "It was my pleasure."

"What are you doing here, Drer?" I demanded.

"Making sure nothing went awry. Are you well?"

"I am as right as a peach in May."

He frowned and then nodded. "I understand." Drer stepped toward the hatch. "Now that you have returned, we can proceed with the murder investigations."

Hadrien glanced at me. "There have been more deaths?"

"Yes," I answered. "I'll fill you in later."

"I will take my leave of you now. If you require my assistance, please do not hesitate." With that, Drer was gone.

I turned to Hadrien. "I was going bonkers without you, me China mate."

His hand came up to caress my neck and cheek. "I thought I'd bit the big one, Philipa. Thanks for saving me." I didn't get in an answer because he kissed me again, and the greeting went straight into a sexual meeting.

Later, after having spent our emotion on the reunion, we huddled together in the bunk, and Hadrien started talking quietly.

"It was a strange sensation, Philipa. I channeled through dimensions trapped by the whiplash energy of the creation force." He paused to squeeze me. "I now think I understand how the causal planes work."

"Are we just a tiny mote in God's eye, then? Nothing more than foolish microbes?"

"Yeah, we are, but I can be happy with that." He sighed. "There are infinite planes, and I perceived several thousand of them. Foolish microbes were not meant to experience the depth and breadth of creation."

"You seem sad."

"I am. I can't quite explain it, either. Maybe it's depression that hits you after you've spent days trying to survive."

"Maybe it's the fact that all the mystery in the universe is now gone to you. You know how it works."

"But why me?"

"Why you? Does there have to be a reason for foolish microbes to get tangled up in eternity?"

Hadrien studied me, and his gaze reflected an aged quality I'd not seen before. "Is there a reason? After what I experienced—yes, there has to be a reason."

It was my turn to study him. The Hadrien whom I'd known and loved before his trip through the universe was no longer there. A different Hadrien had emerged, one that was so far advanced of me that there would never be any way for me to catch up in my understanding of how everything worked. Loss settled over me like a glossy coverlet. Our meeting had been predetermined for just this event, and that knowledge yanked at my heart. I'd been used by creation. "I'm glad I could save you, Artie," I whispered.

"When you switched on your implant and stepped into the creation force, it was if my unit acted like a homing device. It pulled me straight to you."

"But I'd opened the door while you were gone."

"You didn't step through."

What he said was like a rock banging me in the head. "You told me to come to Argos, didn't you?"

"I screamed at you with everything I had. I'm glad you heard me."

"Do you mean if I'd stepped on through, you could have latched on and come home?"

"No. You had to be able to pass through time dilation to do it."

I rolled over and sat on the edge of the bed, pausing to rub the grit from my eyes. Grit in space. Dirt followed you everywhere, hanging on like old suspicions. "Artie, I don't doubt your intelligence, but you're not the techie type. How did you figure all this out?"

He crawled across the bunk to sit beside me, his thigh touching mine. "I had help. You know that little orange fellow I latched onto before disappearing?"

"Yes."

"Well, his name was Tharsiah. He's pretty well-versed in quantum and dimensional physics. Did you know that these little whackers can achieve time dilation at an individual level?"

"I figured as much when they ran off with you. How did Tharsiah manage to carry you all the way back to Argos?"

"That little trick he does to travel around in time and space has a field range. I was caught up within his frequency and transported immediately."

"Why didn't he return you to the Baderes instead of trapping you on Argos?"

"The Argos are a complicated lot, Philipa. They're assigned frequency ranges and they can only go in and out at certain points along the path of time. If they invade numerous points, they set up too many paradoxes. Too many paradoxes throw the balance off on the galactic scale."

"So Argos aren't foolish microbes like the rest of us. What they do affects the fabric of creation."

"More than Humans do, at any rate."

"Why couldn't you find someone else to help you? We were taken right down to see Kiumah. Couldn't Tharsiah have done the same thing?"

He shrugged. "I didn't have time to ask."

"Why not?"

"Because after about an hour at the Gates of Everywhere, I almost died."

"What?" My tum clenched.

He nodded. "I looked the Grim Reaper right in the eye. I could feel myself fading as I begged Tharsiah to help me. I was in pain, Philipa. My entire body raged at what was happening to me." Hadrien stopped speaking to pull a ragged breath. "Each molecule in my body seemed to be changing, and I experienced every transformation. I'm lucky Tharsiah came up with this plan as fast as he did."

"Kiumah said there was some sort of technical difficulty with Tharsiah's navigating ability. Dark matter was preventing him from blipping out."

"Your friend, Kiumah, may have been the cause."

"What do you mean, Artie?"

"Tharsiah is a freedom fighter from Argos."

"Freedom fighter?"

"Yes. A splinter group of terrorists who oppose the Argos mandate of interference in dimensional proceedings. They think their leaders should do away with the butting-in routine. Kiumah's folks have been trying to put a stop to the terrorist proceedings."

"So you think Kiumah was trying to prevent Tharsiah from returning to Bohdan, and he did it through a part that he passed on to Duriken Sunteel. She installed it, and that trapped Tharsiah?"

"And probably any Shimbang inside the space station."

I rose just to get away from his heat. "I'm sorry you had to go through all this, Artie."

He shook his head. "You can't change destiny."

I turned to regard him, seeing more of a man than had left me. "Do you know your final destiny?"

"No."

He said it with such finality that I wondered if he knew and was trying to spare me any future heartache. Hadrien switched subjects before I could belabor the question. "The Argos have a problem with their planet's suspension halo."

"How do you know this?"

"By eavesdropping on the dimensional telephone. The Argos communicate by using the fluff of dimensions."

"Yes. The orangey who met us at the space dock made a call to Kiumah in that fashion. What kind of problem are they having?"

"It seems that the halo is moored in place by anchors set in different dimensions. They were using Bohdan and its moon as a fastener. When the satellite jumped orbit, they lost significant stability in the sheath."

"Why don't they just find another mooring point?"

"They did." He stared at me until his gaze forced its way into my thought processes.

"The space station."

"Cheap, but powerful enough to handle the load. And someone else was doing all the work."

"They were going to come in to take over the pie."

"But the Shimbang were trying to foil them."

"Do you think one of the Shimbang convinced his host to kill Sunteel just to piss off the Argos?"

"I don't know. They're not the only ones who want control of the station and that part of space."

I nodded, and despite this revelation, I headed for one of our backpacks sitting in the corner. "Hungry?"

"I should be starving having jetted between extremes, but I'm okay. I think I need to fully ground myself in physical reality for a few more hours. Then I'll probably be so hungry I'll eat the lining of the suitcases."

I unzipped the sack and crawled around inside it.

"It was hard on you, too, wasn't it, Philipa?"

"Yes, but it never could have been as hard as what you went through. I realized I love you and I'm chained to you in more ways than just that one."

"It's not a bad thing as far as I'm concerned."

"It's not a bad thing for me, either."

"But?"

"But what do I do when the links in the chains finally break apart?"

"Nothing. There's nothing either one of us can do."

I found a tin of sardines. I dropped into the chair, keyed open the can, and began to pick oily fish out with my fingers. Hadrien watched me closely, wearing a characteristically fierce look. He finally stood to address me in a serious tone.

"There's more."

I stopped fishing. "What?"

He slid into the tiny chair next to me. "I think we're part of the plan on this caper, and Theo might be hanging off to port ready to snare us."

"How so?"

"We're unique individuals who have come to the attention of the Senerians, the Argos, the Idealians, and the Bohdans. It's best that we creep along with guns drawn." He pointed to his holster, which I'd hung on the bunk post. "But then, it seems that you instinctively knew this."

38

According to Hadrien, we'd become celebrities among the alien races of our own galaxy as well as a few in other dimensions. We could do what no other Human had been able to achieve: We could blend with the creation force without the aid of a vehicle other than our own naked bodies. Because we could do this, we could literally snake our way through time and space. The only problem, of course, was that we didn't have a bloody clue as how to do it on a regular basis, but the folks who thought they might force their mentor duties upon us were starting to nip at our heels from all sides.

Hadrien decided the best use of our time would be to examine Marctori's body without the services of Idealian, Bohdan, or Senerian benefactor. I wasn't keen on sniffing alien bile, but I was relieved when I realized that I couldn't have accessed some dimensional pathway to kill this bloke. If I had, Hadrien would have been back home sooner than he was because we could have communicated early on. Killing a Senerian froggy was low on my priority list. That meant Drer had lied.

We stood in the ship's sick bay meat dryer and counted seven gurneys with bodies. All were Senerian, and each looked like a Granny Smith apple that was ready for doll-making. I set my logos calculator on the counter and switched on the overheads while Hadrien pinned the hatch from the inside.

"What the bloody hell happened here?" I asked.

Hadrien moved to one of the bodies and pulled the drape from around its torso. He looked clean from where I stood, like he'd died of natural causes and not some grisly big knife. I tried to be brave about bobbering in the middle of a field of dead aliens, and so I yanked the covers off another corpse only to find something surprising. It was the Senerian who had given me the kiss of time. I must have whined or something, drawing Hadrien to my side.

"Do you know this one?" he asked.

"Yes. She's the one who gave me power to go to Argos and collect you."

He nodded. "She saved our lives."

"Yeah? Well, what killed her?"

When he didn't have more of an answer than a shrug, I scanned this group of poor sinners and then made a startling find. "That bloke in the back on the left. He tried to sell me hot air and hard bread back on the station. I didn't know that he'd shipped out with us, too."

"Then we've either got a murderer aboard this vessel, or these stinkers went down from a virus or something."

His words sounded flat inside the cold box. There was no echo, no movement of air, and this heaviness descended upon me.

"Why go to all the trouble to kill innocent sulters?"

"Revenge?" Hadrien said. "Insanity? Duty to an assassin's contract? Maybe they were simply in the way."

"That last reason I'd believe, now that I have a better understanding of all the slime surrounding us."

"Yeah, these aliens are all bog dwellers, Philipa. Don't get cozy with any of them. The only reason we're not lying on one of these racks right now is because we have talents that they each want."

That was the penny in the peach pie, now wasn't it? How were we going to keep ourselves from becoming the crumpets for the alien tea?

I turned back to my calculator and booted it up. I'd collected personal info on Marctori and converted it so I could create a horoscope for him based on the planets in the Sol System. Marctori was born on December 7, 2222. That date would have placed him on the outbound side of life if he had been a Human, but if he could somehow manipulate time, he could have lived far into the future.

His birth date signaled a completion of spiritual matters; the ending of an old incarnation and the preparation for the new cycle starting with his next birth into materiality. Taking a moment, I did a quick transit of his sun and moon and found that over his life he'd attained influence through the generosity of others, had periods of mental uncertainty and depression, and times when he rode high on promises to deliver. Still, what seemed sensible for a Human rarely computed for an alien, so I could have been bumping into an iceberg of inconsistency. The unexpected twist to his death left me stumped. What had he done that he'd deserved to die by violence? Did his death mean something to this investigation, or was it just a coincidence?

I glanced up to notice Hadrien getting a bit close to one of the cadavers. "What are you looking at?"

"I'm not sure." He straightened, spun around, and then headed for a large, white metal supply cabinet. It wasn't locked, which aboard this filthy rattletrap was no surprise. He rifled around inside the cupboard until he produced an energy resource meter—Earth issue.

Hadrien turned to the body and held the gray, boxy meter over it, scanning the skin above the snaking feed tube that jettisoned from the Senerian's navel. He moved slowly, grunting as he studied the scanner's readout. I joined him, feeling like I might chuck a little bubble and squeak at the smell. "This guy is full of unera."

"Unera?"

He marched over to the next body, did a scan, and came up glowing. "What would you say if the next Senerian we test possesses a heavy concentration of unera in his tissues?"

"I'd say there is a good chance that all of them would have it because they must have each been involved in a similar activity. Back in the Stone Age on Earth, people who made copper tools ran around with high levels of arsenic in their bodies. Whatever they were doing could have contributed to their deaths."

"Or their deaths may have covered up something that shouldn't be going on."

There was an examination light attached to the gurney, so I bent the gooseneck down so I could get a better look at Marctori's bread and butter. In the harsh lamp glow, I saw that his skin glowed orange and golden, iridescent and sparkling. Just like Kiumah's hide had glowed.

"Artie, did your little Argos buddy glow?"

He nodded but kept his focus upon the meter and the next body.

"Why?"

"Why, what?" he said absently.

"Why did he glow? Was it species specific, or did something he do cause the glow? The pattern of color and sparkle on this gent reminds me of Kiumah and his glittering skin."

I finally managed to snag his attention. He glanced up to squint at me. "Somehow related?"

"Marctori brought products from the Argos to Sunteel. It may have been that these sulters were involved in its delivery."

We decided our best course of action had to do with finding out what we could about unera. Hadrien followed me back to our quarters, where I dug out my *Alien Compendium* and looked up the word.

Imagine our surprise when we discovered that it wasn't a chemical or a poison but a by-product of genuflecting to the god of time.

I read it out loud while Hadrien dug through our food baggie. "Unera is an expository light transmission emitted during time dilation conflicts. Unera embeds in the nuclei of cell matter, transmuting its color. It also embeds extra atomic patterns into the structure, enabling changes in any organism. These changes are unstable and most affected with long-term unera die because of time/space incontinence."

"So, what in the universe does all that mean?" he asked.

I shook my head. "It might be a similar situation to what we experienced on Argos." I started reading again. "Unera occurs in holding pools of time dilation. Many species across the galaxy collect from these pools, and many more are said to keep artificial wells of time for resource purposes. Many species have evolved with time/light cellulature, and in some cases, it is introduced into a willing organism through a symbiotic union with hive-sentients such as the Gin-li, who are capable of creating stress fields for harnessing neutrinos as well as gravity and, it is thought, dark matter." I paused when a new idea hit me. "If Marctori brought dark matter to Sunteel, then he may have used these crewmen to contain the product," I said. "I'm pretty sure the stuff doesn't come in a box."

39

We kept close to our cubbyhole aboard the Zanru, and when we pulled into the Bohdan System, we noticed it was cluttered with traffic. Standing at the viewing porthole in our quarters, I counted three silver disks flanking us.

"Do you recognize the hull markings?" Hadrien asked.

"That's Regerian."

He glanced at me and scowled. "Oh, oh. Crustacean trouble."

"Yes, nasty mincers, they are. The question begs to be answered, too: What are they doing here?"

"I've heard they're up for taking over the star systems in the southern quadrant of the galaxy. We're a little far from their home turf, wouldn't you say?"

A quiet tapping from the hatch made us both spin around.

"Who?" I called out.

"It is Va-qua-nua. You sent for me."

Artie pulled his side arm, took his weight low in his thighs, and nodded for me to cycle the hatch. Va-qua-nua squeezed into the room before I had the door open all the way. He quivered as he stood there staring at us while Hadrien replanted his gun into his holster.

My partner is a good blend of intuition and fierceness. He saw how his presence seemed to disturb Va-qua-nua, so he turned back to the viewing porthole and acted like he was ignoring him.

After the alien sat down, I came right to the point. "Va-qua-nua, what errand did you do for Rold back on Argos?"

The little whacker took a loud swallow before answering. "I delivered a message to an individual residing there."

"Who was the person?"

"A being by the name of Tharsiah."

Hadrien whipped around from the view like someone had bit him in the bum. "Tharsiah. What did he do with the note?"

"He read it and then returned to give me a small plastic box."

"What was in the box?"

Va-qua-nua sighed. "Cellular agitators."

"And that would be?"

"The Idealians use these agitators to stimulate certain cell growth. If, for instance, an individual wishes to stimulate his charisma, he will ingest these agitators. They are amoebic mechanoids called the Gin-li. They are special sentients with many powers."

His confessions stopped us both in our tracks. How did we get so bloomin' lucky right out of the gate?

Hadrien was the first to pick himself up from the surprise. "Does the process work for them?"

"Yes. As far as I know, it does."

"So why did he have to get the agitators from Tharsiah?"

He paused, studying the tips of his fingers. When he did answer, his voice was soft. "Their transport and use are illegal in all Idealian sectors. I am assuming that Tharsiah has contacts on the black market. Because Gin-li are sentient and when ingested, they are forced to enter into an unwilling symbiosis with the creature in which they inhabit."

"They're not flushed from the body?"

"No. They remain with the host for the rest of his life."

I stepped close to Va-qua-nua and studied him. "I'll bet they're a real problem on Istos, huh?"

"Well, yes."

"Why?"

"Because there are more and more defects birthed into the species. Parental units want to help their offspring to compete and survive."

"Is that the only reason?"

He hesitated again, as if speaking the words burned the roof of his mouth. "No. Many believe the agitators can aid in the resurrection of the material in Idealian cells that is analogous to the cosmic strings found across the galaxy."

I raised my head and let my attention skid over to Hadrien. He'd sat down on the edge of the bunk. His face was all hard edges in the dim light cast by the system's star. "Are you saying that they are looking for a door into time and space?" I said.

"On an individual level, yes. They see it as their only salvation before the planet strains to the breaking point with the rigors of resource depletion."

"The government wants this kind of free thinking stopped?"

"Yes."

"Why? Does the symbiosis really work?"

"Most of the time, it does not."

"What happens when it doesn't?"

"I do not know."

"How many of these agitators did Rold purchase?" Hadrien asked.

"A king's ransom. I am surprised by one such as he.

His monetary recompense is not great enough to afford him these creatures on his own."

"So someone is working with him. Or someone paid him to take this chance."

"Perhaps."

"What would Rold want with the Gin-li?"

Va-qua-nua sighed. "Immaculate Rold has many reasons. He could use them as a weapon, you know."

"How?"

"The ingestion by some species causes instant death through incompatibility. This mostly happens with the carbon-based life forms, but there are those Idealians who should avoid their introduction. That basic fact is the sore spot among the mechanoids. Many die from trying to join with the Gin-li. Still, if I were Rold, I would ingest them myself so that I could carry on a normal life again. He desires it more than anything else, and the daily contact with the Idealian who was responsible for his misery would make a perfect act of revenge."

"You mean one of the mechs aboard the station diddled with his innards?" I asked.

"No, one of the mechs aboard this ship diddled with his innards."

"Who?"

"Dr. Drer, of course. He works directly for Jandel Sajan, carrying out the cultural culling. Did you not know this?"

My mouth had dropped open, and I suddenly felt dirty remembering all the times Drer had put his stubby fingers on my body.

"Where does he keep these Gin-li right now?" Hadrien asked.

"In a transport locker in the sick bay. It is the only cold storage aboard the *Zanru*."

I changed the subject, just so I could stall for time to

digest the news tidbit he'd given us. "Any bloody idea why the Crusties are hanging around us like fish sucking on a shark?"

He glanced out the window and shook his head. "I am assuming that my people called them in to right this dead-end investigation."

"Your people? I thought what little cohesion you had was lost when your moon took an arcing orbit away from your planet."

"True. We have been at the mercy and generosity of other species. But because we chose to serve the Idealians does not mean we are not without influence."

"Yeah, well how cohesive is your species?"

"We have a communications network."

"Telepathic?"

"Empathic, actually. We each feel strongly on this issue with the Baderes. After all, our ancestors built it. If the climatic changes caused by the moon's escape velocity had not overwhelmed us, we should be the ones to do the recovery work in our own station."

Hadrien snorted, stepped to an empty chair, and mounted it pony style. I glanced his way, seeing the haggard look in his face. Whatever he might admit to, one thing was clear: He was overwhelmed on a mental level. The enforced rapture of the creation energy had done a lot to him, and I was sure that most of what it had done was wrong. Hadrien needed repairing.

He always did have a short temper, but now it was like the final gasp of a star ready to go nova. I didn't know how he'd gotten stuck in this breath of ferocity and except for not interfering when he did his bleedin' cock-of-the-walk shit, there was no way to help.

With every admission that Va-qua-nua made, Hadrien gained a little spark of meanness. "You bastards set us up, didn't you?" he rumbled.

The alien jumped in his seat and very nearly piddled

on my pumps. His head bobbled, his lips blubbered. Words swelled his mouth, but all that came out was stink. Finally, he regained control of himself, answering in a cracking voice, "The Regerians are our allies. They come to help solve this case."

"Since we arrived, we've counted quite a few cups and saucers," I said. "Now why would you need all that firepower to solve the murder of an Idealian?"

He shook his head. "I do not know."

"But you are an empath. What do your feelings tell you?"

He didn't answer until Hadrien came to a quick stand, knocking the chair away as he placed his hand on his gun. Stepping up to the rotter, he leaned close despite the sewage stench issuing from Va-qua-nua's nervousness. "You know, when I held on to the Argo, my particle mass changed, and I was forced to slide through the universe on a nonstop trip for days. When I finally got back to this dimension, I'd seen things, heard things, smelled things, and felt things that continue to put me off my supper. If you pricks had anything to do with that, I'm going to kill one of you every chance I get."

"That's vile and inappropriate. You gain nothing by doing that."

"But I do. I gain satisfaction. You know why? Because in all the causal universe, there's no such thing as Heaven. It's all Hell, right straight up the line to the friggin' top. I might as well split as many Bohdan atoms as I like. There isn't any rhyme or reason to this goddamned monstrosity we call existence. No praise and no punishment that isn't already installed and waiting for you. So if I feel like sending someone to the great beyond, then I'm going to do it." Hadrien took a hard inhale before casting a sly look my way. I searched for that smile he could wear in his eyes, hoped that all he said was just some belligerent bobbie act, but there was no sparkle there. He must have known I read him because he turned his attention back to Va-qua-nua. "I think that if your people have influence, then you should stop whatever battle staging is going on."

"I cannot," he whispered. "There is too much at stake, and I am but one voice in a million."

It didn't look like he could move so fast, but Va-quanua jumped from the chair, sidestepping Hadrien and leaping to the hatch. He cycled it no wider than my shoe and wiggled through it.

"We're in big-ass trouble, Philipa. There's going to be a war fought, and we're trapped in the middle of it. In fact, I think we're probably the prize, now that Duriken Sunteel's experiment failed. Theo, the apex, the Argos, the Senerians, and now, it appears, the Regerians got their eyeballs on us."

"Do you think the Bohdans are going to have the Crusties overrun the facility and take back the planet?"

"I don't know. What do they want with the planet? It's a lifeless rock."

"All species need a home world."

"Well, there are millions of them out there. At least one or two are nicer than Bohdan. Whatever it is has nothing to do with that planet."

I nodded and moved to the porthole. Two more Regerian disks had joined the *Zanru's* escort.

What had the charts predicted for the coming days? I couldn't even remember.

40

In this dimension, we experience height, width, and depth, all with the facilitation of time. In the interplanetudes, time is solely associated with the speed of light traveling through our causal plane. Time enables us to perceive our world in three intradimensions. This concept is sublime, yet it is so logical that it borders on the ridiculously simple. Why it has taken all of our Human evolutionary capacity to grasp this notion is a mystery in itself.

As I sat there on the bunk in our quarters, I attempted to calm my nervous nellies with a little omletting. I never seem to meditate with any sense of style, but then, being British, it's a little hard to let go of the conservatism that keeps our conscious thoughts in control of our sensitivities. Still, while relaxing in this manner, I manage to snag a passing thought or two. They plop into my lap like buzzard shit falling from the sky, and they ooze around until they start to wet my underknickers. It's then that the discomfort turns to enlightenment.

In this case, I realized that my causal plane was established on the realities of geometry. Spheres, tori, cylinders, cubes. Because I was a being who could judge distance using light, I could perceive depth and size. I could see the shadows presented: soft and shimmery or hard and sharp. For the first time in my life I actually perceived my surroundings as they truly were.

If I looked hard enough, I could escape the tiny mathematical equation that encompassed the totality of my dimension. I could actually experience the sparkling base of atomic structure. When I was encapsulated within zero point gravity, I managed to exist outside the normal bounds created by the time/light architecture of my causal plane.

I saw with all my three dimensional viewpoint a place filled with right angles. Squares, rectangles, triangles. Spheres sat at an angle, forming a shadow of lines and the perspective view of the horizon was composed of angular lines that shifted to a single point in the distance.

What the scientists said was true: Time moves through eternity at right angles. Light is time and time is light. It takes time for light to hit an object and bounce the reflection of it to our eyes. If you would just cast an eye to the room you occupy, it's easy to see that there are no shadows that do not fall at right angles.

To fail to understand geometry is to fail to understand life.

Hadrien moved into my immediate angles, leaned over, and kissed me full on the lips. Then, as though he'd just turned up the pilot light on the stove, he went ahead and began preparing dinner by gently pushing me back into the bed before rolling in next to me. Sighing, he tested the meat by poking me with his own understanding.

"You know, the whole thing—all the dimensions with all the universes—are the same. What occurs at this level doesn't ripple through the causal planes. At least, I don't think so."

"Are they independent of each other?" I asked, snuggling into the crook of his arm.

"Yes and no. I suppose it's one of those weird paradoxes that the Human brain has trouble with. What occurs at this level occurs in all other causal planes at the same time because the dimensions essentially fill the same spaces. But we're limited to our perception, so most of the causal planes are not in our purview."

He sounded like an old schoolmaster and it made me smile.

"What's funny?" he murmured.

"Nothing. I'm just glad to have you home in this neck of the dimensional woods."

"Glad to be here. For now." He kissed me again, but I pulled away.

"The Argos' use of Bohdan as an anchor for their suspension halo didn't affect the other planes did it?"

"As far as I can tell—it did and yet it didn't."

"That's makes a lot of sense, Artie."

He chuckled.

"What do you think the real reason is the Regerians have sent in their pigeon chippers?"

He studied me. "Pigeon chippers?"

"You know, armed ships."

"I don't know, but like you, I doubt it had anything to do with helping the Bohdans."

"It might be that Theo has caused too much trouble trying to lay this network."

"Theo." The sound behind Hadrien's words carried a lethal value. "He's jerked us right straight out of our socks, and we let him. Now, there's a man who doesn't understand the law of patience."

"The law of patience? It sounds like you've been reading up on the interplanetudes."

"Well, I have. But I figured it all out when I was doing the walkabout around the universe."

I shifted slightly to see his face better. He was all angles and shadows himself. "Go on. Tell me."

"We talk about having or needing patience, but patience is part of our dimensional perspective," he answered. "Time functions as an inhibiting factor in our causal plane. Think about it. Light travels at 196,000 miles per second. It takes that long for us to perceive an object in our dimension, so in reality, we use patience on a continual basis. We are always in a state of readiness as we receive the data mirrored back to us. Unfortunately, Theo can't wait."

I grinned. "That last part oversimplifies it, doesn't it?"

"Not really. The old bastard wants to be out in front; he wants to look back to what is to come. He thinks he can do it, Philipa, and I think he believes we're part of the answer. He wants to find out where time starts, and he wants to go there and control it. Don't you think it's the ultimate ego trip—one our beloved emperor would seek to do? If he didn't want the secrets of time, then why would he have gotten so involved here, and why would he have repeatedly sent emissaries to Argos?"

"But we don't know for sure if time has a starting point. And if it does, what makes time?"

"We're discovering that certain species can control time." He suddenly rolled off the bed and assumed a schoolteacher's stance, his right elbow tucked into his left hand, his fingers stroking his chin and mouth in abstract reflection. "I think the creation force is a collateral effect of time-making."

"Slough? Garbage frequency? Noise? I can't get me head wrapped around that one, Artie."

"As a matter of fact, the noise scatters as it continues through the causal planes. I'm sure of it."

"How so?"

"The folks on level two have the ability to perceive width and height but no depth. Time and light is still focused, the angle of trajectory is spinning sharply.

There is simply not enough time for these people to perceive depth. In our dimension, level three, we can see depth because the angle that time is traveling is a little longer and wider than the guys get downstairs. The farther and wider time moves, the more diffuse the light becomes. While energy is in the next dimension from our own, it experiences the wavelength to include a new perspective of shadow." He paused before adding, "The atoms slow down or something, but reflections become alive in this causal plane."

"If we're patience personified in this dimension, then what are they?"

"They are less affected by time because of the dispersal of light transmitting through their plane. I think of them as folks on sabbatical. They have enough time to perceive, and yet they do so slowly. The people inhabiting the fifth dimension kneel to the differences in comprehension."

"It all comes down to the amount of time they have to perceive the phenomenon," I said.

"Yes. Now you've got it. The right angles to eternity are getting longer. Without going into it, I'd say time is the factor that runs the whole show. It's God, if you choose to believe it that way."

Hadrien dropped his counselor's stance and slid onto the edge of the bed. He took my hand, kissing it gently, but when he caught me face on, I saw he wore that wild-eyed squint. "I'm glad I can perceive you now. And eternity is not what most people think it is."

I was about to tell him that if nothing else, he came back from his trip with a snootful of enlightenment and deep thinking, but the communication unit went off before I could utter the words. Fay-et's pinging voice pumped into our room. "We have just been contacted by Progenitor Anu."

"What did he want, Engineer Fay-et?" I called out.

"He wanted you to know that there has been another death aboard the Baderes."

Hadrien dropped my hand and stood again. "Who this time?"

"Administrator Telroni."

41

When we arrived at the Baderes, we discovered
Idealian, Senerian, and Human warships had arrived
upon the scene. It was like Piccadilly Circus on a Friday
night. There were strange folks everywhere, from big,
crunchy-skinned Regerians to hulking Humans. I heard
a lot of loud talk, loud growls, and loud mechanical
pings as we debarked the *Zanru* to step into the unload-
ing terminal. We were instantly met by Anu, who could
not seem to shake two Humans dressed in dark blue
cammies. I instantly recognized them: Terrapol, Theo's
personal army of ball-busting coppers. These blokes
were Hadrien's home boys and glancing at my partner,
I saw the distrust lurking in his features. We'd been
badly used by Terrapol in the past.

"What the sam hill is going on here?" Hadrien demanded.

Anu answered before his colleagues could comment.
"It would appear that we are on the brink of intergalactic
war."

"Over what?"

The Idealian stepped away from the Humans to address us in a huddle. "I am not sure. No one is sure. Our
governments are tootling their horns, but all we are getting at this level is white noise. Before we continue into
the station, tell me one thing."

"What's that, old boy?" I whispered.

"Who called you in on this case?"

"We received a dispatch from the Senerian government."

"Are you sure?"

"Reasonably. Why?"

"Did it come by way of your home world?"

Hadrien scowled. "Yes, it did, as a matter of fact."

"Are you saying it didn't fly straight to us from Seneria?" I said.

Anu shook his head. "Your planet's government knows something about this situation and decided to send you in to see what it was all about." With that, he spun on his heel and marched away. The two Humans approached us, sticking out their hands in greeting while the taller, balder of the two politely gave up their identities.

"I'm Agent Lee and this is Agent Karbrose."

Hadrien fueled like a star ready to burst. "Why are you here?"

"To help you get to the bottom of this murder investigation."

My partner's explosion happened in the next half second of right angles to eternity. He drew his side arm, took one quick step toward Lee, and before I could stifle a gasp of surprise, he had the bloke in a neck lock with the gun to the bobbie's head. "I want the truth," Hadrien snarled.

Karbrose made a move to defend his partner, but I'm not anything if I'm not good at fortifying my own defense. Two quick kicks from me disarmed the clamper and gave him a broken honker as he fell into an unconscious heap on the deck. Aliens came charging in— Crusties, Senerians, Bohdans, and Idealians—but rather than advancing on us, they merely encircled our playground fight.

Hadrien pushed the ragged edges of the manila mailer.

He squeezed Lee's neck until the guy choked. "What are you doing here?"

"If you'll release him and come with me where we can talk privately, you will receive your answers."

I flipped a look over my shoulder. Imagine my surprise when I saw Xan Nen, Emperor Theo's prime barrister, standing at the edge of the crowd, wearing the long, vermilion robes of his office. I paused to stare at him and that long, black ponytail of his. He wigged his eyebrows at me, pulling on a leer that told me we were in big-footed trouble.

"Goddamn it!" Hadrien barked. "Theo is at it again, Philipa!"

I nodded. "Let go of him, Artie. They got us like a load of old cobblers. We're not going anywhere."

Hadrien grunted, flung Lee to the deck, and replaced his side arm. He took me by the upper arm to steer me toward Nen. When we got to within a meter of the alien interlopers, Hadrien wadded up a loogie and spat at the nearest Crusty. It was amazing how fast a path was cleared for us.

I could understand Hadrien's temper. The rage built in me with each step we took, but nipping at the heels of my anger was a fantasy vision. I saw myself clearly in my mind's eye—killing Theo.

We passed from the debarking terminal to the embarking terminal and entered the *Misha*, a warship from Earth. As our trip progressed, we picked up more and more clampers until we were surrounded by guards. It seemed that we barely left them behind when we cycled the hatch behind us inside Nen's quarters.

Having moved from the filthy to the antiseptic to the truly grand, I almost popped a blood vessel at the differences of perspective that packed all the geometry of my causal plane. Silks, brocades, burled wood, gold-encrusted—it was a frickin' treasure room.

"Please have a seat," Nen offered politely.

I thought Hadrien might object just so he could maintain a state of combat readiness, but he fooled me by flopping onto a sofa. There really was bloody little we could do about this situation, combat ready or not. I joined him, making sure our bodies touched just for the strength we transferred to each other.

"I apologize for the difficulties you have endured over the last few weeks," Nen said, sliding into a chair.

"Theo is behind this, isn't he?" I said.

"Well, yes. My presence would indicate it to be so."

"What's going on, then?"

"Ah, that is complicated."

"Come on, Charlie Chan," Hadrien snapped. "Spit it out."

Nen tossed him a look that contained a live hand grenade, but his answer was smooth and even. "The emperor and his court were aware of this project that the Idealians, Senerians, and Bohdans were concocting. We knew it involved pulling a planet back into alignment using a combination of sciences that included zero-point gravity. Theo invested heavily in this interest through the Idealians. In fact, the Idealians were very willing to supply the live bodies if we could manage the technology."

"You're kidding," I said.

"On the contrary. They have lost a great deal of their power and technological understanding. Here they are, probably some of the most impressive silica-organic life forms on this side of the galaxy, and they don't have a clue as how to fix the machinery on their own planet."

We stared at him, and when we didn't jump on his opinions, he continued.

"That's right. Where do you think they got the funds to pull off this fiasco? Istos is on the verge of collapse. If you ask me, it's their indomitable practicality that has brought them to the brink of devastation. They have no imagination and no creativity."

"But they're tight with the Bohdans."

"Tight? Well, let's say the Bohdans feed off the Idealians like piranha chewing on a cow."

"So when Duriken Sunteel came up dead, and the experiment went tilting away, Theo watched his money roll into a big, black cauldron of silica goo," I said.

Nen nodded. "Precisely. It then came to our attention that the Argos were snarled up in the affair. They wanted the experiment stopped."

"Why?" Hadrien asked coyly.

"We were hoping you could tell us."

"Well, we don't know," he lied.

"Come, come, Investigator Hadrien. You and Astrologer Cyprion are tops at what you do. You could not have visited the center of the galaxy and come away empty-handed."

"We were a little rushed for time," I said. "You are aware that Humans have a limited survival window on Argos."

"We have heard that."

"I got me partner back. That's all."

Nen studied me. "We believe the Argos wish to stop this experiment at all costs."

"They could if they wanted to."

"Why don't they?"

"I think the old saying goes: Give the dog enough rope and he'll choke himself."

"Yes, yes," Nen said, rising. "That was to be expected."

"Why all the firepower?" Hadrien asked. "What's going on behind the scenes?"

Nen strolled to a crystal-laden bar and paused to chose a pink-colored liquid. As he poured a tumbler of refreshment, he grudgingly explained, "It seems that each government is accusing the other of manipulation. The Senerians and the Idealians are practically at war, and the Bohdans fear the Argos infiltration and complete subjugation by the Humans, so they have summoned the Regerians. We had not thought the Bohdan were so strong."

"Yeah, that's a big problem with us snooty Humans," I said.

"I am here to try to avert the war. Anything you can tell me may help."

"Why don't you tell us something first?"

He squinted at me and then tilted the glass to his lips. After taking a deep suck, he bobbed his head my direction. "What is it you want to know?"

"What's so bloody special about this sector of space?"

"If we knew that, do you think Theo would actually send you two in? He would overrun this scraggly lot of aliens to gain control. No one knows what's so special—not us and not them. I have a feeling that there are very few people who do know. They are the ones who we need to deal with."

I felt the hot breath of suspicion on the back of my neck. "What's the real reason we were sent here?" I asked flatly.

Nen smiled. "All right. Honesty from our side. If you can't trust the home team, who can you trust?"

Hadrien grunted but didn't interrupt.

"It's simple, really. Theo knows about the alien implants you wear. He wanted to determine the absolute range of them. That's why you thought you were going in on your own. The emperor decided it would be a good test of the devices."

"How would he have known anything?" Hadrien said.

"Our informant would have relayed everything to us. Actually, he has relayed everything to us and the word on your units is positive."

I stood slowly, the feeling of betrayal wetting my thoughts. "Just who is your informant?"

Nen shook his head. "Can't you guess? Why, Dr. Drer, of course."

42

Drer. I had expected that there was more than met the diode with him, but an informant for the emperor of Earth? When would Theo learn that some things just seemed too convenient? His compunction for immediate gratification had gotten him and us into a bloody lot of trouble in the past, and here he was, trying to gratify himself again by spanking our hides. No wonder Drer had shown up and stuck close by me. To think, I'd almost started to consider him as a friend.

Nen parked us into available quarters aboard the station close by the *Misha*, so he could easily grab us in case he needed to bug out quickly. Two large guards pinned us behind the hatch, shutting down the first of many possibilities for escape. Nen underestimated us and our abilities.

I guess I don't like to believe these things about my own government, but it was true. We were a couple of herrings being pickled by our illustrious leader, who was blind to the damage he caused in a relationship that could go against him in a frightful way. If we ever got free of this predicament, I swore to myself that I would do something I should have done when I had the chance: make Theo suffer.

I flopped heavily on the black leather couch sitting in the middle of the room. Hadrien thunked in beside me, wrapped his arm around my shoulders, and drew me close. "We're baked," he whispered.

"I'm not going to let that conniving old wank turn us into lab rats."

"He already has, Philipa. We just didn't realize it until now." He sighed. "Now we'll never find out who killed Duriken Sunteel."

His statement made me pull from his embrace so I could swivel my attention onto him firmly. "Why do you even care?"

"Because I don't want to see the Milky Way Galaxy blown off the dimensional map. And to be honest, any one of the players in this situation probably has the power to do something foolish. The quicker the murderer is found, the quicker this place will go back to normal."

"Yeah, and we'll go back to Earth."

He nodded. "That seems pretty much a given." Hadrien paused to stretch. "I've been as stiff as an old piece of pine since I settled into this dimension. It must be the gravity."

As I watched him, I had several errant thoughts go through my noggin, and one of them stuck. "Artie?"

"Yes?"

"What do you think happened to all that dark matter that Sunteel bought from Marctori?"

"I'm thinking the Senerians paid with their lives to deliver it."

"Yes, but what did she do with it once it got here?"

He frowned and then shook his head. "I don't have a clue. How do you store the stuff?"

I shrugged. "Do you think it's still here?"

"Now, that's a real good question, Philipa. What could you do with it?"

He didn't get a chance to respond because the station started quaking at the very next moment. Hadrien grabbed me to him like I was a lifeline into Heaven, and we rode out the rumble for a full minute. Pictures were knocked from the bulkheads, and bowls on the counter vibrated to the deck, crashing into fragments of cheap crockery. The shake was so violent that it caused a metal cabinet to burst at the seams and spill its contents of metal mugs into the small sink. When it was finally over, we just stared at each other.

"This place gives me the creeps," I said.

Hadrien swallowed hard. "I'm with you on that. I wonder when this bastard is going to blow open and spit us all into the vacuum of space."

"It felt like we were trying to pull something, like the experiment was still going on without us knowing it."

He thought a moment. "You know, you're right. Maybe Sunteel locked onto the moon in hopes of dragging it out of the path of something else."

Funny how the Human mind works. We're considered the worst kind of vermin in all of the galaxy because we have the unique quality of associational imagination. Someone says something, and our brain takes it and creates a new product from it. In this case, Hadrien's words had sharp points that stuck in the soft slush of my gray matter. "It's possible that Sunteel was trying to do more than one thing in this experiment."

"You mean she was trying to please everybody?"

"Why not? The Senerians seemed to be line-of-sight folks, in that there species' telepathic powers don't work at relatively long distances. Maybe certain things block their boinking abilities, and they hope to get this moon nudged out of the way of something. There may be some long term benefit in doing exactly the opposite of what they express.

"You've got a point. The Argos wanted the station to remain where it was to moor their planet's halo and could have exchanged something important to Sunteel for the Idealian take in the situation. And the Bohdans just want their planet back. What would Theo want?"

"What Theo always wants: power."

Hadrien rose and disappeared into the back room of our prison chamber, but I was only vaguely aware that I was alone. I stood and patted down the pockets on my cammies before I found my astro-cards. Pulling them out, I slapped the deck onto the glass coffee table fronting the couch and began arranging them into a circle of twelve.

"What are you trying to find out?" Hadrien asked, stepping back into the room.

I smiled to myself. When I'd first met Hadrien, he'd had little regard for soothsaying with astrology or the cards, but now he automatically accepted it as a matter of course. Instead of answering him, I pointed to the cards. "This indicates that the people involved are trying to rebuild stability through negotiation. The negotiation involves the oppression of unity. There's trouble stirring. Indolence brings recognition of collaboration toward commitment."

I studied the cards and suddenly had one of those illuminative experiences that brand you right in the solar plexus. "Theo and Earth are in big-arse trouble, Artie."

"How so?"

"Because the Idealians, the Bohdans, the Senerians, the Argos, the Regerians, and the Shimbang have aligned themselves against us."

Hadrien stepped behind me to gaze over my shoulder. "It's as bad as all that?"

I collected the cards and threw down another twelve, skipping my gaze over the circle before jumping to conclusions. "It's worse than we think. What if the aliens aligned against Earth are feeling like their purpose is ruined?"

"They might do something about it."

"A drastic something. These passionate feelings are changing the strength of balance. Theo's losing ground, and as much as I hate the old bastard, this isn't a good thing for our planet."

I threw down several more cards.

"So what do they tell you, Philipa? Can you read the way the light is falling right now?"

Well, that was the question, wasn't it? I read the cards to myself: Practicality enhances ego by increasing anger and completion. Strength fulfills liberation through fortune of cruelty's prosperity.

This litany could go three ways to Monday Mass, and so I was forced to rely upon my intuition. I turned to study Hadrien. He watched me with a soft expression. "We've got to interfere. If we don't, it's good-bye, Charlie."

"We're two people. I say we forget interfering and get the hell out of Dodge," he said.

Unfortunately, destiny, like the emperor of Earth would not be denied. Fate was sealed and with a kiss for luck, the beginning of the end came at hand as someone tapped on the hatch.

43

*The visitor happened to be a guard pushing a din-*ner cart into our quarters. He growled something about the fine smell of the food and how his dinner was going to be all gruel and beef chips. After he left, Hadrien picked off the silver cover to review the offering of saffron rice, tender lamb, and baby onions. We stood there staring at the provisions, each realizing that it had been way too long since our last decent meal.

"Think it will poison us?" Hadrien asked.

"Why would they go to so much trouble? Naw, not poison—sedative." I sighed, changing the subject. "I wish they'd deliver our luggage in. I feel like me bric-a-brac is hanging out."

Hadrien grunted, but instead of clamping the lid down on the tray, he tossed it on the deck and picked out two plates warming in the cart's service drawer. He spooned off the food and handed me a dish. The aroma begged my belly to pay attention. A second later, I jumped into my sense of taste at the same time I studied the cards. Hadrien joined me on the couch.

It was obvious that we couldn't talk out loud about any escape plans because surveillance cameras were poised to get a closeup shot of our backsides, and electronic listening devices hid in nests of wire and filament throughout the room. We had been in a similar situation before, and over the months of our association, we developed an astro-speak method of communicating.

"We have Saturn dogging us," I said. Translation: *We can't wait.*

"The scales are ringing heavy," he answered. Translation: *It's all out of balance. Who do we trust?*

I scooped rice into my mouth and talked around the food. "All the houses are available. I'm thinking our best bet would be Virgo." Translation: *Everybody stands to gain by our association. The sign of Virgo represents practicality and machinelike precision. The Idealians fit the bill.*

"How do we disentangle ourselves from the Mars influence?" Translation: *How the bloody hell do we escape in the midst of a growing war?*

I shook my head and spooned up more rice. Something made me stop for a moment and stare at the little, yellow oblongs. All this brain-wrenching thought about the nature of reality had whacked out a piece in my frontal lobe because I sat there counting the bits of rice. Seventy-five oblongs, and the light fell at right angles to the heap. Small made big. Small got lost in big. Many atoms composed a single entity. Noise. The universe was composed of noise, and noise disrupted surveillance devices.

The cards had spoken to me in a way that only I could understand. We stood in the light, able to look up the barrel of time by identifying what was coming next.

I dropped the spoon onto my plate. It clattered and pinged, making Hadrien glance at me.

"What?" he mouthed.

"Noise," I whispered, aiming his line of sight to my wrist.

It took him only a moment to understand. The alien implants were not foolproof. At a certain adjustment of the units, the frequency went wild and created a barrage of noise that would foul up electronic equipment within a range of fifty meters. It would park blinkers on the cameras and earmuffs on the audio bugs, allowing us to conceal ourselves for a few minutes from Theo's scrutiny. Unfortunately, it would cause one of us a great deal of pain.

I took on the cause for liberation by pressing the stud on my wrist. It was a half-power setting, not enough to thrust me into zpg but enough to start the burn that traced up my arm and into my body. Hadrien scowled but didn't waste a moment of this precious sacrifice. "How can we get out of here, Philipa?"

I spoke through clenched teeth because moving my lips would hurt more. "We need to get to Fay-et, and we need to have her phase the station into the creation energy flow. When she does, this room will enter the flow, too, and frig up the surveillance system, making it possible for us to walk through the walls without our guards seeing it."

"Fine," he growled. "How do we contact her?"

I took a deep slug of air, trying to soothe the heat building through my torso. The burn singed every cell in my body. "We'll open a window." The full impact of the frequency squeeze engulfed me, and I couldn't help crying out. Hadrien grabbed me, slapping his hand over my mouth before he released my pain by palming the stud in my wrist. The heat left immediately, and so did all my jets of energy. I slumped back on the couch, but Hadrien drew me into an embrace to make prying eyes ignore me. We sat this way until he sensed that I was back from the brink.

"You'll have to open a window," he murmured.

I nodded. What he said was logical. I would have to make the dimensional structure while he kept the noise up to conceal our efforts.

Amazingly, when the pain left, it was as if I'd never experienced the burn. Two minutes after Hadrien had closed down my implant, I couldn't recall what the agony felt like. I leaned forward to eat some more food and to study the cards. Was Fay-et the help we needed? Or were we turning to the wrong person?

We scarfed all the food on the tray and pounded on the hatch for the guard to come fetch the waste. It was the same footsore soldier who complained before. He was always watching over something, he complained.

"Guard duty won't in all likelihood get you killed," Hadrien said casually.

The man glanced at him. "No, it won't," he answered. "And I make sure of it." He paused to pat his side arm. "I shoot first, ask questions later. Always have and will always continue to do so."

"Now there's a brave peckerwood," I muttered as he left.

Hadrien snorted and grinned at me. There would be no bribes for that sentry. "Ready," he whispered.

"Aye. Let's."

With that, I slowly sank down on the couch, working up my energy by downing more gulps of air as I prepared to convince Fay-et that we needed her help before Hadrien could no longer endure the implant's blasting power.

He sank to his knees by the coffee table, adjusted his own stance, and then nodded. "On three," he whispered.

"Three," I said.

Hadrien activated his stud at half measure, while I punched my clock to form a window into the creation force. The hole began as a ripple in the atmosphere and grew quickly, the edges shimmering with a soft pink glow, but the picture I received was hazy. I needed to focus on the Idealian by remembering her face, her mannerisms, her sounds, her life energy signature. The signature was an unconscious understanding, and when I concentrated on seeing her ugly mug, the mirror into eternity started to clear. I found Fay-et. Surprisingly, she stood at the space station bridge, surrounded by Idealian compatriots. Obviously, they weren't giving up control of the Baderes.

I reached into the creation force with my thoughts, and doing so, it made me realize that it was, indeed, true. We were manifest into a landscape of height, width, and depth, but while our perception was limited, our thoughts weren't. Our thoughts didn't need light. Our thoughts were not governed by time itself. They were the essence of who we were. A sentient soul stood at the center of the universe, and that sentient soul was a part of every person to manifest in creation.

Fay-et reacted like a bull, swinging her ponderous head from side to side. She took several steps from her post at the command console and glanced around. Returning, she adjusted one of the wires lacing her cranium. I called her name again in my mind, introducing myself. Fay-et spun from the computer, hands on hips. *What?* she thought.

I smiled. Even her mind responded in pings and clicks.

We need your help. I sent images to her through this shifting vortex in the creation force, hoping that by some chance in Hades, her mechanical adjustments were tuned to receive me clearly. When done, I swung my perspective to take in Hadrien. He sat still, his eyes closed, barely breathing. His long blond hair fell away from his face, and by the golden glow of the light, I could see the bulging of tendons and veins in his neck.

Help us, Fay-et. You could yet do something to save the universe.

In ten standard minutes, she thought. *I can only set the current control for sixty seconds. Any longer would damage many people and many ships. I will be waiting for you off the port bow of the station at the eleventh minute.*

Hadrien proved to me that he was still breathing because he drew a sudden intake of air and snarled against the pain flooding him.

I made quick thank yous to Fay-et, washed out the window, and released him from his torment. He sagged the second I punched his life force back in, gasping, and sucking in long drafts of three-dimensional existence. "I'm really starting to hate these little jaunts into zpg," he whispered between slugs of breath.

When I was sure he was recovered, I told him, "We wait until the tenth house circles around."

He nodded but didn't speak.

I gathered up my cards. It would be the last time I saw them, and they were like old friends to me. Still, they couldn't cut through walls in the same way I could.

Fay-et was good to her word, and whether she was helping us for gain or hinder didn't matter. What took the prize was the fact that we'd stripped to our jaybirds and stood by the bulkhead waiting for the shift. I'm sure we looked like we were going go at a toss in the sack and this made me wonder how many spy eyes enjoyed my naked body.

At T minus ten, Fay-et sent the station into a dimension shift. That silky feeling of confidence and peace swam into our awareness, and to add to the sweetness of it, we activated our implants with nothing more than our thoughts. We stepped into the bulkhead where the atoms of the ship melded with the atoms of our bodies. It was one big vibratory celebration. That is, until I lost my interdimensional equilibrium and found myself stuck where I stood: half in the bulkhead and half out.

44

*It was my worst nightmare. I had become entan-*gled with creation by becoming trapped inside the wall. Here I stood, unable to draw enough of my energy together to pull through the weighty material and step into the Idealian run-pod stalled off the port side of the Baderes. We had planned on jumping from the station to a waiting shuttle, but if I didn't tear lose from this snare, I would spend eternity as fleshy pieces of a titanium bulkhead.

This kind of snarl had worried me but had never happened in my other trips into the creation energy. It could only have been caused by the forced dimensional shift of the Baderes, causing me to drag along pieces of the third dimension. If I could have taken a physical breath, I would have probably puked from the panic. I tried to calm myself, but as if a topper on the ice cream sundae, I discovered that I was alone. There was not even a wispy sign of Hadrien.

Blast him! Bopping off like he was some old hand with this kind of interdimensional flaking! I tugged with my mind, but the gelatinous feel of zero-point energy was too gluey for me to proceed through. It was then I heard the pinging voice surrounding me.

"Help me!"

Help you? I thought. *Who are you? One of me facets?*

"No. I am Sunteel. I am trapped, just as you are, in a layer of dark matter."

Well, spank me blue. Was I such a nut as to have a
fantasy at a time like this? I stalled my fear just enough
to wonder if I'd lost my peeping mind. *You're trapped
inside the atomic structure of the Baderes, aren't you?*

"Yes." A moment's hesitation and then, "Part of me
resides in the Baderes. Most of me does not."

Where's the rest of you?

"I am spread across all boundaries. I am flowing to
the end of the universe. Help me to find release from
the station."

*Sister, I can't even figure out how to release meself
at the moment. Why are you stuck in the space station's
heavier substances?*

The voice clicked in, pinging like every mechanoid
I'd come to know. "I am caught for the same reason you
are trapped. The station was lined with compressible
dark matter. You have attempted to make this connection; I have heard you speaking about it." There was
another short silence before the voice clanged in again.
"Dark matter is abundant in the universe. It is also creation energy negative. There is no vibration flowing
through this force. It is antitime and antilight. I have
been trying to communicate with you to tell you where
my essence resides."

*You bought the dark matter from the Argos, and the
Senerians somehow used their time cells to contain it.*

"It was the only way it could be delivered."

All those blokes are dead.

"They knew the danger. They did it for money to feed
their families. Do not be concerned with their paltry
lives. They gave nothing to the universe but heartache."

With an imperious attitude like that, she deserved to
be glued in the wall, but thinking about it got my own
panic juices flowing. I didn't want to be stuck with the
likes of her throughout eternity. *How do I get through
this mush?* I demanded.

No answer came. No evidence that I hadn't lost all my brains from the stress of this kind of travel.

Suddenly, I popped through the bulkhead the same way as a Fudgsicle is pushed from the wrapper, but on my way out, it felt like globs of me were left behind. I was squeezed straight through the eternal layers of the causal planes, but despite the agony of being sieved through dark matter, I plopped out into the vacuum of space. My momentum drove me straight through the bulkhead of the Idealian run-pod waiting to ferry us away from Theo. When I sparkled back into dimensionality, I found Hadrien, Fay-et, Rold, and Drer.

I was overwhelmed by the fact that I was in my causal point of origin. This shock clobbered me and I sobbed into my lap. At that moment, there was nothing I feared more than dying.

The second I landed on the ship fully formed, I noticed Fay-et at the helm. She gunned the engines and departed the parade, hurtling like an eight ball heading for the side pocket. I felt Hadrien's comforting hands, but his attention wasn't aimed at me and my whimpering. His voice came slowly into my awareness. "Drer. Why did you deal us over to Theo?"

"Because I did not believe what the Earthers claimed about you, and I wanted to see for myself." There was a dull moment of heavy clicks and pings as everyone faced off. Hadrien knelt to help me sit up.

"Are you all right?" he whispered. "Are you hurt, Philipa?"

"I got blasted by dark matter," I croaked, wiping away the residual fear with relief.

"Dark matter?"

"Yes," I answered. I used him to stand up, and when I did, I showed them all my peach-colored glory. "Compressed dark matter expands. It was used to fill the bulkheads of the station. Obviously, it's not done growing, since you passed through without a problem. I seemed to have caught a whole glob of it."

Hadrien's scowl told me of his concern. "How'd you free yourself?"

I shook my head. "I think it was the fact that the Senerian had given me time with her sloppy kiss. Otherwise, I don't have a clue."

Rold stepped forward with a couple of human-sized cammies. While we slipped into our clothes, he took command of the explanation. "We were all privy to the secret."

"What secret?" Hadrien growled.

"We were going to turn that space station into a null-point time bubble."

I glanced at Hadrien and shrugged. "What would that do?"

"Any Idealian who possesses an active cosmic string component in his or her DNA could enter the bubble and go anywhere and any time in space."

"I thought your DNA strand didn't work."

"It does—for a few. Sunteel was one such person. That is why Gasba gave up her IDT node. It was logical because Gasba is one of the many whose DNA wasn't functional in this area."

"You were thinking of slipping the yoke on zero-point energy, weren't you?" Hadrien said.

"Yes. We did not want to have to rely upon this conventional conveyance. As you know, most creatures are constrained by it."

My brain hurt from that one. "Why would you want to slip the creation energy?"

"To see what is there," Fay-et offered. "To touch the true face of the divine."

Drer stepped up to me. "To get clear of this natural force would allow us a view that would go all the way to the beginning of time itself."

"But why do you need the view?" Hadrien asked.

Rold sighed and then slid heavily into a flight chair. "We believe that there is another energy source available to us beyond the creation force. Many have thought it simply myth, but there are those who believe that we each survive in the butchered frequency of a force more eloquent than we could ever have imagined."

His words dug me a great big grave full of awe. I turned to stare at Hadrien, and he looked at me with a thoughtful frown. He'd pegged the truth while whisking through the causal planes. Somewhere, somehow, someone was making time, and we lived in the midst of the noise produced as a by-product of the process.

"All right," I said. "Why the blazes are you going to so much trouble to prove this point? You're a species who's overused your allotted resources on Istos. Shouldn't you be concerned about finding another planet and getting your people ready for evacuation?"

"There are reasons that species become extinct," Drer said flatly. "One of those reasons is that they do not deserve to live any longer. They have lost the zest for life, so, therefore, they surrender it in ways that are totally repugnant to the balance of the universe."

"Well, that holds true for the lot of us, governor."

"Correctly stated," Rold answered.

"So, you're saying that you wanted to form the bridge to exit the creation energy."

"Yes. It would have been successful had we not received the foul goods from Marctori."

"The dark matter," I said.

"Yes. The dark matter was supposed to decompress at a consistent. This product did not obey specified calculations. Apparently, it was not entirely dark matter, though it simulated it."

"What was it?"

"We do not know. After several hours, we realized that nothing was happening."

"So Sunteel contacted Marctori and cursed him over it before she demanded a new shipment."

"In a word, yes. Sunteel had been promised a new delivery. Marctori brought it, and she had approved it."

"Obviously, another bad batch."

"I am sure he intended it to be so. He lost much in this dealing." Rold shook his head. "Sunteel was in a hurry and did not wait the allotted time for the dark matter to decompress so we could fully analyze the load. When we reached fifty percent on the boards, she called it a success."

"How were you containing it?"

He smiled. "With zero-point gravity, of course."

"Well, I've got news for you, mate," I announced. "You've got holes in the galley. It's probably leaking, and it's going to start affecting this star system."

He nodded. "Undoubtedly."

"Why was Sunteel in such a hurry?" Hadrien asked.

"She had been ordered home by the apex."

"Why?"

Rold bit his bottom lip, and I was caught staring at this very Human reaction that served to signal the creation of a lie. "She had filed for legal separation from Sajan. He was upset. The action had caused damage to his reputation. There was much arguing in the ranks of court."

"Then he could very well have killed Sunteel to save face."

"He was evacuated to the run-pod on the evening we left Duriken to her fate. His concubine was with him."

"He's powerful. Didn't he have any say in the matter?"

"None. He held no authority over Sunteel."

I glanced out the viewing porthole to see the image

of the station drop out of sight. "Where are you taking us?"

"We have something to show you on the planet's surface," Fay-et answered. "It will enlighten you further."

45

*While we buckled into our flight harnesses, Had-*rien pounded Drer with the question that sat on the tip of his thoughts. "Why'd you set us up, Drer?"

"Sometimes, one has no choice," he answered, shifting his weight in his chair. "Ask Rold. He's a slave to limited options."

Rold didn't reply. Instead, he shifted his view out the porthole. Sitting there with not much more than a zipper between me and them, I could feel the cold rush of the run-pod's environmental as well as the frigid attitude that spoke volumes about Rold. "You hate each other. Why?"

"The people have had enough of population control and the likes of Sajan and Drer. Those who are trapped in poverty are culled and cleansed. The rich control our world and make our decisions."

"The rich are educated," Drer said. "The poor are not."

"You lose over half the population by using that as an excuse," Fay-et called out. "The poor have brains and possibilities, too. You negate some of your finest resources. How stupid the rich are, even with your education."

"I don't want to hear about mechanoid choices," Hadrien growled. "I want to hear about Drer's alternatives."

Drer scowled. "Your species' brutishness is showing.

Do you realize the term *mechanoid* is considered vile by my kind? It is an insult."

"Oh," Hadrien said. "Like your species isn't brutish? Look at yourself, Drer. Look what you did to us."

"As I see it, you are in no position to demand anything. You are the ones with the limited choices at the moment."

Hadrien bit at the reins on that one, but could do nothing more than agree. "At least, enlighten us."

"It will not change your attitude about me. It will only worsen it. I am not sure I wish to do that."

"We already hate your friggin' guts because of your contemptible actions," I explained. "It won't matter anyway."

Rold swung around to stare at Drer. "If you will not enlighten them, then enlighten me."

Drer turned an ugly mechanoid sneer onto him. After a moment, he dropped his expression and cast his gaze along the deck. Rold swiveled back to the console.

"I knew you were a coward, Drer," he said flatly. "This proves it."

"How dare you make judgments? You have been cleansed so your line no longer proceeds. You are like litter in the gutters on Istos. It is only through Duriken Sunteel's belligerent, noisy force that you were brought onto this project in the first place."

Rold said nothing. This silence didn't do much to swell my knickers with confidence. I was glad that Drer changed the subject by switching his attention node onto me.

"I will tell you why I informed on your activities to your beloved emperor."

"He isn't our beloved emperor," Hadrien snapped.

Drer smiled. "Of course, he is. Across this vast galaxy Theo of Earth commands respect. The mere mention of his name is enough to cause nervous disorders in some species."

"We know Theo has influence," I said. "But certainly not that much."

"More, if you can imagine. How did he get to be so powerful in a universe already filled with power? He is the great manipulator. Theo creates great wealth for many planets and in return earns great wealth for himself."

"Yep, that's hit 'em-in-the-purse Theo, all right," I answered. I had always suspected Theo's reach to be enormously long throughout the galaxy. The old man had not let his MBA credentials go to waste. Unfortunately, increasing his personal gain had blinded him to the needs of his own world and his own species. He was a creature of excess, and he drew his resources from Mother Earth, herself. "Let me guess. Your government is up to its shimmies. What did he nick you for?"

Rold swung around to stare at me. "I did not understand one word you just said."

Hadrien laughed, even if it was a chuckle smoky with darkness. "You owe Earth. I'm guessing the haloshield that surrounds your planet is the big reason."

"It was in disrepair, and we had no resources to rehabilitate it," Rold said.

"Did Theo come in and finance the gum and glue?" I asked.

Drer smiled again. "Yes, the repair bills. Theo did not stop there, either. On and on he went, shipping in food, water, building materials. Before long, we were totally dependent on him."

"In return, he wanted schematics, information, engineers, and anything else he could get on the construction of the sky dome."

"That is absolutely correct," he answered. "How do

you know this? Are you that intimately acquainted with your emperor? Most of what I have told you has been conveyed only to the top levels of our society. It is a secret we did not wish to expose."

"That is why we are at civil war," Rold fired. "It will get worse, Drer. Those of us who live at the fringes of hope on Istos will have our day. You and your kind will cease lying to us because you and your kind will be dead."

Drer ignored him. "Some of the lower-level administrators were asked to work with the Earth government in exchange for the funds to repair the energy grid. I was one of them."

"Why you?" I asked.

"He knew he could trust me and because I am a biotechnical analyzer and not, in the truest sense of the word, a doctor. Your emperor paid me well to learn the secrets of mechanoid species throughout the galaxy. It was a natural request for him to ask me to look after you."

"So, you have silica cousins," I said.

"Yes. Many, many cousins." He paused to shift in his flight seat. After he did, he spent a moment considering the both of us. "Organic-silica species are far more numerous than those created from organic carbon compounds."

For some reason, I couldn't even imagine it. It just didn't jibe with my sensibilities, but set against the awesome diversity of our dimensional universe, it made sense. "Theo is worried that you blokes are going to take over the fleshies."

"You know him well. How is that?"

"I'm his personal astrologer."

Drer frowned. "And you didn't see his lack of integrity?"

"Oh, she saw it," Hadrien answered. "We both did.

What neither one of us fathomed was just how far the old bastard could go."

"If it is any consolation, you two have entered a higher place in this dimension."

"What higher place?" Hadrien demanded.

"With the inclusion of the alien implant, you became mechanoid. The fact that the implant is becoming part of your lifestyle and is not a daily hindrance to your carbon-based forms makes you one of us."

I wouldn't say it wasn't a daily hindrance, but I suppose my mouth fell open at this stark realization, because my tongue dried out from the swift rate that I sucked air down my throat. Drer was right. The implants enabled us to do more than the average Human. Hadrien had learned to use his to survive, and I had learned to use mine to give me power and strength. If I had the opportunity for it to be removed, would I give up this Waki'el technology, or had it become so much a part of me that it would be like ripping my hand off at the roots?

"Astrologer Cyprion?" Drer murmured. "Are you ill?"

I shook my head, finally clamping my lips together.

"Then you understand why I did this?" Drer asked.

It took me a moment before I could take a deep breath to speak, and when I did, my voice sounded flat, even to me. "Because you were told to. Not because you give a fig about us."

"I am part of the power structure on my planet. That means I obey my superiors."

"The lower part of the power structure," Rold reminded him.

Drer ignored him to speak directly to me. "I serve authority, just as you do."

"You're not serving authority now," I said.

"No, he is not," Rold said.

"What's that supposed to mean, mate?"

"That means I am Rold's prisoner," Drer answered.

Maybe I wasn't as mechanoid as I thought I was because it occurred to me that Drer didn't seem very concerned about being a prisoner.

"Rold," I called out. "Why and how?"

"He's the poster boy for the revolution, Philipa," Hadrien said.

"That is essentially correct," Drer answered, settling back into his chair. "I am the truth that seals the opposition's conclusion. Once my story gets out, it will be a long night ahead."

"What makes you such a big fish?" I asked. "You haven't done all that much. A little spying? Big deal."

"Do you not see?" Drer said. "I have been their prisoner for many months."

"You've had free run. You could have gotten away."

He shook his head. "My DNA has been harnessed."

"Excuse me?"

"Do you remember when you asked me about the cosmic strings available in our cells?"

"You said they were inactive, a holdover from another time. You lied."

Rold snorted, but instead of speaking, he watched Fay-et execute a banking turn to bring the run-pod into the planet's atmosphere. The light inside the shuttle turned pink from the sunlight lancing off ammonia molecules.

"Perhaps I just omitted some of the facts." He paused, and when I didn't cut him any slack, he pulled a long, deep breath. "The strings make it possible for us to move between the dimensions in a similar matter as the Argos use." He frowned, nodding slightly. "Centuries ago, there was an Idealian leader who decided that freedom was dangerous. He ordered DNA harnesses to be installed in all Idealians during that time. My species is quicker to adapt than most, and once the unit was inserted, it soon became a working part of our systems. Within two or three generations, the harnesses became a natural part of our bodies. We were completely controlled by our government, unable to experience unrestricted movement within our lives."

"We became pawns," Rold added.

"So the door to the other dimensions was shut down by some greedy-arsed beggar who would be king," I said.

Drer winced. "Yes. We allowed ourselves to be mutilated, and it was probably the beginning of the end for Idealians."

Hadrien popped into the conversation. "But now you need this ability back because you've got a dying planet, and you're trying to develop methods that will get around the harness. Why not just take a ship offworld? Why go through all the time and space stuff?"

"We are a poor planet. There are not many ships and little fuel to operate them with."

"Theo wouldn't provide the ride, huh?"

"No. But he has promised to help. My government thinks that Humans will be the next species to gain the ability to move between the causal planes and to travel in time. You must realize that whatever information I gave your Emperor Theo, I also gave to my own apex. He knows about you, too, and has great interest in your safety."

These admissions were starting to hurt my head. "But, if your DNA is harnessed and so is Rold's, what's he got over you to keep you his prisoner?"

Rold swiveled his chair toward us and threw Drer a slight smile. "I have the frequency code that controls his inhibitor. If he doesn't do as I wish, I will enter the code into a small pocket computer and wait for his DNA to stop replicating altogether."

46

As we fell through the pink atmosphere, I leaned toward the porthole in the run-pod so I could get a close-up eyeball of Bohdan. It was a world whose icing had slipped. Even from where I sat, I could tell that the planet's mantle had succumbed to stresses the moon had forestalled with its gravity. Glaciers creeped up the southern sector, filling rust-colored oceans with enormous ice cubes. Whole continents had gone jumbled, some places desiccated by the caustic ammonia mist that hung in low clouds around mountain peaks. Closer up, I saw the old remnants of civilization—high rises, market malls, roads, abandoned vehicles—but most of all, I noticed the vast number of cemeteries, with metal mausoleums flashing gold in the sunshine. This place was a grave robber's delight and a paradise for your average bin diver and scrap hauler. Could that have been Bohdan's appeal? Was Theo dealing in junk, or was there real treasure to be found here?

Fay-et landed the run-pod in a central desert, secluding the shuttle in a canyon that was rimmed by twisted, black volcanic travertines. The gully she chose was a tight fit, and yet the light lancing in at odd angles slowly revealed a sparkling landscape. When she unrolled the pod's hull armor, we were treated to a narrow view of Bohdan's secret beauty. Glancing up, I saw the shimmer of the planet's rings; glancing toward the the ground, I saw the glitter of gems.

The stone creating the walls of the canyon was
smooth and blue, flecked with gold and laced with silver.
In places, the rock twinkled like an azure sky, looking
for all the world like sapphire and turquoise. Closer inspection showed that the lava spat by the travertines ran
in runnels down the canyon's sides, and where it had
cooled, the rock had turned into sawtooth ridges of clear
white gems. Could this be Theo's greedy interest here
and the Baderes just a means to an end?

Rold stood and marched to the center of the shuttle
to address us. "This is why the Idealians are here."

"Gems?" I asked.

He snorted and smiled, but that pinging quality to his
voice still made its way through his words. "These gems,
as you call them, are virtually worthless to most species.
The Bohdans crush the rock for road and building construction. It is nothing more than beautiful gravel."

Okay, but did Theo see it this way? "So why did we
stop here? To enjoy the beauty?"

Rold shook his head. "It is a justification for Idealians.
It is one of the reasons we have such a high stake in the
commodity known as Bohdan."

"What's so special about the dirt and rocks?" Hadrien
asked. "And how would you know? You're just an immaculate."

Rold scowled—a big, ugly look that cautioned Hadrien to remember his place and his physical size. "You
do not understand me or my kind. How dare you make
assumptions?"

"Well, we've gotten a pretty good dose of you folks
for the last couple of days."

"Because he is an immaculate does not mean he is
without power," Fay-et said. "He would have more
power if he so chose."

I studied Fay-et for a moment. "There's a family thing
going on between you two, isn't there?"

It was her turn to scowl. "How did you deduce that?"

"The way you talk to him. You could be his mum."

"His mum?"

"Mother."

Rold's mouth fell open, and Fay-et's was right behind his. "This is impossible," he whispered.

"Is it true?"

Fay-et unstrapped herself completely from the flight harness and took a step to stand by Rold. "He is my son. Yes, you are correct."

Hadrien glanced at me and shook his head. "I wouldn't have guessed that."

"It is true. I am a progenitor, and my first child is an immaculate."

"Must make for a rough time at family reunions."

"It does not make for an easy time; that is true."

"So, there is hope for a unification of some kind here on Bohdan?" I asked.

Rold swept his gaze toward Hadrien. "Your partner is perceptive. I have not met a Human like her before. Most are belligerent, self-centered, and narrowly focused."

Hadrien smiled. "She's the dame of the ball, and don't you forget it."

I rolled passed the kudos to demand some answers. "What's so special about this place?"

Rold opened his mouth to answer, but Drer stole his thunder. "It is exactly like us," he said.

"Exactly like you? Do you mean it has the same silica elements as your bodies do?"

"That is correct," Drer answered.

"Well, excuse me for being the chump here, but so you share the same vibration as dirt. We carbon-based life forms mimic the structure on many worlds, but we don't go off and get excited about it."

"Do you not see?" Rold snarled. "We have believed

for many centuries that we were a bastard life form, composed from an organic source and enhanced by silicon implantations."

"That would mean that mechanoid evolution wasn't tinkered with in the beginning. Your clockwork innards are supposed to be there."

"Yes," Drer answered quietly. "This planet kept itself in perfect balance by gauging environmental needs through sensing fibers that occur naturally in everything around you. It proves that Bohdan and all mechanoid life forms in the galaxy are natural species and not manufactured."

"Are you looking for positive PR from this discovery?" Hadrien asked. He paused to squint at Drer. "Tell us the truth. Are you really more interested in harvesting the living planet for the repairs needed on Istos?"

"We could do many things allied with the planet and the living resources here," Rold said.

"That's sort of cannibalistic, isn't it?" I whispered. "A bit like chomping on your own leg to get it out of a bear trap."

Rold shrugged. "I never said that we would have trouble exploiting any life form. That is not the problem."

"Your government disagrees on how the life form should be exploited," Hadrien jabbed.

"That is it."

"So, whose side was Sunteel on?" I asked.

"Her own," Drer said. "She took funding from everyone; she disobeyed orders from her government, disavowed her mating ties, hastened alliances when they met her own agenda."

"What did she want to prove?"

"That she was a goddess," Rold answered quietly.

"Well, she done that," I answered. "In a manner of speaking."

My words suddenly brought everyone's attention onto me.

"What do you mean?" Hadrien asked.

I grabbed a lungful of air before launching into the improbable story. "While I was stuck in the dark matter, I communicated with her. She's there, and she's spread across the universe like light itself."

Drer's face furrowed darkly among his tubes and wires. "It cannot be."

"Why not? You don't understand how the reality works any more than the rest of it. Duriken Sunteel stepped into forever, mate."

"Then she's alive," Hadrien murmured.

I shook my head. "As far as I can tell, Duriken Sunteel is technically dead. It's her essence that still remains alive. But if you think about it, none of us ever die. That essence still remains. It's just converted. After what you've been through, wouldn't you say that death is nothing more than a movement from light to shadow? We're there in the same dimension we always were; we're just invisible to the naked eye."

"Only Duriken is spread like jelly across the causal planes."

I nodded. "Probably just like you were. The real nilly here is the fact that the dark matter has trapped a lot of her atomic structure within the Baderes. She can't be saved, as far as I can tell. At least, I don't know of any way it can be done. Even the Argos were having trouble flicking in and flicking out of the dark matter. But the fact remains the same. Someone tried to off Sunteel. They botched it, but they tried, nonetheless." They all looked at me like I had a big green booger hanging on the end my nose. It didn't matter, though, because there wasn't time to wipe the snot off with a further confusing explanation. We were abruptly joined in the canyon by a contingent of Crusties—and they didn't look like they were in for teatime.

"Holy mother of the god," Hadrien whispered. "We're not only baked. We're boiled, too."

He said that right. Obviously, Uranus, the planet of the zodiac known for its cruelty, was just about to drop a load of gravity poop on top of us.

Rold moved like a metallic Olympian by stomping to the shuttle's equipment locker to fetch out breathing masks and gloves for us. "Just in case we need to abandon ship." Fay-et turned once more to the controls, igniting the engines at the same time she closed the viewing portholes.

"Does this metal ball have a deflection source?" Hadrien asked as he climbed into his gear.

"No," Drer answered. "If we are hit, then we will crash to the planet if the damage is extensive."

Hadrien glanced at me. "Well, we didn't specify where to get off when we left Nen and his imperial pooches."

The Crusties traveled slowly up the gulch toward us, using the sure-grip treads of dune rovers. These tanks barely squeezed through the narrow passage and scraped the canyon walls to shatter the delicate lacing of crystal formations.

"Cover your heads and faces as much as possible," Drer said, helping me with the hood on my cammies. "The air is caustic and will eat skin to the bone."

Lovely. Just a summertime bike ride in the country, it was.

Fay-et lifted off deliberately like she was floating out of a no-parking zone at the gates of Buckingham Palace, but before I knew it, she'd turned into a snarling morning commuter. I felt the recoil of the run-pod's main weapons battery as she fired down the cut at the Crusties. The force was enough to slam me hard against the chair. She lobbed two more catapults, and once we could breathe and talk, I was all over her like chopped liver on a bed of metallic onions. "Why are we sitting here hovering? Get us the bloody hell out of here!"

"I cannot," she said. The firing pins take much of the pod's internal power. I must let it initialize before I can launch into space velocity."

In the dead silence that followed this unbreakable, mechanical edict, the Crusties fired upon us. The punch landed square on the hull and sent the pod careening, until it smashed into wall of the gulch. Another slam brought a curse from Fay-et. She strapped into the flight chair quickly with one hand while she typed coordinates into the flight console. The engines stewed like my mum's Sunday dish of tripe and potatoes.

Rold joined her at the helm console and fired—two short raps from our belly guns. The punches banged through the shuttle, nearly shaking my teeth right out of my gums. Drer sat in his flight chair looking as nearly unconcerned as a vicar giving an old sermon. What was death to a creature who had already been effectively shut down? Amid the pounding, little battle, I wondered if he wasn't the reason why Sunteel's body was a lifeless corpse.

The Crusties lobbed a mortar at us, and it took, shearing off the nose of our craft. It was all over but the fall, and fall we did, straight down into an ammonia-laden hell.

The shuttle dropped in the same fashion as a cow flop and we hit—a wet turd in a field of clay. Our pod somersaulted and bounced, and I struggled against the g force pinning me to my seat. Rold was flung from his chair. I heard the sound reverberate in my mind more clearly than in my ears. The mechanoid launched toward me, a huge boulder, and the only thing that saved me from being flattened by an Idealian bowling bowl was that my flight chair cracked under the pitch and yaw to shove me into Hadrien. My partner grabbed onto me by hooking his hand around the strap of my harness. I clawed at the handles of his seat as we intertwined our legs. Unfortunately, the rolling sent Rold straight for me again, and this time, he hit me like a square peg forced into a round opening.

47

I took a knock to the bread loaf, and the next thing I knew, I was lying under a vaulted ceiling of clear white crystal and smooth indigo rock. Light filled this chamber: gentle, calm blue light. The chilly air had numbed my nose. Reaching up to rub circulation back into the tip, I realized that my mask had been stripped from me, and I lay there buck bear in the breathing department. The notion that I inhaled ammonia vapor made me sit straight up. I took a short snort, testing air that I had obviously swigged down for at least an hour.

"Welcome back," Hadrien said.

I swiveled my attention to find him sitting against the wall.

"Want some water?" he asked. "Real H_2O?"

I stopped testing the air to test my throat with a swallow, finding that I was drier than a summer in Khartoum. Hadrien didn't wait for me to respond. Instead, he crawled over to hand me a gray plastic canteen.

"Where did this come from?" I asked, after wetting the dirt on the back of my tongue.

"Nen," he answered.

Well, Friar Tuck. "We've been swindled slicker than peat on moss, haven't we, Artie?"

He managed a smile but lost it the moment he nodded.

I took another slug. How wonderful the water would have tasted if I'd had an Earl Grey tea bag to dunk into it. "What happened after me bell was rung?"

"The Crusties charged in with pincers snapping. I crawled over to you, and there for a minute, I thought I'd lost you." He let his gaze slide off the floor. "It still might happen."

Despite the sluggishness of my thoughts, I clearly recognized heartfelt concern. "I'm harder to bag than that, Artie."

He shook his head. "No, you're not. Neither am I. The thing that's bad is we're just now getting around to realizing how vulnerable we really are."

I couldn't waste words and emotions on thoughts of insecurity. "You said that Nen was here."

"He is. The Crusties called him down from the station. I think those nippers are working both sides of the train tracks."

"Allied with the Bohdan and the Earthers."

"And the folks who have a better offer will come out the fortunate winners in this mess."

"I wonder what they want out of it all."

"Probably the same as everybody else. A renewable resource that is sentient."

I took a minute to sight around the cave. It glowed with ambient light, providing enough illumination to see the little crow's feet at the edges of Hadrien's eyes. "I wonder what it would be like to go interdimensional through this stuff?"

Hadrien shivered. "I don't think I want to try."

I shook off the idea growing in my noodle to focus on the danger at hand. "What's Nen going to do with us?"

"Who the hell knows? We're Theo's prize pigs, so I don't think it will include shackles. Although sedatives might not be out of the question." He sighed and dragged his arse back to the crook of the wall. I heard delicate crystals shatter as he slid over them. "Right now, I wouldn't mind a nice, long sleep."

"Where are we?"

"In a cave."

"I know that. Where is everyone else in relation to us? Where are the metal heads?"

He pointed into the blue haze curling through the cave. "I don't know where they took Rold and Drer, but everyone else is around the bend. Fifty meters, maybe less. I could hear them talking while you snoozed. And if you're thinking about conventional means of escape, you should know there's a Crusty guarding the end of the tunnel." Hadrien leaned his head back and sighed again. "Did you know that the Bohdans lived underground for the most part?"

I climbed to a wobbly stand. "Of course not. But I'll bet if you get more than two or three Va-qua-nua types together in a closed system like this, it's going to start smelling like the inside of wank within a week."

"It's not a closed system."

"Oh?"

"The rock filters the air. It must somehow regenerate using the chemicals found in the atmosphere."

"How did you find this out?"

"I asked Va-qua-nua."

"He's here too, huh?"

"That squirt of an alien follows everybody around. Now it seems he's Nen's best buddy. At least until a new one comes along. You know, Philipa, that little bastard is capable of shutting down Sunteel. If an Argo gave him a little help, it wouldn't have been hard at all. He's bad news."

"I don't think he was very fond of Duriken Sunteel, either."

"And I don't think he was too keen about Administrator Telroni. I've got a feeling that the murders around here have something to do with him."

"But he was aboard the *Zanru* when Telroni came up mustard."

Hadrien grunted but didn't offer any more possibilities.

I stepped to the wall in an effort to appease my growing curiosity and the glimmer of evil thoughts. True, I should have been thinking of a way out, but I had a sudden idea of how I might best assassinate Theo, and strangely, images of Duriken Sunteel's last moments kept boiling up through the stew of my revenge. "Are Bohdans natural to this environment, do you think?"

"Some stories have them coming here. Others place them on this pissy world from the start. What are you driving at?"

"If they are natural to this world, then they will be composed of the same material as the planet. They seem to tolerate ammonia in their atmosphere, and yet they have no trouble breathing oxygen."

He climbed to a stand using his back to slide up the wall. "So these fellows could be the spawn of this planet, and they don't appreciate folks trying to take it over."

"What better place for an exploding bomb?"

"Yeah, but the Argos won't let anything snap the balance that they seem to think they control. If they want the station for their own business, it's too bad Bohdans."

"What if they can't do anything to avoid a tilt in the scales?" Before he could answer, I touched one of the crystalline structures decorating the rock. I don't know if I expected an instant, magnetic attraction with these pointy blokes, but what I got was par for the course: nothing. No reaction. No noodling of the old noodle. No psychic, telepathic, or emphatic twinges. No indication of life, as we knew it, existed in the facets of the gems.

"The Shimbang were behind the dark matter screw up aboard the Baderes," I said. "You realize that, don't you?"

"Yes, it occurred to me."

"I wonder how many dimensions they're messing up with their envy of the Argos?"

"All of them."

"Puts a new twirl on the old way of carrying out galactic conflict." I pulled my hand back. "I wonder how well the war is going in the other causal planes?"

"I wonder how you'd fight it in the first place."

Good point. I didn't bother to answer. Instead, I ignited the Waki'el implant. The burn shot through me like the five ten rolling into the station. It exploded into my ears, and the echo just kept ringing through my body.

Hadrien stepped up to me. "Don't do it, Philipa."

"I have to know, Artie." With that, I pumped the device to full power and shoved my hand through the cave wall.

It tickled. I'd never experienced this kind of sensation before while in the midst of the creation force energy. Over the months, I'd learned that when moving into zero-point gravity, I could sense the essence of others sharing the realm with me. It was usually akin to passing through water. If I moved through a life force, the water might be rough and violent, telling me that the nature of the species was in upheaval. If I trotted on through a life force that was blown out of pacifism, it was a gentle wave and a greeting. I pulled my hand out and hit the stud with nothing more than a thought to disconnect. When I fluttered into the material dimension all the way, Hadrien pounced on me with a question.

"How did it feel?" Hadrien whispered.

"This planet is feather soft, Artie. It's old, too. Parchment old."

"Did you get a feeling for sentience?"

I shrugged. "I'm not sure."

"What do you think you are doing?"

The voice startled the both of us, and I flipped around to see Nen approaching me. I levied my thumb over the button under the skin of my wrist, ready to face off this warthog of Theo's. "You better watch your step, you blunderbuss of turds."

He stopped. "You are in no position to confront me in such a disrespectful manner."

I poised my finger over the stud. "Come closer, you hog-lipped arse, and I'll show you what I can do. Eternity is a long time to sit and wait out my anger." I paused and rubbed the implant with the tip of my thumb. "I swear to you, Nen. I'll take you and everyone in this room with me, straight into the rock of this cave."

"Impossible," he said, spit flying from his choppers.

"No, not impossible."

I glanced beyond Nen to see who had interrupted our showdown. Va-qua-nua stood there. "Finally, a bloke who talks sense."

Nen debated the possibilities for a minute before surrendering. He took several steps back. "Truce," he murmured.

What the bloody bay was I going to do, anyway, but give in? I lowered my arm like it was a gun. "Where's Drer and Rold?"

"In the custody of their own government. It is where you shall be heading, too."

"Excuse me?" Hadrien said.

"Theo and the Idealian apex have come to a working solution to some of the problem. You will finish the investigation on the murder of Duriken Sunteel, but you are effectively still detained. Progenitor Anu will be your keeper while you complete this project."

After hearing this piece of rubbish, I thought hard about punching the trigger and pulling the lot of these bastards into the wall with me. I would have, too, if it hadn't been for the fact that I hate being squashed like a raw egg between Mars and Saturn and will do anything to transform this alignment.

48

We were once more installed in our quarters
aboard the Baderes, but this time, we had a live-in watch
dog by the name of Charlton Yarb. He carried a big gun
and the rank of colonel in the emperor's army. Yarb also
walked around with a pair of deep-set eyes—the kind
that seemed to have enough penetration to see through
fabric—and he kept his gaze fixed upon me. I did my
best to ignore him, to the point of tripping over his feet
as I passed by his chair.

Upon our return, my logos calculator and cards were
waiting for me, so instead of resting, I set out a plan of
action. At first, I was concerned with finding Sunteel's
killer because something told me this bloke would enlighten me in areas that included my abilities to walk
into forever, but after an hour of listening to Yarb's
wheezing breaths, I changed my tack and decided to plan
Theo's assassination instead.

I'd been a real rodeo clown to think that the emperor
would allow Hadrien and me to walk away with our
skills, talents, and implants. As long as the old barnacle
lived on the material plane, there would be no peace of
mind for my partner and me, and though I calculated
cold-blooded murder, I rationalized it. After all, we deserved freedom and personal sovereignty. Theo's
ruthlessness had taken those things from me for a long
time. Eventually, I would end it, and at that moment of

deliberation, I was sure that I would never feel a milli-
meter of remorse.

Hadrien finally left his staring match with Yarb to
walk over to the table where I sat. He pulled up behind
me to massage my shoulders, and as he did, he studied
the horoscope displayed on the calculator's screen.
"There's a chunkin' fire square going on in the middle
of that logos," he said quietly. "Whose is it?"

I smiled. "You're getting to be a right dilly pink on
this stuff, Artie. Pretty soon you won't need me to interpret anything."

As if motivated by spontaneity or some macho move
to show Yarb that I was, indeed, his woman, Hadrien
kissed me deeply. When we broke apart, I glanced at
our guard, who studied us. He didn't remark on it but
just continued to watch us. Hadrien slid into the seat
beside me and pointed to the screen. "What's going on?"

"This is a picture of the current situation. I calculated
the time and place for the drawing of species to this
point here on Baderes Space Station. There's a lot of
heat going on between the Crusties and the Bohdans.
They're both pulling Mars forces while opposing part-
nership energy."

"So Va-qua-nua was lying," he murmured. "I had expected it."

"If my interpretation can be trusted, yes, the little
knacker was feeding us a load of sea bilge every step of
the way."

For some reason, he went at my lips again, breaking
down my resistance to work. I couldn't help it; I
moaned, and it fueled the fire I felt growing inside of
Hadrien. He kissed me like there was not going to be a
tomorrow for us, and with all this mess, he might have
been right. Of course, the minute he pulled back, he shot
his gaze straight to Yarb, saucing him with that wild
squint of his. This was some kind of male cock-of-

the-walk bullshit, and I spent a hard moment fighting an aggravated reaction to it. I wasn't anyone's personal love slave, not even Hadrien's. Yarb reacted by shifting his position in the chair and taking a good, hard look at my boobs. I almost spent my annoyance by blurting out my suspicions about this foolish game, but my partner interrupted me by turning his attention to the screen again. "What else?"

I pursed my lips, frowned at him, and snorted, finally letting this rooster squabble go. "The Idealians and the Argos are not the best of friends. There are inconjuncts floating through the charts."

"Meaning?"

"Meaning that they may be polite to each other out of mutual need or understanding, but they will never be allies unless the stakes are the same."

"But that can't be, because the Argos have the ability to commune between the dimensions unaided, and the Idealians don't."

"But the Idealians may not be far from achieving something similar. Maybe that worries the Argos enough to try to stage a conflict with the players. Set two sides at war, that gets rid of only half your problem. Set four sides at war, and you could eradicate the challenge."

"Unfortunately, they didn't see Theo coming."

"That's me take on it, all right. The worm squeezed into the midst of this bleedin' battle and has been slowly chewing away the underpinnings. Now everyone owes him."

"The Argos don't."

"Yes, but Theo's been sniffing around their neck of space, probably making himself an imperial-sized nuisance." I sat back in the chair and studied the chart. The Crusties' sudden presence slammed across the logos like a comet circuiting the night sky. I tapped the calculator into go mode and waited for it to chug out the figures for the next twenty-four hours. When it displayed, the Crusties were gone. "Do we know anything about the Regerian home world?"

Hadrien shook his head. "Not me."

"I do." Yarb's voice stabbed into our conversation, but at that moment, I was kind of relieved that it had.

"What do you know?" I asked.

He put a little drama into his presence by sliding slowly from the lounger to walk to the table. He glanced at the screen like he knew what the bloody hell he was looking at.

"I've never been there myself, but I've talked to folks who have. They told me that the Regerians come from a world just like Bohdan."

"Meaning what?" Hadrien demanded. "It's the same size, has the same kind of ring system, similar atmosphere—what specifically?"

"All that and more. You know that chitinous hide they have?"

"I always thought it was some kind of shell."

"It's silica."

Hadrien flipped me a look. "The Crusties are comprised of the same thing as their planet."

"That's what I was told. And they're limited because of it."

"Why?"

"Because they need a certain protein available on their world. I think it must be some sort of by-product made by the planet."

"Maybe they work like the Gin-li," I said to Hadrien.

Yarb nodded. "Yeah, that's possible. Anyway, they can't go off the beaten path unless they have enough provisions."

"And it's bleedin' hard to find the protein on most carbon-based planets," I said.

"That's what I understand."

I popped a glance at Hadrien, who stared at me with a twist to his brow while Yarb continued.

"They need refueling outposts," Hadrien said. "And Bohdan is along the way."

"But the route might have been closed to them for a while, given the planetary stresses and changes," I said.

"Now they see an opening and a possibility." Hadrien sat back. "I wonder how far away Earth is from here?"

I shook my head. "Not far enough."

"Crusties are known over a good portion of the galaxy," Yarb mentioned. "They've conquered a few systems in their time. I'll bet you the emperor is keeping more than one eyeball on the critters."

I nodded. "If that's the case, then they're pretty pissed off about everybody being here to disturb their provisioning link. They're probably wondering if Theo's going to make a power grab and hold this station for ransom. It would put the brakes on Crusty expansion on this side of the galaxy."

"Make 'em pay for the use of Bohdan," Hadrien said flatly. "That would be just like that old son of a bitch."

I tossed a hard look at Yarb before tapping the calculator's screen with my knuckle. "Theo might be barking up the wrong tree. He might not get a chance to spend all this new money he expects to get from the Crusties." If I had anything to do with it, he wouldn't.

49

Before we were allowed to leave our quarters and pursue the investigation, Hadrien and I were squeezed, poked, and mashed by Theo's private physician, Irma Quiggly. She was a saucy wench—raven-haired, voluptuous, beautiful—and she had a way of staring at Hadrien that made me want to smack her right between the mascara pots.

Quiggly's assistant was a beefy bloke named Wallerson. He'd at some point assumed medical responsibility for me, and instead of listening to my protests on the matter of an examination, he simply picked me up and threw me on the sofa where he ripped open the snaps on my cammies to place a stethoscope monitor over my heart. The thumping that issued from the pickup gave me away. I should have belted this old boy for his insolence. I had a martial arts background. Why didn't I use it?

Wallerson pulled my lids back, checked the whites of my eyes, and then moved his fingers down my throat to determine the fitness of my glands. I thought he might be done, but the badger fooled me. Instead of letting me sit up, he ran his fingers through my hair and tugged harder than he should have. I let my questions about restraint dissipate and bringing my foot up, I kicked him in the bread loaf with everything I had in me. When the force drove his ugly mug my direction, I balled my fist and popped him straight in that pouty kisser of his. Wallerson went down like a load of Saturday's wash. Our tussle attracted Yarb's attention, and our watchdog bounded around the couch to stop short.

"What happened?" he asked stupidly.

I stood, egging the colonel on. "Do you want a piece of me? Come on, you flaming rube. I'm in a mood that's black enough to make me send your arse to a moon halfway across the galaxy."

"You're not that strong," he said. "Don't fool yourself."

Something really snapped in my brain, and I reached for the stud on the alien implant. The only thing that stopped me from punching the button and nipping up Yarb was Hadrien.

My partner wrapped me in his arms, stilling my anger with his embrace. He kissed the top of my head and massaged my neck while holding off the animals with a hard look. "Don't waste your life on this guy," he husked. "Saturn and Uranus square Mars."

Yes, they did. Active cruelty slowly moved our course along.

I tried to escape his hold, but Hadrien kept me firm, obviously waiting for the silence and stillness to create meaning in their minds. Finally, Quiggly spoke in her proper British accent.

"Well, it would seem that Dr. Wallerson is incapacitated at the moment. Colonel Yarb, would you be so kind as to have him removed?"

Yarb nodded and started yammering on his walkie-talkie.

I glanced at Hadrien, but he didn't return my look. Instead, he crushed me harder to his breast.

After Yarb ordered the stretcher for Wallerson, Quiggly surprised me by changing mules in the middle of this polluted stream.

"I suppose you would like to examine the body of Administrator Telroni," she said.

This time Hadrien did toss me a frowning expression and released me.

I fumbled to close the snaps on my cammies before answering. "Yes, we would, and we'd like all the information you have."

Quiggly motioned to Yarb before marching to the hatch. "I don't have that much information. According to the duty medic, who I might add was an Idealian, Telroni was found in his quarters. He was sitting at a table with his hand in his lap."

"Did you perform an autopsy?" Hadrien asked.

"No," she answered. "Not my purview."

"Not in my purview" translated to: "I'm not touching any of these filthy aliens."

We marched to the Baderes ice box, detained several times by Crusties, Idealians, Senerians, and Humans. Quiggly got us through each blockade by flashing a red badge that she wore about her neck. Whatever was going on at the space station was being controlled from a single source: Theo.

Quiggly selected a freezer in the locker room, rolled out Administrator Telroni, and dashed back the sheet protecting the corpse. "It's a beautiful sight, it is," she announced.

The Senerian's right side was exploded. A gaping, blackened hole, thick with brown goo, was the first clue that Telroni—with the murderer's hand—had been murdered himself. One arm was a stump, and the severed hand had been neatly balanced across his thigh.

"What happened?" I asked.

"He was found shot to death," Quiggly answered. "It appears to be a manchower wound."

"Manchower?" Hadrien said. "You're talking about a rifle that's illegal on this side of the galaxy."

"Manchowers can be bought on the other side of the galaxy. Don't forget that."

"The Senerians run manchowers," Yarb offered. "Hell, I hear they will sell the nuts and bolts right off a ship flying through zero-point gravity."

Hadrien stepped up to the cart and flicked the sheet off the rest of the body, exposing long, spindly legs and reproductive organs that looked like a clump of pink grapes. Telroni's corpse was a pallet of bruises, nicks, and circular burn marks. "He appears to have been tortured."

"Yes," Quiggley said.

"But why?"

She shook her head. "He knew something."

Hadrien snorted but didn't crack her with his sarcastic wit. Instead, he studied the body a bit more closely than I would have liked him to. "These burn marks look like they come from a laser probe."

Quiggly wigged her eyebrows. "Quite possibly."

My partner turned from the cadaver, walked boldly to the equipment locker, and fetched an analyzer. "Why was his hand sliced from his body and laid to rest with him?"

"Some alien symbolism, no doubt," Quiggly said.

Hadrien returned, clicking on the monitor when he reached the table. "Alien symbolism. Maybe he was heavy-handed or had his hands in things that didn't concern him. Or maybe the killer just wanted to cut off his hand for emphasis."

Quiggly frowned. "So if you have an idea what it means, why did you ask me?"

He paused, openly studied her face, and then replied in a no-nonsense tone, "The other deaths contained no symbolism. At least none that we saw."

"Maybe Telroni's demise didn't have anything to do with this case, Artie," I said.

With that, he turned away from Quiggly and flashed me a confident smile before he bent to the job before him.

Quiggly's nostrils flared. "All these aliens are in collaboration in one form or the other. What are you hoping to find?"

"Unera readings," he answered casually.

"Unera?"

"Yeah. Have you ever heard of it?"

She shrugged and backed away from the body. "No. I never have. What is it?"

"Well, we're not at all sure about that. It might be what happens to Senerians after they die, or it might be something that kills them." He straightened, casting her with a disapproving gaze at her sudden distance from the corpse. "Do you think it might be contagious?"

"You're talking about alien physiology. I'm a Human doctor. If that monitor picks up evidence of unera, then it must be a virus of some type."

"Why?"

"Because the analyzer measures that sort of thing. You never want to get too close to a virus unless you know what you are dealing with."

Hadrien made a show of studying the monitor. "This thing tells you what chemical substances are present in the tissues."

Quiggly blew him off like a raspberry atop a tart by turning to address Yarb. "Colonel, please roll Administrator Telroni back into the freezer when they are done." She suddenly walked away, her shoe soles clicking loudly on the metal floor.

After she was gone, I turned to Hadrien. "What was that all about?"

"I don't know. There is one thing I'm sure of, though. She's no medic. More like a weasel for Theo."

I thought Yarb might protest, but he remained silent

while my partner skimmed the tool over the body.

"He's clean." Pausing, Hadrien squinted at me. "Any expansive thoughts on the subject?"

Sometimes, my brain functions at a half-second delay, but when enlightenment finally smacks me in the brain-pan, I get off my knobs and act on the inspiration.

I waltzed my way over to the refrigerator and, opening it, I glanced in like I was looking for a little leftover boiled beef from Monday supper. There were medications, ointments, and a red box wrapped with a white medical restraining strap. A blue delivery tag was still snapped to the package. "What have we here?" I pulled the box out and read the note. "This was Telroni's property." Hadrien and Yarb joined me at the box.

"What's inside of it?" my partner asked.

I shook it and found that it sloshed. "Liquid." I flipped the box over, and right there on the bottom was a warning: *"Do not expose to bright light. Gin-li solution with active compounds and components."* It looked like we might have found the reason Telroni was dead.

50

We decided it was time to talk to the Idealians, and so we dragged Yarb with us to see Anu. The investigator had a command post set up on the bridge, and when we arrived, we found him staring out of the viewing porthole at the conglomeration of ships meeting for the afternoon war recital. He glanced at us as we walked in, frowned, and then turned his attention back toward space.

I stomped straight up to Anu and blocked his view. "Do you realize this place is crawling with Gin-li, and your folks are right smack in the middle of the mud puddle?"

He scowled. "Who told you that?"

I handed him the box of thawing critters that I'd found in the fridge. "Telroni might have had the market around here, and someone killed him for the goods."

He took the box with his thick, stubby fingers and gently caressed it. "It was not necessarily an Idealian who murdered him for this prize."

"Why not?"

"Because all the species gathered here have the ability to assimilate Gin-li."

"Humans, too?" Hadrien said, stepping beside me.

"Humans, too."

"I know of one Idealian who is buying the Gin-li," I said. "I don't know if it's for personal use or if he's trafficking in it, but we need to talk to him, and we think you need to come along to enjoy this conversation."

"Who?"

"Immaculate Rold."

Anu snorted. "Please. He is a nobody. He is unimportant."

"He's part of a growing army of civil disobedience on your world, Anu. I'd think you'd want to pick these blokes off each time you came up against one."

My words finally pumped a little interest into those tubes encircling his bread loaf. He handed the box to me and stood, a movement that was remarkably graceful, given his bulk. Pausing, he stared hard at me. "Rold risked his life to help you. Now you betray his trust. That is despicable, Astrologer Cyprion."

Okay, I'll admit it. I hadn't thought of it in those terms. After having been recaptured by Nen, my only concern had fallen to self-preservation and more than a few fantasies of revenge. I didn't even care that I was ratting on Rold? I studied the mechanoid for a minute before belting out the truth. "It's just the way the light is falling, Anu. The devil will get his due."

He snorted. "Devils. What a ridiculous concept." With that, the Idealian clomped away, and we were forced to scurry after him.

We entered the enormous mechanoid ship called the *Vargus*. It was like I expected it to be: cold metal, slate-colored plastics, all presented in a heavy, industrial look that was enhanced with enough colored lights to make a person squint. The Idealians were lumbering and huge, and aboard the *Vargus*, they seemed twice as hulking and slow. Yet, for all their heavy-footed noise, they moved with amazing dexterity into tight passageways, maintaining equal alignment so they didn't bang into the bulkheads.

We finally entered a soaring passageway of titanium girders and molded aluminum. It was the main backbone

of the ship, a half-kilometer-long expanse that joined the
forward to the aft. A quarter of the way along this route,
Anu stopped before one of the hundreds of nondescript
hatches. Instead of knocking, he closed his eyes and did
that mechanoid telepathic rubbish. Yarb glanced at me
with a curious look. His expression turned to surprise
when, seconds later, Rold opened the hatch to stare at
me with a lethal glare. Seeing it, I knew Anu had said
something about Human deviousness in his transmission. So, to prove him right, I kept to the brutish road.

"You might want to take this conversation inside for
a bit of privacy, mate," I said.

Rold said nothing as he stepped aside to allow us all
to enter.

These were his private quarters, and the bulkheads
were decorated with strange, metal artwork laid against
upholstered fabric, the fit of which reminded me of
copper-hued army blankets. The furnishings were heavy
and large, made to accommodate the Idealian girth.
Rold's bony, metallic armor reflected the soft pink color
of the recessed lighting.

"I have done nothing wrong," Rold growled.

"According to the Humans, you have conspired
against the Idealian government and have in your possession illegal contraband. Speak truthfully, Rold. Lies
will only complicate the consequences."

Rold stood there, rocking slightly. I edged close to
Hadrien in case this tank decided to bolt, because if he
had, the boulder would have flattened me, but after a
minute of indecision, he sat down on an enormous couch
and buried his head in his hands.

We each situated ourselves around the room. Hadrien
and I came to rest in the seat of a single chair. My
partner was the first to speak, his voice sounding heavy
in the oppressive atmosphere of guilt.

"We know you fetched a pricey box of Gin-li while

on Argos. Someone had already paid for the mother lode, and when you saw a chance to go pick it up, you managed to get a box without going through Captain Marctori and his sulters."

Rold raised his head to cast a glance toward us. "Yes. I stole them. It is true." He stopped speaking long enough to draw a loud breath. "And if you think you have proof, think again. They are gone."

"Did you ingest them already?" I asked.

"Yes. And I'm feeling stronger than ever."

"You have committed a felony offense against our penal code, Immaculate," Anu piped in.

Rold's dark, gritty laugh made me flinch. "Has it not occurred to you that those who live a miserable existence as second-class citizens do not care one whit about your laws? One day you shall find that the title of progenitor no longer protects you from the truth. You cannot keep stripping people of their birthrights. I want mine back, and the Gin-li will help me accomplish this. It is too late, Anu. You cannot arrest me at this point."

The Idealian investigator almost looked uncomfortable as he shifted his weight in the chair. When it was obvious he wasn't going to push the matter, I took over the interview.

"Who paid for the mother lode, Rold?"

The Idealian lifted his head to study us in turn. "Dr. Gasba."

"Drer's mate?"

"That is correct."

"What was she going to use them for?"

"She was hoping to regenerate her ability to enter zero-point gravity."

"That was because she willingly gave Duriken Sunteel her IDT node," Hadrien said.

Rold frowned and used his thumb to scratch his face

under a clump of wiring. "Willingly? I do not understand. Who told you that?"

"Dr. Drer, of course. You know, the one who you keep prisoner."

"Prisoner?" Anu abruptly barked.

"Prisoner," Hadrien answered. "It has something to do with his DNA harness. This fellow here seems to have the numbers that can turn him off. Permanently."

Anu swiveled his attention to take in Rold, but surprisingly, he didn't even reprimand the mechanoid. I jumped back in before the subject could slide away to political posturing. "Was Dr. Gasba forced to submit to the surgery to remove her IDT node?"

"Yes."

"How do you know?"

"She told me. We had a close relationship, even though she could not admit it to anyone."

A hatch in the back of the room cycled, and Fay-et stepped through to interrupt the proceedings. "Gasba despised Sunteel," she announced. "She was sensitive to the plight of the immaculates. Sunteel thought everyone was beneath her. When Drer operated on Gasba, she swore she would get revenge."

"You think Gasba killed her?" Hadrien asked.

"I do not know," she murmured.

"How did Drer feel about the whole situation?" I said.

Fay-et joined us in the sitting area and plopped down heavily next to her son. Placing a hand upon his knee, she squeezed gently—something that a mother might do—but with the metallic fingers, it just looked weird. "He expressed anguish. Drer believed that an IDT node should be taken from an available immaculate instead of a progenitor. Had there been anyone aboard the station with authority over Sunteel, then his wishes would have been granted. Since Sunteel was in command of the project, it was her decision, and for some reason, she desired Gasba's internal property."

"It is because she expressed love for me," Rold pinged. "She did not want to see any harm come to me."

A general pause in the discussion followed this admission. My thoughts went back to the day aboard the Baderes when the station had phased into zero point gravity, killing Gasba. Had Sunteel been able to cause this malfunction at the moment we discussed her murder? Had she been trying to alert us to the truth? Or had she simply been trying to silence the Idealian doctor?

Hadrien started up again. "I was under the impression that Sunteel had been aboard the station for several months."

"That is correct," Fay-et answered.

"When did her IDT go bad?"

"A few days before the experiment commenced."

"And you said Dr. Drer performed the surgery."

"Yes. He flew in on a personal transport to undertake the project."

Hadrien swept me with a look. "He said he came in after Sunteel's death to help his mate during the murder investigation."

Fay-et shook her head. "He was here three standard Earth days before the event. I know; I serviced his shuttle."

"So, he was here when the experiment began," I said.

"That is correct. He evacuated the station at the same time the team left." She shook her head again. "He was open about expressing his love for Gasba. It did hurt him to see her abused by Sunteel."

"Was Gasba aboard the transport with you, or did she evacuate the station with her mate?"

"She was with us. In fact, she was monitoring all of Sunteel's processes by remotely linking with her through the Baderes."

"Couldn't her life force have been pulled into zero-point gravity along with Sunteel's?"

"It was a possibility, but Gasba pulled out of the link a full standard minute before the switch was hit."

"Then there was a moment's worth of dead time when no one was in communication with her or the station."

"Correct," Fay-et answered, adding a breathy ping to her response. "The link remained open, though. If any of the other monitors had signaled a problem, Gasba would have tapped back in."

I stood up as the dawning truth hit me. "This link. Could someone have jumped on the line in the interim and formed a meld with the Baderes and Sunteel?"

"Yes, it is possible, but they would have to use a linking unit aboard the station."

"Did anyone actually clear Drer for departure?" I asked.

"I did," Rold answered quietly.

"Did he leave immediately?"

The Idealian pulled a pinging breath. "As far as I know, he did."

"Weren't you checking the station's exterior cameras?"

"Just before the implementation of the experiment, all scanning devices were turned off." He sat back on the couch to study me. "Drer might never have left."

51

Drer. He certainly had the moral scruples for mur-der; spies, informants, and cads always did. The fact that Rold and his revolutionary compatriots controlled the doctor through his DNA harness gave him another reason to kill Sunteel. He couldn't hit the group all at once, but he could hit them individually. By murdering Sunteel, he chose to express the emotion of anger he felt at having to purloin his mate's IDT to help this female who disobeyed the apex and who treated folks like a bunch of mechanoid dairy cows.

The Idealians were complicated blokes, but the justifications for murder were always as vile and as base as they could be. No species, however enlightened they thought they were, could escape this one certain fact: The universe was born of violence and we were its spawn.

We sat in Rold's quarters while Anu used his mechanoid telepathy to locate Drer. While he did, I silently berated myself for trusting this person. I'd learned long ago to be suspicious of aliens, but I'd let my better judgment be clouded by the possibilities of friendship.

All that we lacked, according to Anu, was a confession of guilt, and the matter would be closed. We would be on our way, hauled back in electronic chains to become Theo's lab rats. Adding this to my personal feelings of betrayal, it was a bitter pill to pop.

Hadrien's thoughts had gone to Telroni's death instead of to our futures. "Drer couldn't have killed the Senerian administrator. He was aboard the *Zanru* with us."

Rold spoke up. "Telroni did a brisk business in illegal trade. Any one of the sulters could have killed him for any reason. As the one in charge of the station, he was not above claiming kickbacks and defrauding his own government. Telroni got what he had coming to him. He knew about the delivery of dark matter to Sunteel. He approved it."

"And a bunch of sulters died transporting the dark matter for Marctori."

"Then Drer must have killed Marctori," I said. "The pissant tried to deflect suspicion onto me."

"Sunteel paid Telroni and the captain to find the people to help us keep it quiet. Drer may have blamed Marctori as one of the people connected with the source of his unhappiness and discontent."

"I told you he could not contain his emotions," Fayet added. "He probably has a bad capacitor flow to his logic center."

"Or it might be even more simple," I said. "He may have wished to keep Marctori quiet."

Anu abruptly interrupted us. "Drer is aboard the space station in the launch bay. He is ready to depart and apparently is demonstrating his displeasure. The personnel in that area have been evacuated."

Hadrien jumped up. "Let's go stop him." He paused to pat his side. "I wish I had my gun."

"I have guards dispatched to his point. Drer will not escape."

Famous last words were never more inaccurately uttered. We all stumbled into the main corridor and, as we did, we were all flung hard to port. I knocked against the bulkhead with a splat and hung there for just a minute, sensing the deep, rumbling vibration of a ship that had been hit squarely in the belly with a torpedo. Anu climbed onto his communicator and bellowed: "Command! What is happening?"

Harried voices, static, pings, grunts, and twitters answered his plea for information. A response finally vomited through the online noise. "We are under attack! The Human ship has fired upon us with no provocation! We are hailing the *Misha* now!"

"Hold your return fire," Anu ordered.

After a moment, the *Vargus* yawed and settled back into place just before the warning Klaxon sounded. The Idealian bridge command made a new announcement that I couldn't hear above the din. Minutes flicked by as we wound our way back to the Baderes. I thought I'd go deaf from the noise, but I heard Anu clearly enough when he stopped in the middle of a cramped, dark access way. "The Earthers claim not to have fired."

Hadrien and I looked at each other. "It's the Argos," I said.

"Or the Shimbang," Hadrien barked. "Tell them to hold their position. Let the Crusties and the Senerians know, too. We wouldn't fire first. There's too much money riding on this deal."

Anu nodded and slipped into the mechanical warble of his native language. Before he was done speaking, he was pushing his steps toward the Baderes's docking bay.

The station had been thrown into chaos by the explosion. When we entered the commons, I glanced up toward the panoramic view through the immense portholes. Instead of seeing the beauty of the planet and its rings, I saw the scorched underbelly of the *Vargus* sitting in its berth.

People ran in all directions along the Baderes's main corridor—Crusties, Senerians, Idealians, and Humans—each person trying to escape an unknown outcome. One of the Regerians hit me going the other way, and the

force of his collision plopped me on my bum. Hadrien
yanked me to a stand with no word spoken. Just as we
entered the docking bay, it seemed that Sunteel's ghost
had ideas about slowing down the trouble, because the
station unexpectedly phased into the creation energy.

Calm, lazy, dreamy atmosphere met my best efforts
to concentrate. I swam forward, but all I really wanted
to do was float with the euphoric feeling. Had it not been
for my partner pulling me along, I would have stopped
to enjoy the bliss without any concern about trapping
Drer.

In a way, Sunteel helped. By shoving us into zero-
point gravity, she exposed a whole group of invading
Argos through their energy signatures. The little orange
terrorists were everywhere, popping in and out of view.
Even Anu saw them, because he stopped his forward
march to stare at the intruder.

As abruptly as it all had started, the creation vibration
ended, pulled back like some cosmic blanket. We each
plopped into dimensionality, and the second we did, the
Idealian investigator was on the horn trying to forestall
disaster between our peoples. Another impact rocked the
station, but I couldn't localize it. All I could do was hold
onto Hadrien while he held on to the treelike stability
of Rold. We ran through the quaking structure until we
came to Drer's transport, a boxy conveyance that made
most Human shuttles look like a carp compared to a
whale.

The zone had cleared out with the first problems, and
the bay doors were shut and locked down tight. I don't
know what happened to Anu's guards, but the metallic
bastards hadn't shown up. Anu drew his side arm, closed
his eyes, and obviously commanded Fay-et and Rold to
move into flanking positions. They fell away, and Hadrien grabbed my arm to pull me close. I was momentarily stalled by the heat of his body and the musky smell

of his perspiration. My partner was back with me, fully in this dimension, braving the possibility of eternal death of his current form. Yet he made sure that he was a step ahead of me, acting like a Human shield.

The deck was sandy. Yes, dirt and grit followed a person everywhere. Sweeping my gaze across the floor, I saw a thousand footprints, each one going in a different direction. Suddenly, the Klaxon was deleted, and we stopped moving in unison, listening hard for any signs that, we the stalkers, had become the stalkees. I heard no unauthorized pings and dings, but then all the noise and heavy vibration had caused my ears to ring.

Anu stepped beyond Drer's transport, spinning on his heel toward the shuttle's bow while holding his side arm high. We slipped up behind the Idealian investigator only to be greeted by Drer, who leveled a big, black manchower at us.

"Drop your weapon," Anu ordered.

Drer chose to demonstrate the depth of his emotion by spitting out an answer laced with dark passion. "Do not make me laugh."

"You are under arrest for the murder of Duriken Sunteel," Anu thundered.

"Am I?" Drer hefted the manchower a little bit, and I found myself staring right down that wide, round barrel. "If it had not been for these Humans, you would never have known. The government is ineffectual, as usual."

Anu snarled, answering in their Idealian language. Drer, however, ignored him to focus on us. "What gave away my secret?"

"You're a bloke who has nothing to live for," I answered. "It made sense."

He snorted. "Only to a Human would that make sense."

"Drop your weapon!" Anu bellowed.

We clearly understood Drer's response. He pressed the firing pin on the manchower, and the gun exploded into noise, fire, and vibration. I slammed my weight into Hadrien, and we both barely missed being singed by the volley. Anu, for all his size and bulk, jumped to his right, using a titanium support beam for cover. The energy bolt dissipated on the far wall, denting the metal and scorching the deck below the impact site. Smoke fizzed from the crater in the bulkhead, stinking up the bay with the smell of fried electrical parts.

Hadrien and I rolled clear, using the shuttle's belly ramp as protection from Drer's aim. We were defenseless, Theo's thugs having taken any weapons we might have had. I glanced at Yarb. He stuck with us like glue, and he held tight to the one rifle we had on our side.

"Open the bay doors, and I will be on my way," Drer roared.

"No!" Anu answered. He stepped from the cover of the girder to lob a couple of laser bolts at the doctor. Drer sidestepped the investigator's clumsy efforts and fired again, the impact banging into the support. It melted the metal, the outcome of which was a grinding moan issued by the roof beam. This bloody mechanoid was deadly serious.

Rold stepped forward, holding a palm-sized computer. Fay-et hissed at her son, but he ignored her.

"You know what this is, Drer," Rold called out. "I have placed your DNA code into the processor. I need do nothing more than execute the program, and you will not even get the mockery of a trial as promised to you by our government. Put your weapon down and surrender."

"I will not," Drer answered quietly. "You and your comrades have manipulated me for far too long. It ends here, and it ends now." That said, Drer raised the manchower and pressed the pin.

Rold was not as limber and fast as Anu. He tried to miss the volley at the same time he tried to press the button on the computer, and he failed miserably at both. Drer's aim was true, hitting Rold in the midsection and opening him like a hole in a square doughnut. I saw wires, tubes, blue blood, smoke, and the Idealian's surprised expression as he crumpled. The palm computer flew from his hand to clatter between Drer and me.

Yarb came to life momentarily, shooting a couple of rounds from his rifle, but he cooked like a girl when it came to hitting anything. Drer swiveled and aimed our direction. Hadrien and I wormed under the belly ramp on the shuttle, the blast from the manchower echoing as it passed over us on its way toward Yarb. The shot splattered through the colonel. I heard a truncated scream before the rifle clattered to the floor followed by the man's headless body. Hadrien crawled toward the gun, dragging it to him by the bloody stock.

That really put my knickers into a bobble. I could see the handheld computer lying on the floor just meters from me, but it might as well have been on the other side of Bohdan for all the good it did us.

Anu tried again. "Stop this course of action, Drer, and I promise your execution will be swift and painless."

Drer laughed. "Painless? I have spent an entire lifetime living in pain, and you think it concerns me in the matter of my death? You are a fool, Anu. You are a pawn, a pawn who has no common sense."

He raised the manchower and lined up the melted post that shielded Anu. One more hit, and the ceiling would collapse on that side of the bay. I felt Hadrien move behind me. Glancing back, I saw him rise above the lip of the ramp, place the rifle on his shoulder, and target Drer, but before he could take a shot, Duriken Sunteel stepped into the melee.

A vibration built slowly around us, shaking the con-

tents of the entire landing bay. Cardboard supply barrels
fell from stacks to roll along the deck; plumbing materials scattered and bounced along behind them. The rumble moved through the entire bay, expanding within the
bulkheads until the station screamed under this advance.
Hadrien used the opportunity to plink a round at Drer,
and Anu followed his lead. Drer unloaded the manchower at his fellow Idealian, but the volley went wide
and impacted the bulkhead.

The shaking abruptly turned into a violent quaking.
Ceiling tiles split from snaps on the overhead to crash
down around us. Hadrien forgot the gun and launched
for cover beneath the belly ramp. Drer fired at Anu and
took several steps in our direction. His trip was leading
him to the forgotten computer.

Sometimes, I don't know where my courage and fool-
hardiness come from, but this time, it was set on go. I
slipped from my hiding place and rolled toward the unit.
Drer hefted the manchower in my direction, growling a
threat as he did. Anu popped a shot at him, and it was
enough of a disturbance for me to grab the computer. I
punched the execute button. When I did, the shaking
stopped completely.

So did Drer. His mouth flopped open, his fingers
twitched, and he dropped the manchower. Anu ducked
falling objects and rushed from his cover to kick the
weapon out of Drer's reach, but it was obvious that the
launching of the numbers had stalled the doctor's DNA
in midreplicate. He sank slowly to his knees before he
announced his death with a thundering bellow.

52

The soldiers showed up right on time five minutes later. Hadrien and I had held our positions in the bay and, after seeing Nen and his crew arrive on the scene, I silently kicked myself for not having hightailed it off the station in Drer's shuttle. Yes, I know, we wouldn't have gotten ten meters without Theo's dogs chasing us, but it was a missed opportunity to give the old man trouble.

Drer now appeared frozen, his subarchitecture grown inflexible, his tubes no longer pumping juice into the joints in his head. Dark fluid seeped from his open mouth, and his face held the rigid contours of a person whose final seconds had been unbelievably painful. Here had been a being who for just a few minutes, I'd thought of as an ally. I was a real sucker for the porky and that thought pissed me off. It must have shown in my own expression as something akin to indigestion because Nen rushed up to me.

"Are you two all right?" he demanded.

I glanced down to my hand. I still held the computer, the weapon that had killed a person. The words never came out of my mouth. Instead, I pitched the unit as hard as I could on the deck, yowling in sudden realization of what I'd done.

I was an astrologer, not a bounty hunter. I was paid to give people hope about their lives; I wasn't commissioned to execute them, and yet, here I was, the dame

of the ball, as Hadrien called me. I'd done the deed
because nobody else could have.

"Astrologer Cyprion?"

Nen's words wormed into my thoughts, and the nasal
sound riding the vowels gave me a sudden, tanker-sized
headache. "Leave me alone, you alley wank." I circuited
away from him but bumped into Hadrien before I got
very far. He stopped my trajectory by enfolding me in
his arms.

"It's okay, Philipa," he cooed.

"No, Artie, it's not."

"You need rest."

"So do you."

Before I could say anything further, Hadrien released
me and turned his attention to Nen. "This place is crawling with Argos. I'll bet my soiled shorts that they were
behind the attack on the Idealians."

The barrister gathered up his maroon robes, frowning
slightly, as if he were about to shoot a lie our way. "We
had a malfunction aboard the *Misha*. The port guns
opened on their own. You say we have been duped by
the Argos? How do you know this?"

"We saw them," Anu said, approaching him. "They
have a large complement here. There seems to be nothing to do about their invasion, either."

"Ahh, now that's where you're wrong," Nen answered. He plastered on a smile. "We have developed a
way to detect their presence. It was one of the reasons
that we've been trying to gain access to them."

"They can still undermine the station," Anu countered.

"True, but I don't think they will. I'm sure that our
leaders will create a treaty whereby everyone can share
in the bounty. The Argos will get their anchor, the Regerians will have a viable provisioning outpost, the Senerians will be allowed to administrate the whole thing,

the Idealians will get their wish for autonomous recognition, and the Bohdans, well, the Bohdans just might get to go home."

"What about the Humans?" Hadrien snapped.

"The Humans get to make money," Nen answered quietly. "Everyone is happy." He turned toward me, but he lost his pleasant expression as he did. "As for you two, the emperor wanted to be informed the minute this mess was finalized. He wants to congratulate you personally."

Well, scoobies and muck. "I don't need to hear his phony bullshit, Nen. We won't take the call."

"Yes, you will." He snapped his fingers, and four large guards stepped up to us. "Install them back into their quarters aboard the *Misha*." Nen paused to sling another hard look my way. "We leave for Earth immediately."

Anu poked his way into the crowd. "A moment, please." He held out his big hand. Hadrien and I took turns letting him pump our arms in a crushing attempt to show his thanks. It was awkward, yet it was the perfect try at peace. "Thank you for helping us to discover the killer. Whether by default or deceit, you were the perfect choice to help us foil Drer and avoid war."

"No thanks needed, mate. You were on the right road. It would have eventually led to the same conclusion."

He grunted. "Probably not." Anu turned stiffly and marched away. I followed his retreat until one of the guards stepped into my line of sight to block his hulking form. We did an about-face and allowed ourselves to be led away to our fate.

Once back in our quarters, Nen followed us inside with a sentry. He didn't make excuses for this invasion of privacy; he instead went to the communications console and dialed up the emperor. Hadrien I flopped onto the couch, knowing full well we wouldn't escape the coming sugar-sweet song that Theo sang to us while he committed reprehensible acts behind our backs.

His face came to full color on the large monitor decorating the far wall, and I could see every wrinkle, pimple, and white nose hair. When he realized we were safe and sound, the old barnacle grinned like the madman he was.

"As you can see, your majesty," Nen began, "Cyprion and Hadrien have won the day. You were correct about their skills. They've gained much in service to Earth."

"Philipa," Theo said. "Artemis. I'm glad you came through this problem unscathed."

"With no bloody help from you," I snarled.

He lost his grin. "All right. I deserved that. I apologize for not telling you anything up front."

"Why don't you apologize for stripping us of our freedoms?"

"Now, now," he soothed. "I'm emperor. If you are born on planet Earth, then I technically own you."

"You don't own me, Theo. You never will."

"On the contrary. The only place you can go is to bug out into the creation energy, and while you may think you can escape that way, you're wrong."

"Why?" Hadrien asked, without adding the obligatory "sir" to his question.

Theo ignored the impropriety to answer him. "Because the same process that lets us monitor the presence of the Argos will allow me to follow you, wherever you may roam. The minute you pop back into materiality, I've got you." He stopped to smile again. "Now, be good children and do as you're told. Nen, I'll expect your report at oh eight hundred hours." He signed off without so much as a good-bye.

I glanced at Hadrien. "Baked, boiled, and fried."

He nodded, sighing loudly.

Nen cut the transmission by stabbing the button on

the remote. Seconds later, someone tapped on the hatch. The duty sentry answered it, admitting the same guard who had delivered dinner to us before. This time he returned with a beverage cart.

"This calls for a drink," Nen said brightly. "You must be thirsty."

Come to think of it, I was as dry as the dust of Bohdan. He poured three tumblers of liquid from a crystal pitcher, handing them off to us and keeping one for himself. "A toast. Here's to your successful futures." Nen placed the cup to his lips.

Hadrien glanced at me, and I shrugged. We sipped the drinks at first, but by the third or fourth swig, I started gulping the water. Nen took our empty glasses and stood there staring at us.

It took a couple of seconds, but it eventually hit me. The realization and the sedative. Of course, I should have known we'd be taking a long nap on the return trip. My eyelids suddenly seemed to weigh like a couple of boulders. I blearily aimed my gaze at Hadrien, just to see him pass out.

"You're a filthy wank, Nen," I mumbled.

Then, like the stars at dawn, my awareness slowly faded, my thoughts following into oblivion as I considered ways to assassinate Theo. I'd killed before; I could do it again.

Penguin Putnam Inc.
Online

Your Internet gateway to a virtual environment with
hundreds of entertaining and enlightening books
from Penguin Putnam Inc.

*While you're there, get the latest buzz on
the best authors and books around—*

Tom Clancy, Patricia Cornwell, W.E.B. Griffin,
Nora Roberts, William Gibson, Robin Cook,
Brian Jacques, Catherine Coulter, Stephen King,
Jacquelyn Mitchard, and many more!

**Penguin Putnam Online is located at
http://www.penguinputnam.com**

PENGUIN PUTNAM NEWS

Every month you'll get an inside look at our upcom-
ing books and new features on our site. This is an
ongoing effort to provide you with the most
up-to-date information about
our books and authors.

Subscribe to Penguin Putnam News at
http://www.penguinputnam.com/newsletters

The battle for the future of humanity begins here...

EVERGENCE
THE PRODIGAL SUN
by SEAN WILLIAMS &
SHANE DIX

Commander Morgan Roche of the Commonwealth of Empires is charged with escorting an artificial intelligence unit to her superiors, with the aid of a genetically engineered warrior whose past is a mystery even to him...
__0-441-00672-8/$6.99

"A personal story told on a galaxy-sized canvas. Filled with action as well as intriguing ideas."
—Kevin J. Anderson

Don't miss the second book in the national bestselling series:
EVERGENCE: THE DYING LIGHT
__0-441-00742-2/$6.99

Prices slightly higher in Canada

Payable by Visa, MC or AMEX only ($10.00 min.), No cash, checks or COD. Shipping & handling: US/Can. $2.75 for one book, $1.00 for each add'l book; Int'l $5.00 for one book, $1.00 for each add'l. Call (800) 788-6262 or (201) 933-9292, fax (201) 896-8569 or mail your orders to:

Penguin Putnam Inc.
P.O. Box 12289, Dept. B
Newark, NJ 07101-5289
Please allow 4-6 weeks for delivery.
Foreign and Canadian delivery 6-8 weeks.

Bill my: ❑ Visa ❑ MasterCard ❑ Amex _____(expires)
Card# _____
Signature _____

Bill to:
Name _____
Address _____ City _____
State/ZIP _____ Daytime Phone # _____

Ship to:
Name _____ Book Total $ _____
Address _____ Applicable Sales Tax $ _____
City _____ Postage & Handling $ _____
State/ZIP _____ Total Amount Due $ _____

This offer subject to change without notice.   Ad # 898 (4/00)

NEW YORK TIMES
BESTSELLING AUTHOR
PETER DAVID's
PSI-MAN

❏ **PSI-MAN: MIND-FORCE WARRIOR**
0-441-00705-8/$5.99

Chuck Simon is an ordinary man with extraordinary mental powers. A top secret government agency is aware of his existence—and now Simon has become the most hunted man on Earth.

❏ **PSI-MAN #2: DEATHSCAPE**
0-441-00710-4/$5.99

On the run, Simon hides out in a toxic wilderness populated by mutant predatory animals—and eco-terrorists whose psi-powers rival his own.

❏ **PSI-MAN #3: MAIN STREET D.O.A.**
0-441-00717-1/$5.99

❏ **PSI-MAN #4: THE CHAOS KID**
0-441-00745-7/$5.99

❏ **PSI-MAN #5: STALKER**
0-441-00758-9/$5.99

Prices slightly higher in Canada

Payable by Visa, MC or AMEX only ($10.00 min.), No cash, checks or COD. Shipping & handling: US/Can. $2.75 for one book, $1.00 for each add'l book; Int'l $5.00 for one book, $1.00 for each add'l. Call (800) 788-6262 or (201) 933-9292, fax (201) 896-8569 or mail your orders to:

Penguin Putnam Inc.
P.O. Box 12289, Dept. B
Newark, NJ 07101-5289
Please allow 4-6 weeks for delivery.
Foreign and Canadian delivery 6-8 weeks.

Bill my: ❏ Visa ❏ MasterCard ❏ Amex _____ (expires)

Card# _____

Signature _____

Bill to:

Name _____

Address _____ City _____

State/ZIP _____ Daytime Phone # _____

Ship to:

Name _____ Book Total $ _____

Address _____ Applicable Sales Tax $ _____

City _____ Postage & Handling $ _____

State/ZIP _____ Total Amount Due $ _____

This offer subject to change without notice.   Ad # 900 (6/00)

WILLIAM C. DIETZ

__IMPERIAL BOUNTY   0-441-36697-X/$5.99

Since her brother's absence, Princess Claudia has seized the throne and
brought the Empire to the brink of war with the Il Ronn. Only the missing
Prince Alexander can stop Claudia's plans. And McCade has only three
months to find him.

__GALACTIC BOUNTY   0-441-87346-4/$5.99

A traitor is on the loose. A treacherous navy captain plans to sell military
secrets to the alien Il Ronn. The only man who can stop him is Sam
McCade—an interstellar bounty hunter with a score to settle.

__WHERE THE SHIPS DIE   0-441-00354-0/$6.00

There are only four known wormholes in existence. But the location of
one of them is hidden in a veil of mystery, lost in a conspiracy of murder.
And its power belongs to the first human who finds it—or the alien race
who would kill for it....

__THE FINAL BATTLE   0-441-00217-X/$6.99

Defeated at the hands of the Legion, the alien Hudathans plan to fight fire
with fire. Using copycat technology, they create their own corps of
cyborgs and target the heart of the Confederacy, once and for all.

__BODYGUARD   0-441-00105-X/$5.99

In a future where violence, corruption, and murder grow as rapidly as
technology and corporations, there is always room for the Bodyguard.
He's hired muscle for a wired future—and he's the best money can buy.

__LEGION OF THE DAMNED   0-441-48040-3/$6.99

When all hope is lost—for the terminally ill, for the condemned criminal,
for the victim who can't be saved—there is one final choice. Life...as a
cyborg soldier.

__STEELHEART   0-441-00542-X/$5.99

Prices slightly higher in Canada

Payable by Visa, MC or AMEX only ($10.00 min.), No cash, checks or COD. Shipping & handling:
US/Can. $2.75 for one book, $1.00 for each add'l book; Int'l $5.00 for one book, $1.00 for each
add'l. Call (800) 788-6262 or (201) 933-9292, fax (201) 896-8569 or mail your orders to:

Penguin Putnam Inc.	Bill my: ❑ Visa ❑ MasterCard ❑ Amex _____ (expires)
P.O. Box 12289, Dept. B	Card# _____
Newark, NJ 07101-5289	Signature _____
Please allow 4-6 weeks for delivery.	
Foreign and Canadian delivery 6-8 weeks.	

Bill to:
Name _____
Address _____ City _____
State/ZIP _____ Daytime Phone # _____
Ship to:
Name _____ Book Total $ _____
Address _____ Applicable Sales Tax $ _____
City _____ Postage & Handling $ _____
State/ZIP _____ Total Amount Due $ _____

This offer subject to change without notice.   Ad # 519 (8/00)

NEW YORK TIMES BESTSELLING AUTHOR

ANNE McCAFFREY

❑ FREEDOM'S CHALLENGE   0-441-00625-6/$6.99
"A satisfying culmination to a saga of desperate courage and the desire for freedom."
—*Library Journal*

❑ FREEDOM'S CHOICE   0-441-00531-4/$6.99
Kris Bjornsen and her comrades have found evidence of another race on their planet. Are
they ancients, long dead and gone? Or could they still exist...to join their fight?

❑ FREEDOM'S LANDING   0-441-00338-9/$6.99
Kristin Bjornsen lived a normal life, right up until the day the Catteni ships floated into
view above Denver. As human slaves were herded into the maw of a massive vessel,
Kristin realized her normal life was over, and her fight for freedom was just beginning...

❑ THE ROWAN   0-441-73576-2/$6.99
One of the strongest Talents ever born, the Rowan's power alone could not bring her
happiness. But things change when she hears strange telepathic messages from an
unknown Talent named Jeff Raven.

❑ DAMIA   0-441-13556-0/$6.99
Damia is stung by a vision of an impending disaster of such magnitude that even the
Rowan can't prevent it. Now, Damia must somehow use her powers to save a planet
under siege.

❑ DAMIA'S CHILDREN   0-441-00007-X/$6.99
Their combined abilities are even greater than those of their legendary mother. And
Damia's children will learn just how powerful they are when faced with another attack
by the mysterious enemy that Damia drove away...but did not destroy.

❑ LYON'S PRIDE   0-441-00141-6/$6.99
The children of Damia and Afra Lyon stand ready to face their most difficult challenge yet—
against a relentless alien race that is destroying life on entire planets.

Prices slightly higher in Canada
_____

Payable by Visa, MC or AMEX only ($10.00 min.), No cash, checks or COD. Shipping & handling:
US/Can. $2.75 for one book, $1.00 for each add'l book; Int'l $5.00 for one book, $1.00 for each
add'l. Call (800) 788-6262 or (201) 933-9292, fax (201) 896-8569 or mail your orders to:

Penguin Putnam Inc.	Bill my: ❑ Visa ❑ MasterCard ❑ Amex _____ (expires)
P.O. Box 12289, Dept. B	Card# _____
Newark, NJ 07101-5289	Signature _____
Please allow 4-6 weeks for delivery.	
Foreign and Canadian delivery 6-8 weeks.	

Bill to:

Name _____

Address _____ City _____

State/ZIP _____ Daytime Phone # _____

Ship to:

Name _____ Book Total $ _____

Address _____ Applicable Sales Tax $ _____

City _____ Postage & Handling $ _____

State/ZIP _____ Total Amount Due $ _____

This offer subject to change without notice.   Ad# B363 (7/00)